# POLAROID
# MAN

# POLAROID MAN

*by* Michael Cormany

*An Irma Heldman/Birch Lane Press Book*
*Published by Carol Publishing Group*

A Birch Lane Press Book
Published by Carol Publishing Group
Birch Lane Press is a registered trade mark of Carol Communications, Inc.

Editorial Offices
600 Madison Avenue
New York, NY 10022

Sales & Distribution Offices
120 Enterprise Avenue
Secaucus, NJ 07094

In Canada: Musson Book Company
A division of General Publishing Co. Limited
Don Mills, Ontario

Manufactured in the United States of America

10   9   8   7   6   5   4   3   2   1

Carol Publishing Group books are available at special discounts
for bulk purchases, for sales promotions, fund raising, or
educational purposes. Special editions can also be created to
specifications. For details contact: Special Sales Department,
Carol Publishing Group, 120 Enterprise Ave., Secaucus, NJ 07094

Library of Congress Cataloging-in-Publication Data

Cormany, Michael.
    Polaroid man / by Michael Cormany.
        p.   cm.
    "An Irma Heldman/Birch Lane Press book."
    ISBN 1-55972-069-7
    I. Title.
    PS3553.06525P6    1991
    813'.54—dc20                          91-6694
                                              CIP

# POLAROID
## MAN

# ONE

It was 4:00 A.M. I was sober as a judge, bored out of my skull, and there was a roar in my ears louder than Niagara Falls. A girl with no hair and black lipstick was hitting on me. A blonde better looking than Michelle Pfeiffer was ignoring me. A fat middle-aged man with a ponytail to the middle of his back kept assuring me I could trust him, Full Frontal Nudity's check would be in the mail Monday morning.

Off the top of my head I could think of a couple hundred places I'd rather be. I asked myself, who the hell booked us into Johnson City, Illinois, anyway?

Johnson City isn't the middle of nowhere, but I bet you could spit there from the city limits. I sat at the bar in the Crazy Alm Nightclub, slurping Diet Pepsi from a two liter plastic bottle and chainsmoking Kools. The club was dark except for two long black lights above the bar and a purple spot over the stage sixty feet to my right. It was empty if six people didn't count.

I was sitting at the bar in the Crazy Alm because a year ago, prompted by financial desperation, I'd answered a "musician wanted" ad in *The Reader*. Since then I'd been playing lead guitar for a band called Full Frontal Nudity, a name we stole from Monty Python because we figured those words on a marquee or a coming attraction poster would sucker in hordes. Yeah! It rarely did. For three sets we rocked the Crazy Alm. Two encores. Brought the house down with an extended, killer version of "Boogie at Midnight."

But that was an hour ago. The equipment was back in the vans. Van number one with Dave, Priceman and LeRoy was long gone. I wished to hell I was because the total silence

1

that enveloped the room now was such a contrast to the wall of noise the band generated for five hours that the buzz in my ears was a palpable, painful thing.

The friendly girl was maybe twenty-two. She sat on the stool next to me. Except for a single curly lock in front, her head was shaved so only a five o'clock shadow of stubble showed. She wore tattered jeans, a black T-shirt with DRUGS SAVED MY LIFE across the front, a black leather jacket and biker boots. Black lipstick completed the look. A skinhead. I get along fine with the ones who aren't racist. They love rock 'n' rollers. There's lots of skinheads in Chicago, but I bet it played out here like a fart in church.

This one was cranked over the brim. Through the constant hum I half-listened as she babbled intensely about the ties in "self-destructive, but creative spiritual energy" that linked all the great rockers starting with Elvis and continuing down through John Lennon and Keith Richard and Sid Vicious. Then she started naming names I never heard of. That happens often now. I'm a musician who doesn't pay much attention to the music scene anymore.

She stopped every few minutes to sniffle and rub her nose or take a long pull on one of the three menthol cigarettes she had going. After twenty minutes of the rap, she jerked her stool around so she faced my left side and said, "So, you dig how I look?"

With no hair, black lips, and sitting under a black light she was certainly a sight. Without looking at her I said, "You make a definite statement, but take it easy on the go-fast."

She ignored that, said, "I think it's so shallow, so middle class to always try and look your best. Your prettiest? This preppie look makes me sick. There's so many other effects to strive for. I dig having people go like, 'Oh, my God' or 'Jesus!' when they see me. I wanna stand out from the crowd, I wanna shock. You're a rocker. What's your opinion about it?"

I said, "I don't have opinions anymore. And if I did have opinions I wouldn't expect anybody to be interested in what they were."

She said, "You're too cynical, man. Must be all that time

on the road. God, I envy you. You really got the life."

I looked at her, then at the Pepsi bottle and said with some heat, "This *looks* like the life?"

She said, "I think living in Chicago and playing in a rock and roll band like Full Frontal Nudity is life on the edge. I love that feeling, that philosophy. Being on the edge."

"It's a job, that's all. I like to play, but mostly it's a job."

"But it's like, a cool job, right? Fun?"

I jerked my head at the stage. Our singer, Justus Walker, sat on the lip of it, daubed with purplish light, his arm around the shoulders of a horse-faced brunette. I said, "It'll be daylight in an hour and a half and I'm two hours from home. I'm drained. All I wanna do is crawl in bed and go to sleep. When I do, birds'll be chirping and I hate falling asleep when birds are chirping."

The girl said, "But—"

I talked over her. "But before I can do that I gotta sit here and wait while that arrogant putz over there who thinks he's Jon-Bon-fucking-Jovi tries to convince that chick to perform oral sex on him. I got a humming in my ears so loud they actually hurt. I wrenched my back lugging the amps up the stairs out back of this joint. The van broke down on the way out and I fully expect it'll do the same on the way back. Plus I'm trying to stay sober because—well, just because." I looked at the girl and tried to smile. Said, "Fun is not these things."

I looked again at Justus and his "date." He whispered in her ear. She tittered drunkenly. Justus cocked his head and shook it slightly so his long blond hair shimmered.

I muttered, "For Godsakes, Justus, turn on the charm, make your play—something, so we can get the hell out of here."

Thing was, anytime except 4:00 A.M., Justus wouldn't of spit on this girl if she were on fire. But he considered no gig official unless he could brag about an act of fellatio on the way home. Even by rock singer standards, Justus was an unusually conceited, self-absorbed, adolescently-arrested prima donna. He should've been fired months ago. But he could sing—a little—and he was a pretty boy. It never hurts a rock band to have a pretty boy out front, especially Full

Frontal Nudity. The rest of us looked like the offspring of Andre the Giant and Moms Mabley.

The bartender-owner of the Crazy Alm was the fat man with the yard-long gray ponytail who promised to send my check first thing Monday morning. He sat at the first table from the bar, ten feet to my left. The blonde sat across from him. The fat man kept yawning. He was tired and bored too and he wanted to lock up and go home. But Chicago bands draw well downstate and he didn't want to offend this Chicago band by telling its singer and guitar player to get the hell out.

I'd been sneaking glances at the blonde in the mirror behind the bar. She'd been following the conversation. Now she said, "Well, guitar player, then why do it?" Her voice was cigarette and alcohol husky.

I twisted the stool left to look full at her. Made a more complete visual inspection. Okay, maybe not *better* than Michelle Pfeiffer, but not much shy. She had the almond shaped eyes, long golden hair, cheekbones like giant marbles, the perfect V jaw and large luscious lips. I said, "Why do what?"

"Why play in a band if it's such a drag?"

I said, "I'm getting too old for this, that's all. Twenty years ago it was a blast."

The skinhead girl said, "How old are you?"

"Thirty-eight."

She said, "That's not old. Keith Richard is over forty now. Chuck Berry's about sixty."

"I made the money they do, it'd still be a blast."

The blonde said, "The money's no good?"

"Ask him."

The owner patted his belly, shrugged. "He ain't gonna retire on it."

The blonde asked, "You work a day job?"

"I got a private investigator's license and an office on the North Side. But mostly I do drudge work for Cook County, deliverin' writs and subpoenas for ten bucks an hour. Been close to a year since I had a case to speak of. And that one the woman I worked for ran off to Mexico and never paid me."

"What's the problem?"

"The problem is one-man detective agencies are getting squeezed out of business by monster outfits like Lloyd's and Lawrence. They got scores of agents, they got massive computer systems hooked up nationwide, they got state of the art surveillance equipment and bugging devices. Some of that hi-tech stuff costs more than a Van Gogh painting."

"What do you 'got'?"

"Hi-tech-wise, I got a Corona manual typewriter, a file cabinet and a telephone. Also a rusted out green Skylark. And a rabbit, but he ain't much help."

"You don't 'got' much, do you?"

"That's why I'm lugging the Gibson around again. I only know how to do two things—snoop and play chords."

As we talked the blonde's expression changed from idle curiosity to something like interest. She said, "What's the name?"

"Dan Kruger."

"Of your agency."

"Same."

"You work outside Chicago?"

"Sure."

"Would you work in Johnson City?"

"Did tonight, didn't I?"

"What's your fee?"

"Hundred a day. And expenses if I work outside Chicago."

She winced. I said, "I guarantee you nobody comes cheaper. I'm good, mind you, but I work cheap. That's *my* selling point."

She removed a Bic pen from a purse on the table and wrote quickly, tongue clenched between teeth, on a drink napkin. She stood, reached over the nightclub owner, and handed me the napkin. On it printed in large cap letters was ANDREA GALE. Below the name was a phone number and a street address. She said, "Call me tomorrow. I can promise one day's work. Maybe two."

I put the napkin in my shirt pocket and nodded. As I did I heard a shriek and the loud smack of palm against face. I spun right, saw the brunette striding away from the bandstand, maneuvering between tables toward the door. Justus stood where he'd been sitting, rubbing his cheek, acute embarrassment all over his pretty boy face.

I drained the Pepsi, grinned like an idiot. I had a job with a beautiful blonde and Justus wouldn't be saying shit on the way home.

Sometimes the rock life is like, fun.

# TWO

I got to my apartment on Fremont Avenue at 6:00 A.M. Fed Bugs some bunny chow, smoked half a joint till the roar in my ears diminished to a dull throb and was dead out of it by six-thirty. The digital alarm clock read 9:02 when the phone next to my bed bleated me awake. I punched it off the nightstand, pulled the receiver up from the floor and rested it next to my ear.

A low-pitched female voice said, "This is Andrea Gale. From the Crazy Alm? Last night? You didn't forget me, did you?"

The brain waves were about ten percent, but a picture of Andrea Gale came in strong and clear. I mumbled, "It wasn't last night, it was this morning. Five hours ago to be precise. I remember you, Andrea. I was just about to call."

"I bet."

"You at the address on the napkin?"

"Not now, I'm at work. But Saturday's I get off at ten. Don't forget me, okay?" There was an urgency in her voice that hadn't been there in the club.

I said, "Youth is a wonderful thing. What a crime to waste it on children."

"What?"

"Closing a bar and going straight to work. I used to do it when I was a cop. Long time ago. Give you some idea what kind of cop I was. What work you do?"

"Factory. Assembly line. But I won't be doing it long. I gotta run, I'll be home no later than 10:15. You'll be there, right?"

"What's this about?"

"I'll tell you when I see you. But it's important. Trust me."

"I'll be there at noon." I pushed the receiver back on the floor. "Maybe."

I'm definitely not a youth anymore—sometimes I wonder if I ever was—and two and a half hours sleep don't cut it. I ate three whites, poured a pot of black coffee on top. As I swallowed coffee I watched Bugs scamper around the kitchen. Bugs is my partner, kind of. A black and white French Lop rabbit I rescued from a dumpster behind a bar, Bugs' primary job is to protect the apartment while I'm out sleuthing or on the road with FFN. But he likes to get out in the field once in a while and it had been a cool spring, which meant I wouldn't have to worry about him cooking in the car, so when I was ready to go, I scooted him into his traveling cage and carried him to the Skylark.

I drove to the Crawford Hotel on Dearborn. Johnson Jensen sat in his red canvas folding chair by the newsstand on the corner. The chair has MR. JENSEN, SUPERSTAR and a huge gold star stitched on the back.

Johnson Jensen has long, wild white hair to match his long, thick beard. Looks like those old paintings of God. He sells newspapers and he drinks wine. That pretty much covers it. We go way back. Many was the time I paid two bucks for a *Sun-Times* so he'd have the scratch for a morning MD 20/20. He was always too grateful like winos are. I always acted as though we were best of friends and best of friends stood by each other in mornings of need.

But there wouldn't be any more mornings of need for Johnson Jensen because eighteen months ago he hit six numbers at seven o'clock on Saturday night and the Lotto pot was five million dollars. He had to share it with a retired plumber in Rockford, but that still left two and a half. Which made him the perfect person to hit for a loan.

Two point five mil didn't change Johnson Jensen. He still operated his newsstand and he still craved The Dog because he was old and that was all he knew. But he discovered new pleasures. Once or twice a month, he staggered to Bishop's Wine Seller on State. The yuppies who work in the Loop stop there after a hard day in front of the computer terminal to purchase just the right wine to go with the chicken bourbon flamed with oregano or whatever the hell it is yuppies eat. Johnson Jensen would buy two bottles of the most expensive red wine they had. Cabernet, Beaujolais, Chianti, the hell with that; all that concerned him was the color and the price. While the store clerks and the stock traders watched in horror, Jensen would take forever to extricate the cork from one of the bottles using the dollar twenty-nine screw he carried in his Sally Bomber overcoat. After he removed the cork, he'd drain that sucker in two or three long gurgles and toss it aside like a burnt match. Then he'd go outside, sit crosslegged on the sidewalk, and sip the second bottle, smiling a loon's smile that exposed his three yellow teeth. He'd ask the yups as they entered the store if they could spare a C-note because he needed a drink. He'd hold the bottle up to show how empty it was getting and let them read the label. Then he'd laugh like hell. Eventually the police would show, but even they couldn't keep a straight face. They'd drive him back to the Crawford and tell him to leave the beautiful people alone.

Telling his friend Santiago to watch the stand, Johnson Jensen went inside the Crawford to his room, came back with ten twenties so crisp they'd cause paper cuts. As he counted them out he said, "Still on the wagon, Danny my boy?"

I said, "Four weeks and three days."

He shook his head sadly. "World must look mighty bleak. How you feel?"

"Except for not being able to sleep worth a damn, pretty good actually."

He scratched his nose and smiled. Said, "See, I know the reason for that. Bein' sober after you been drunk a long time, that's a high itself. You just hooked on a different high, that's all. When the novelty wears off—"

I said, "Ah, encouragement. I need all of it I can get."

I put the two hundred in my wallet and walked to the car

feeling like a rich man. Which in itself is a sad commentary on my life.

I rode the Tollway for a long time through sporadic soft showers, smoking Kools and talking a blue streak to Bugs after the speed kicked in. Told him we were on our way to meet a beautiful dame. Bugs was not impressed, but then Bugs rarely is. He stays on a very even keel.

At 11:45, we entered Johnson City. Pop. 108,247.

Just inside the limits between a McDonald's and a Pizza Hut was a Clark station. I parked at the full service island because I needed directions as well as gas. A fuzz-faced kid with a patch on his green shirt that said Chuck hurried out. I joined him at the back of the car by the tank. Bent over, hand squeezing the trigger, he said, "How's this baby run?"

"Combustion engine fueled by gasoline."

He made a face. People always say they can never tell when I'm making a funny. He said, "Just meant, she's pretty old—"

I said, "It was a joke, son. A joke, I said. Know where Third Street is?"

"No, sir, I don't. I been here only a few weeks and I don't plan on being here many more." He looked toward the station office. Shouted, "Hey, Audrey, you know of a Third Street?"

Audrey was a nail-thin white-haired woman wearing a red poncho and blue jeans, sitting on a metal folding chair just outside the office. A white poodle in a pink sweater sat at attention on her lap. She petted the dog and bent her head slightly to talk in its ear. In a baby carriage next to her, another poodle stuck its head up over the side, ears alert, watery black eyes open wide.

Audrey took some seconds to think it over, then said, "Go straight to the third stop light, take a right, and I believe it's six blocks." She sounded annoyed.

I waved and looked at Chuck. "Where you leavin' to?"

"Home. Mississippi. I don't like the weather and people up here. They just—" He let it drop as the realization set in that I was probably a "people up here." He said, "You from 'round here?"

"Chicago."

He winced and shook his head like he felt sorry for me.
He looked behind us to make sure no one was there. Said in
a hushed voice, "I heard tell there's lots of colored in there.
Lots of Mexicans too."

I laughed and Chuck shut up and didn't say anything else.

Audrey's directions were right on. It was exactly six blocks
after I turned that Third intersected with Madison.

The address was a three-story dark brick apartment building. The kind that has forty-eight identical apartments
carved in it with the forty-eight sliding glass doors leading to
the forty-eight patio balconies that run along the side. These
kinds of apartment buildings always remind me of those
mountains in the Southwest with the Navajo caves. Or
maybe it's the Pueblo caves. Except this mountain no doubt
had sculpted landscaping, a swimming pool and tennis
courts, laundry facilities in the basement, planned social
activities—neat stuff like that. The Navajos only had
ladders.

This one also had the standard buzz-in security system.
On a waist-high glass-covered table the residents were listed
next to their apartment number. I ran my finger around
until I came to GALE-FARRELL. I figured Farrell for the
boyfriend. Envisioned a rock hard, square-jawed jock with a
sweater tied around his shoulders.

It was 11:59. Punctuality makes the detective. I waited
one minute, then firmly pressed the tiny gold button next to
their names. Waited for a garbled voice from the speaker in
the table or the bleat at the door, but there was only silence.
After some more presses I went back to the Skylark. Said,
"Don't forget me, okay?" to Bugs in a smarmy voice.
Matched another Kool and waited.

At 12:20, I followed a young couple in who had a key to
the main door. They nodded and smiled and held the door
open for me like I lived there. I nodded and smiled back.
That's another thing about these buildings. For all they
knew I did live there.

Andrea Gale's apartment was the last one on the left
down a long dim hallway on the first floor.

I knocked, put my ear against the door. Nothing. No TV,

no stereo noises, no people sounds. I twisted the knob. The door was unlocked.

I said, "Damn." I wasn't liking this at all. I hesitated, then pushed the door open.

Andrea Gale was in the living room. She lay on a cream colored carpet next to a nubby earth-toned sofa, face down, arms spread wide. Her hair, a vivid gold in the light streaming through the sliding patio window, covered her face and fanned over her neck and shoulders like a dropped shawl. Her black skirt was pulled up over her hips. She wasn't wearing panties. Red bruises splotched her buttocks and the backs of her thighs. I didn't see any blood.

I knelt beside her, stuck index and middle fingers through the hair and felt the carotid for a pulse. There wasn't any.

I didn't know if Johnson City was patched into a 911 system, but I dialed it anyway on a phone in the kitchen. It was.

# THREE

I felt my pulse. Fueled by speed and shock it scooted like Ben Johnson after a steroid cocktail. My new philosophy was to take drugs only when needed. I needed. I worked the Valium bottle from my jacket and tossed two down with a cupped handful of tap water.

Down a short hall left of the living room was a bedroom, a bathroom, and another bedroom.

There was a gold-framed high school graduation picture hanging on the wall just right of the door in the first bedroom. The graduate was a round-faced brunette. A little overweight, brown eyes, pudgy features, button nose, a private smile on pouty lips. Under a window was a four-drawer bureau with mail on top. The name Lisa Farrell and this address was on all of it. So Farrell wasn't the jock boyfriend, and this wasn't the room I wanted to check out.

I went to the far bedroom.

Andrea Gale's room was done entirely in pastels. Aqua print wallpaper, peach wall-to-wall carpet and curtains, pale mauve-and-gray-striped bedspread and pillowcases.

One look around the room told me that Andrea Gale had one passion in life: looking at herself. Mirrors and pictures of herself were everywhere. There was a full-length mirror on three of the four walls. On either side of the mirrors, model portfolio shots of her at various ages were hung, forming a pyramid around the mirror.

Propped, framed snapshots taken at parties and picnics sat atop the dresser and nightstand. Lisa Farrell was in two outdoor candids. The girls squinted against the sunlight and wore short shorts, T-shirts, and goofy drunken grins. A long-haired, fish-faced male was in two more. The rest were only of Andrea.

On a writing desk in the corner of the room, a white princess phone weighted down a pile of papers. I set the phone on the floor.

On top of the pile was a ripped-in-half scrap of steno paper with my name and home phone printed in the same oversize childish scribble that was on the napkin in my pocket. Below that was a mixture of junk mail, bills, receipts, advertising fliers, and personal reminders. I went through it all quickly, scanning and setting aside.

There was one other piece of paper besides the one with my name and number that interested me. Another scrap torn from a steno pad. In Andrea's handwriting, EDUARDO TORRES and BUDDY BAKER was written just below the jagged half-circles running across the top of the page. Below the names, BLUE PALM and a phone number. I thought for a second, put this paper in my pocket.

Then I reassembled the pile, making sure the scrap with my name was still on top. I wanted the Johnson City police to know I had a valid reason to be here. My word might not be enough.

I heard the front door open and close. I walked down the hallway to meet the police.

Lisa Farrell stood frozen like a mime ten feet from Andrea Gale's body. She stared down at it, her arms rigid at her sides, fists clenched.

Walking toward her, I softly cleared my throat and said, "Lisa?" Her face swung toward me. She jumped back, her mouth shot open and she screamed so loud I was afraid the windows would crack.

She ran for the door. I sprinted after her and grabbed her around the waist.

Worst thing I could have done.

She sliced her elbows back and forth like a speedfreak doing aerobics. She gasped and sobbed and kept shrieking, "Let go of me, let go!" She maneuvered around so we were facing. She kneed my groin. I tried to catch her fists, but my hands couldn't hold them and she rained punches on my head and face.

The pain in my groin and the exertion of trying to stop the punches made me start to gasp too. I huffed, "Lisa, I found Andrea like this. The police'll be here any minute." I ducked and weaved as I talked.

She clawed my cheeks, spit in my eyes. I was taller and a little heavier, but she had the advantage of thinking she was fighting for her life. I let her go, tried to move away. She chopped my temple with an elbow and I staggered like a drunk.

The tussle had put us in the entryway to the kitchen. She pulled a carving knife from a wooden block of knives on the counter, took a step forward and pointed it at my stomach. I took a long step back. She held it underhand, like knife fighters hold a knife. That way you carve up and the slicee can't block you with a forearm. I did not like the way this one shivered in her hand.

"Who are you, you bastard?" she blubbered.

I raised my hands, nodded my head. Slowly and reassuringly I hoped, but it was probably bouncing around like one of those dashboard puppets. Her saliva was still in my eyes and I blinked rapidly trying to clear my vision. I had to watch that knife.

I said, "My name is Dan Kruger. I'm a private investigator from Chicago and I can prove it. I have ID in my wallet." My voice was hoarse, but at least it wasn't cracking. I didn't need my fright feeding hers. I said, "Andrea hired me last night. We met at the Crazy Alm here in Johnson City. In her bedroom is a piece of paper in her handwriting with my name on it. I was—"

Lisa shouted, "Shut up!"

I shut up.

She started crying harder, sliding close to hysteria. Snot and tears and saliva slid down her face blending on her chin like a shiny cake mix. She wiped some of the mess away with the back of her free hand. Through the shakes, she said, "What's wrong with Andrea? What did you do to her?"

"Nothing, believe me. I found Andrea just like you did and I called the police. They'll be here—"

And they were. I was spun around and pushed hard against the imitation brick kitchen wall. My legs were kicked apart. Someone patted me down like he wanted to break bones and leave bruises. He grabbed a fistful of hair and slammed the right side of my face against the wall while yanking my right arm behind me. My left eye looked into the bore of a policeman's revolver.

Behind me a man using a very composed voice said, "Ma'am, would you please drop the knife?" He repeated the request and I heard the knife land with a soft clump on the tile floor. Her crying sounded muffled now as though her face was buried in the man's chest.

Personally, I was never so glad to have a gun pointed at me in my life.

# FOUR

After they pulled me off the wall and turned me around, I saw three policemen. They listened to Lisa's story, then my story, then talked on their hand talkies and made a lot of phone calls.

It was crowded in the small kitchen. One of the cops took

my wallet and told me to go sit in the living room "for the time being." All of the cops had walked in to take a look, but none were there now. I happen to believe ignoring the corpse is a piss poor way to start a homicide investigation, but who the hell am I?

I sat on the sofa three feet from Andrea's body, blotting the scratches on my face with a Kleenex. I reached forward and flicked hair away from her face. There was blood here, a small puddle under her mouth. Her lips were puffy and her nose was swollen and bent slightly. That's where the blood came from. Lines of it, starting to crust, leaked from each nostril into the puddle. I tried to look away, out the window, but my eyes kept sneaking back to Andrea Gale's marred face and that beautiful gold hair.

The cop who'd convinced Lisa to drop the knife brought a sheet from one of the bedrooms and covered the body, looking at me while he did. I started to think maybe sending me in here was some kind of clever psychological ploy. Like maybe if I was the killer it'd work on my conscience to sit this close to the body and I wouldn't be able to take it and eventually I'd jump up and shout, "Okay, okay, I did it! I confess!"

Then again maybe they just wanted me out of the way.

The cop went to Lisa, put his arm around her and led her to her bedroom. She was still crying. As they walked he talked to her in a low voice. Homicides are such a great place to meet chicks.

A plainclothes detective named McCoy showed up right after that. A bear of a man, mid-forties, dark blue suit that looked slept in, scuffed brown shoes. His face was pitted and lumpy from old acne and he had a rhubarb-colored hook nose that would've looked swell on a lead reindeer. His forehead was high below curly dark hair. He had a beer gut the size of a prize watermelon.

I watched him for two minutes, pegged him as the classic career cop. Here among young men in uniform he was boss man and he gloried in it, self-consciously posing like General Patton at a boot camp. Around the brass, he probably sucked up like a Frank Sinatra hanger-on.

As he talked with the uniforms in the kitchen he took

notes, his face solemn, his eyes swerving often to me. When they were done he walked into the living room, lifted the sheet and looked at Andrea Gale's body for thirty seconds, then floated the sheet back down.

He said, "Good lookin' gash. Nice butt."

I ignored that.

He said, "You in love with her?"

"If I couldn't have her, nobody could."

"Don't talk too smart, pal. Not after you were caught wandering around the apartment with her dead on the floor here."

"I only met her nine hours ago."

"So? You never heard of love at first sight?"

"Heard of it."

He gave me back my wallet. Said, "Still live on Fremont and Waveland?"

"Still do."

"Office still on North Lincoln?"

"Still there."

He removed a 4x6 spiral pad from an inside coat pocket, then a ballpoint pen from his shirt. He read out loud what was on the pad. "My man, Thornton, over there says you claim you met the deceased for the first time at the Crazy Alm nightclub this A.M. around four." He looked up. "What's the deal, bein' there after hours? You work there?"

"Kinda. Last night my band played there."

"What's this band?"

"You know, a rock band. Guitars, drums, fame and fortune, screaming girls."

"You mean a rock band like the Beatles?"

"We got a little ways to go—"

"You're a PI and you play in a *rock* band?"

"Landlord don't care how I pay the rent, just so I pay it."

"Jesus," he said. He shook his head and made a face like suddenly something smelled bad. "So you claim the decreased here asked you to come to Johnson City on a job-related matter."

"Two witnesses heard the conversation."

He made a note on the pad. Said, "Who are these witnesses?"

"One owns the Crazy Alm. I don't remember his name."

"Old guy, wears a scruffy ponytail down to his ass?"

I nodded.

"Donald Gant. Oldest hippie in America. Fifty goin' on nineteen. Describe the other one."

"A skinhead. Female." McCoy looked up from his pad. I said, "Skinheads are kids who shave their heads and wear black clothes and Doctor Marten Brogues. Kind of an anti-style, right wing thing. Gant must know her name if he lets her sit around after the place closes."

"What was the job-related matter?"

"Never found out. She said she'd tell me when I got here but when I got here she was dead."

"Must of been important."

"Must of been."

McCoy turned slightly and stared at the sheet-covered figure on the floor, idly clicking his pen like he was keeping time to a Motown record. He said, "You say she was dead when you got here?"

"That's what I say."

"You sure?"

"No pulse means dead. I think."

"How'd you get in the apartment?"

"Followed some people in the security door. It was about 12:30. I'd know 'em again if I saw 'em. They might remember me. The apartment door was unlocked."

"It was unlocked?"

"I thought that was queer too."

"What in hell'd you do to that kid in there? Thornton says they could hear her screaming when they were still in the parking lot."

"We both panicked," I said. "I wanted to explain who I was and what was going on. I think I went about it the wrong way."

He smiled a bit. "I think so too." The smile died as fast as it came. He hesitated for a bit, then said, "Okay, I'm gonna talk to Gant to verify that she asked you to come out. The boys in there told me your name and phone number is on a piece of paper on the girl's desk. So maybe your story's legit. They called some people in Chicago and it appears you are

who you say you are. So you get the benefit of the doubt.
For now. But consider yourself lucky. Know why? I'm
gonna tell you why. The people they talked to in Chicago I
don't think would volunteer to cosign no loans for you.
Sounds like you've been down so long it probably looks like
up. Even ignoring the murder rap I could hang a B&E and
attempt at assault on your ass if I wanted to be a prick. If I
got the right judge, I could even make it stick. Know why?"

"You're gonna tell me why?"

"Yeah, I am. Out here Chicago is like a dirty word.
Judges in this county would be appalled at a Chicago punk
PI who barges into town without telling anybody he's here
and breaks into a young girl's apartment, then proceeds to
slap around the girl's roommate. Being an ex-Chicago cop I
assume behavior like that is second nature to you, but it
don't go out here."

One more plainclothes man arrived with a Leica 35
draped around his neck. He came into the living room and
lifted the sheet, made a long whistle. Said, "Damn, who'd
wanna waste some fine snatch like this?"

To McCoy I said, "You are some cold sons-of-bitches in
this town. And I'm not sure where this hostility is coming
from. I came to Johnson City for a legitimate reason. I
found a dead body and I nine-one-one'd the police. That's
proper procedure where I come from."

McCoy waved that aside. He moved closer, leaned forward and pitched his voice so only I could hear it. Said,
"There's people in this apartment like you as the prime
suspect."

I laughed. "Yeah, that's the first thing I learned at the
academy too. The murderer always dials 911 then sticks
around with the corpse waitin' for the law. I *know* you
aren't one of those people."

He stepped back, put his arms out in a gesture of "who
me?" He said, "You've made your official statement. And
now some advice, costing not a dime. You stay the fuck out
of Johnson City unless I tell you to come back. You got that?
The person who hired you is dead and you ain't got a reason
in hell to be out here anymore. Our police force might be
smaller than you're used to, but we got all the mod cons.

Even got personal computers on our desks. We don't need no outsider stumbling around, gettin' in the way. I know you Chitown boys think you wrote the book and us rubes have to move our lips to read it." He looked at me for a second, still clicking the pen. The whole time he talked he hadn't sounded angry really. More like irritated. Probably figured I wasn't worth angry. He said, "Guess what I'm trying to say is, this ain't your element, you ain't wanted, you ain't needed. So leave." After a second he added, "I'm telling you this for your own good."

I stood and smiled. Said, "And here I thought you didn't like me, ya big lug ya."

Hansen said, "Waveland and Fremont. That very far from Wrigley Field?"

"Couple blocks."

He smiled a tight, unfriendly smile. Said, "That's not a bad deal."

"It is if you're a Sox fan," I said.

# FIVE

I stopped outside Lisa's bedroom before I left. She wasn't crying now, but her eyes were still red and swollen. She stared at the floor. Two policemen sat with her on the bed, one on each side, talking in low voices. Lisa looked at me, then quickly away. It was a better reception than I'd gotten the first time so I let it go.

It was three o'clock when I pulled out of the apartment complex parking lot onto Third. The on again, off again rain had made the street greasy slick. Cars hissed trails of spray as they passed and their wipers made slow slides across the glass.

I told Bugs about my experience in the apartment. Said, "Afraid we got us an enemy in McCoy. We'll have to keep an eye on him." Bugs looked at me, wrinkled his nose and I knew he was thinking "What you mean 'we,' short ears?" I told him about the paper in my pocket. "I am very curious about Eduardo Torres and Buddy Baker. I might of told McCoy about this note 'cept he had to come on straight off like a hard guy. Now I'm gonna let him find this angle on his own. See if his desktop personal computer bails his butt out on this one. Why do all small town cops have inferiority complexes, Bugs? They think all Chicago law does is sit around laugh at rubes? Yeah, I know I'm acting like a two-year-old because I don't like McCoy and I wanna make him look bad, not to mention I'm withholding evidence. But Bugs? So fucking what?"

We both laughed. You have to be friends with a rabbit a long time before he'll laugh at your jokes.

I found the Clark station and parked at the side of it in a long patch of white gravel. Audrey and the dogs still sat by the door. I walked up to her, my shoes crunching the wet stones. I looked for Chuck but he was gone. A man who looked like Chuck would look in twenty-five years stood behind the glass door.

The man in the door, Audrey, and both dogs watched me approach. I said, "Audrey, the directions were perfect."

She barely nodded. The poodles looked at me, then her, like they intended to follow the conversation. The one in the baby carriage whined a bit. Audrey reached over and caressed behind his ears and he quit.

I said, "There something in this town called the Blue Palm?"

"Fraid there is."

I waited. After a second she said, "Bar. Downtown." She reached under the poncho, brought out a cigarette and lit it. I automatically reached for my Kools. Bad habit of mine. Monkey see, monkey do.

I said, "Wouldn't know an Eduardo Torres or a Buddy Baker, would you?"

"I would not," she snapped. "And if they're connected with the Blue Palm I would not want to. I abhor liquor and anyone connected with the manufacture, sale or consumption of it. If you could of seen what it did to my husband. The Blue Palm is a notorious hangout for undesirables.

Trouble there every weekend. You read about the place in the newspaper every Monday like clockwork."

I asked how to get there. She made a big sigh, and without looking at me, pointed with her cigarette hand. "Back the way you came a mile or so, take a right at Fender Street. You'll see it eventually on Fender after you get downtown."

I said, "Cute dogs."

A smile spread across her face. She sat up in the chair and looked at me like I was her favorite friend. Her voice warm, she said, "Aren't they precious? These are my babies." She pointed to the one in the baby carriage. "That's Lovey. This one is Kissy because that's all he ever wants to do. Kiss, kiss, kiss. Watch." She put her mouth next to his and Kissy licked it, made a yip. The lady looked at me, beaming. "See? Young man, I raised four children, but they're long gone. A worthless bunch, the lot of 'em. Scattered all over the country. I tell you these kids here have been more of a pleasure to me than my human children ever were."

I said, "I got a rabbit. He's over in the car."

"Well, then you kind of know what I mean."

I said I kind of did.


Twenty minutes later, I was cruising downtown Johnson City. Not much left, like most medium-size cities these days. Lots of boarded up buildings and tiny bars and the kind of small-time stores and restaurants that working people dream about owning for years, then watch go belly up six months after the Grand Opening. Had to be a mall nearby. Those things are deadly as cancer to downtown business districts.

The Blue Palm was a dinky brick box between Char's Beauty School and a second-hand furniture store. There was a blue neon palm tree in the front window below a "Pabst on Ice" sign. A narrow driveway ran down the left side. I drove down it, parked in the lot in back.

Run-down bars never look friendly in the daytime, but the Blue Palm possessed all the charm and allure of a locker room in a seventy-year-old YMCA. The room was short and constricted and smelled like a sweat shop. The walls were painted dark brown, adding to the claustrophobic effect, and the only floor I ever walked on stickier than this one was in a porno theater. In one corner, two baseball-capped men were extending a box-size stage with empty beer cases. I wondered how a dive this size afforded a band. There were ten tables, five chairs per, and six stools at the bar. With a shoehorn you could maybe squeeze seventy-five people into the place.

A stout, sullen-faced girl wearing hair curlers asked what I'd have. My first thought was brandy. I could almost feel the warmth sliding from throat to belly, but I said, "Diet Pepsi."

Except for me, the bartender, a bearded geezer snoring at a table full of long-necked Millers, and the two men enlarging the stage, the place was empty. I said, "You guys rock the house down on Saturday afternoon."

She wiped the bar top, didn't look up. Said, "Stick around, Ace. It fills up."

"Eduardo or Buddy here?"

"Torres?"

"How many Eduardo's you got?"

She tightened her lips but didn't say anything.

I said, "It's business."

"Hang on."

She went through a door at the end of the bar, came back and said I had to say what I wanted. I said, "Andrea Gale." She was gone longer this time. When she came back, she said to follow her.

Beyond the door she led me down four concrete steps, then left down a short hallway, past stairs coming from the back, to another door. She knocked on the door twice, pushed it open and motioned me to enter. She left, shutting the door behind me.

The room contained four pieces of furniture. A ripped black fake leather couch along the right wall with a guy in it, a brown desk and chair with a guy on it dead ahead, and a dented brass floor lamp with an orange bulb at the far end of the couch. Behind the desk there were some shelves, empty except for stacked girlie magazines. The walls were papered with tacked on *Hustler* centerfolds. The Blue Palm was one classy bar.

"Eduardo Torres?" I said to the man behind the desk. Eyes like cigarette holes burned in newspaper sized me up. He was nearly as wide as the room.

He didn't answer. He looked toward the couch and said, "Buddy!" The dude who stood up from the couch was also huge; bigger than a Notre Dame lineman. His blond hair was buzz cut and he had a severely demented facial expression. Blank eyes, a punk's smirk. He looked like Curly Howard with a bad brain transplant.

He took two steps toward me, extending a hand as big as a catcher's mitt. He clasped my right wrist and spun me left. He slid behind me, started hiking my arm up my back like he was working a tire jack.

"You're gonna break it," I gasped. I stood on my toes to give my arm a chance. Buddy chuckled like a happy moron.

Torres stood and came around the desk. His head barely reached my shoulders and I'm only five-eight. Next to Buddy he looked like a Singer midget, but his T-shirt was ready to rip at every seam because of his massive chest and biceps. Muscles on muscles is a cliche, but this guy was Mr. America material. He curled a lock of my hair. Said, "So, sweetheart, *you* are what Andrea sends us? Look, Buddy. I think Andrea's friend needs a haircut. You a fucking Apache or something? And what's with these scratches on your face? The boyfriend flare?" Behind me Buddy giggled.

I said, "I think this might be a bad time for you guys. I'll come back later."

Buddy jacked my arm higher. I made a strangled sound and they both laughed.

Torres said, "You better believe it's a bad time, nancyboy. But for you, not us. No doubt Andrea really mean *biznezz* don't she? Sending a skinny fruit like you to put the fear of God in Eduardo Torres."

"It was just a social call."

Torres said, "I got your social call, nancyboy. If Andrea Gale is involved I know it ain't no social call. And I'm insulted as hell she send a doofus like you."

He punched me in the stomach. I doubled over but Buddy made sure I didn't go down. Torres left hooked my jaw. Fourth of July fireworks blinded me.

I was vaguely aware a third punch was coming and I tried to maneuver my head through the colorful explosions out of its way. But Buddy had a fistful of my hair and he held me right there. The punch hit square on my left jaw.

I wobbled out of it for a bit. Felt like you do on a lethargic summer day after too much wine and things start to get fuzzy and then the brain decides to float off somewhere of its own accord. That's exactly how I felt. No pain, just a fuzzy, floating brain.

I heard Torres talking gibberish. I tasted salt, it was a second before it registered as blood. I tried to force some air in my lungs; the first punch had knocked all I had out.

Torres said, "You listenin' to me?"

I said, "You talkin' to me?" I remembered that line was in a movie, couldn't think of which one. Then I thought of Danny DeVito and laughed. I said, "You talkin' to *me?*"

He slapped me. Said, "I tole you to tell that fucking pantywaist Stone and his friend Andrea Gale they better forget about Eduardo Torres. Sábe?"

"Don't know no *fucking* pantywaist named Stone."

He slapped me hard twice. Again my brain floated around, between blackness and the orange tint of the room. I said, "Be honest with you, he don't have a good friend named Andrea Gale anymore." My voice sounded like I'd been sniffing laughing gas.

Torres said, "Dumbass." He sounded disgusted. He cocked his right arm. His fist looked bigger than a basketball.

I woke up slumped over the steering wheel of the Skylark. I freaked for a second, but Bugs was still in his cage, making nervous jerks and kicks, nose trembling like crazy. I said, "You must of scared 'em off, Bugs. Good work."

My face felt like it was made of cement. I adjusted the rear view mirror to get a look at myself. A very ugly man looked back. I had a nose like Jimmy Durante, a Hitler mustache of blood and an upper lip the size of an inflated inner tube. Splashes of red smeared my shirt and jacket.

I was still in the parking lot behind the Blue Palm. I had no desire to go back inside. I solemnly decided McCoy's advice had been sound after all.

I started the Skylark, headed for Chicago.

# SIX

Halfway home the numbness wore off and pain stomped in. Grew until it caused tears. I stopped at the Weiss Memorial ER for X-rays. Jaw wasn't broken, nose was. They packed my nostrils with gauze, put a plaster paris splint and butterfly bandage over the bridge. Prescribed Tylenol-3 painkillers.

I enjoy a codeine buzz now and again so I ate three every six hours not moving from the couch all day Sunday into the night. When asleep, I visited the grotesque, murky dreamworld codeine supplies, and when awake, tracked endlessly up and down the TV dial with my remote. That was a grotesque and murky world too; hard to tell where one ended and the other began. A lost day, but I've had plenty of those.

Monday morning I went to the office I share with Marvin Torkelson. Marvin sells insurance for Midwestern Insurance Group. Makes the kind of money I dream about, mostly by sitting on his butt typing renewal forms. Then once a week he drives around town, has people sign their names at the bottom. He rents me a corner of his office for seventy-five bucks a month.

Marvin and I met when we were thirteen and had everything in common. An awakening interest in girls, a fanatical love of the Rolling Stones, and a passion for *Mad* magazine and baseball, mine South Side, his North. In high school we were inseparable, but over the years something happened. I think it was Marvin grew up and I didn't. He rushed into the real world with a vengeance; I've kept it at arm's length my entire adult life. Now the only thing we have in common is that we've known each other over twenty-five years. Sometimes that's enough. Plus, although he'd never admit it,

Marvin considers me the black sheep kid brother he never had. Fate has decreed I am his cross to bear.

Marvin chuckled when he saw my face. He said, "Some plastic surgery over the weekend?" Another thing about Marvin: his sense of humor is greatly stimulated by the misfortune of others. Probably the *Mad* magazine influence.

The *Sun-Times* lay on my desk, open to page four. Above a photo of a slinky model posing in a short nightie for Marshall Field's, was a six paragraph story headlined POLICE GRILL SUSPECT IN JOHNSON CITY SLAYING. There was a picture of Andrea Gale. Natch. Marvin had circled the article with magic marker.

The story was an interview with McCoy. He said it was believed the murder was the result of a lover's quarrel caused by jealousy. There was a prime suspect already in custody. He couldn't release the suspect's name "at this time." The last sentence said, "The body was discovered Saturday afternoon by an unidentified private detective from Chicago."

I said, "Why do you assume I am this unidentified detective?"

"You make the papers once a year and you were due. When you walked in the door I knew I was right. Who worked you over this time?"

"Two cavemen with more muscles in their eyelids than I have in my entire body."

"It's always two."

"I know. Wish people'd realize they only need one to do a job on me."

"You oughta start liftin' iron."

"Nah, bein' this scrawny, they take pity on me. I get big and strong it'd just freak 'em out. Make 'em really wanna hurt me."

He said, "With that bandage on your schnoz you're just the man for a tail job. You'd be as inconspicuous as the San Diego Chicken at a City Council meeting."

I ignored him, reread the article. Felt twinges of disappointment. A boyfriend was the suspect. On Sunday, my favorite codeine-produced fantasy had been watching burly Johnson City detectives methodically rubber-hose a murder confession out of Eduardo Torres and Buddy Baker.

But those thoughts gradually faded. At eight-thirty, I was deep in the sports section when the phone rang. A man with a severe voice told me his name was Charles Dennison. He was a lawyer and he was calling from Johnson City, Illinois. He said, "I'm calling on behalf of my client, Mr. David Stone."

"Is Mr. David Stone a pantywaist?"

"Pardon?"

"Skip it."

"He's being held on a preliminary charge of murder for the death of Andrea Gale."

"Preliminary?"

"A county law. The police can hold a suspect for seventy-two hours while they build a case strong enough to bring formal murder charges. You are the PI Andrea Gale hired Friday night, am I right? The one who found the body?"

I grunted.

"Mr. Kruger, David Stone insists he is innocent and I for one believe him."

"You for one are being paid to believe him."

"His father has authorized me to hire you at your going rate to prove his innocence. Obviously the police here have their minds made up."

"They can make their minds up all day long, they still have to prove guilt in court."

"Prosecuting attorney claims they can."

I said, "This preliminary thing is probably a bluff to scare Stone into a confession so they can cut a deal. They'll chop the charges in half if he cops a guilty."

"He's not about to confess to something he didn't do. And bluff or not, we'd like you to look into this murder."

"Why me?"

"Maybe Miss Gale told you something when she hired you. Something that could be a lead to the perpetrator."

I smiled into the phone. I love lawyer lingo. I said, "You mean the bad guy?"

He didn't answer. Maybe he was blushing.

I said, "I talked to the woman two times for maybe ten minutes total. She told me nada."

"There's also the fact there are two private detectives out here, but neither will buck the police department. And you *have* been involved from the start."

I said, "I got a feeling I entered this thing a long way past the start. Saturday I was told Johnson City is not a town I want to visit again, let alone work in."

"Mr. Kruger, some people—make that some law officers—now and then suffer from delusions of grandeur. I know who you're referring to. You work for us, there's no trouble from that party. Guaranteed. You know, it's been seven, eight days of hell for David Stone. Last week two punks beat him up. Saturday his girlfriend was brutally murdered and today he's the main suspect for her murder."

Better him than me. I said, "Who beat him up?"

"Claims he never got a look at 'em."

"It a random beating?"

"He won't talk about it."

"I got a good idea who it was and I doubt it was random." I looked at the ceiling, made faces while I thought. I said, "You got a deal. I'll be out early afternoon." I set the phone in the cradle, pretty sure I was making a mistake. But McCoy had frosted me big time and a job is a job.

Four hours later, Charles Dennison, David Stone, and I were talking in a tiny basement cell in the Johnson City jail.

Both men were in their late twenties. David Stone was as tall and skinny as a giraffe's neck. He had hollow cheeks, a permanently curled upper lip, and an intense, arrogant stare. A stare that told you right off he considered himself your intellectual superior. His brown hair was tied back in a short, fashionably hip ponytail. He wore faded blue jeans and a black sweatshirt. Under still slightly puffy eyes were smears of black and blue and yellow.

It didn't take me long to dislike the man intensely.

He said again, "Hey guy, I admit I was there, okay? So fucking what? I admit we had a fight, but she was alive when I left."

"You hit her during the fight?"

"No. Well, I might of pushed her around a little."

"A little?"

"Okay, I pushed her around a lot. That woman could *piss* you off, man."

"What do the cops have on you?"

Dennison said quickly, "Everything's circumstantial. He was there Saturday morning. You heard him admit it. A neighbor lady coming down the hall carrying groceries saw David slam Andrea Gale's apartment door shut and then run towards her. Claims David pushed her out of his way, causing her to fall to the floor, scattering the groceries on the floor. Says he didn't stop to apologize or help. Just kept going. Police say that's because he was fleeing the scene of the crime—"

Stone interrupted, "It's because I was pissed off. I never even noticed this old bitch and her groceries."

I said, "What's the neighbor's name?"

Dennison said, "Cleopatra Bell."

"Cleopatra?"

"Fifty-one years old," he continued deadpan. "Widowed. Lives in 103, the adjoining unit."

Dennison was the perfect prep. Earnest eyes in a boyish face, full head of expensively cut wavy brown hair, Bullock and Jones striped shirt, glen plaid slacks with suspenders, designer slip-on tasseled loafers. I can never figure out if I feel contempt or envy for these guys.

I said, "You lock the door when you left?"

Stone said, "I didn't lock or unlock it. Andrea opened the door when I got there and I closed it when I left."

"What'd you and Andrea argue about?"

"Things."

Dennison said, "He told the police it was over money and a difference of opinion on the status of the relationship."

I said, "She wanted to dump you?"

"Fuck you."

I said, "Why'd you get worked over?"

"Why'd you?" Elvis would've admired this guy's sneer.

"Who did it?"

"Laurel and Hardy."

"PI's supposed to be the smart aleck, not the client. You're the one sittin' in jail. You wanna get out, answer some questions."

"Maybe that question don't pertain to why I'm in jail."

"Maybe it does."

He lit a fresh Lucky with the butt of his previous one. He said, "Honestly, I don't know who it was."

"I always get leery when people start prefacing sentences with 'honestly.' These men say why they beat you up? Kicks? Practice? Didn't like the cut of your jib? What?"

Dennison said quietly, "David, Mr. Kruger is on our side."

Stone smoked the Lucky and stared into space for a bit. "They said it was a message to keep away from Andrea. I was supposed to forget she existed. They didn't say who the message was from. Knowing Andrea it could of been from any male who can get his dick hard and had an extra twenty bucks in his pocket."

"Could it of been from Andrea herself?"

"What do you mean?"

"I mean was she trying to break it off and you weren't liking it."

Stone said, "I don't know what was going on with us. With that bitch anything was possible."

Dennison cleared his throat, murmured, "Now, David." He laughed lamely like Stone was making a big joke. Defense lawyers don't appreciate the accused making embittered statements about the alleged victim to strangers. Even if the stranger is on their side.

I said, "A four-foot-tall, three-foot-wide Latino and a mountain-sized moron looks like Curly of the Three Stooges. Both got muscles like iron plate."

Stone glanced at Dennison, then at the floor. Said, "How'd you know?"

"I'm a detective, remember?"

Stone said, "Yeah, Torres and Baker."

Dennison said, "Dammit, David, why didn't you provide this information to the police? It would appear someone else—oops."

I said, "Yeah, oops. He didn't provide it because sooner or later the police'd ask the same question I just did: Would Andrea have hired the two bozos? If she had—"

Dennison nodded and finished. "And David found out, it

would've given him one more reason to fly in a rage and kill her."

I said, "I knew because right before Torres punched my lights out he mentioned your name. You're positive they never said who the message was from?"

"Positive."

"I'm positive too. Positive you're a liar."

There were more seconds of sullen silence, then he blurted, "Honest to God, they never said. But there's two men I suspect. Headon and Wylie. They've both been sniffing around Andrea. Feeble pervs wanting to get into some young panty. Why can't old people accept their age? You know Lisa Farrell?"

"Who she is."

"Lisa can tell you about 'em. I don't know much."

"Then why suspect 'em?"

"I heard their names a lot lately."

"Doesn't mean they were sniffing. They could be friends of the family."

Stone snorted like a horse.

I said, "Were you and Andrea Gale still a couple?"

"One time we were. Lately, I don't know. I was starting to find out I didn't know her very well at all. But I know I didn't kill her."

# SEVEN

An hour later, Cleopatra Bell and I sat side by side in the curve of a five-piece black leather sofa. A can of Pepsi sat on a cork coaster on a glass coffee table in front of me. To my left the widow Bell sipped gin and tonic from a glass the size of a milk bottle. It was only two o'clock but she was good and toasted. Just the way I like people when I wanna talk.

She wore black stretch pants, a white silk blouse with a plunging neckline, lots of gold jewelry, fire red lipstick and gallons of face and eye gunk. She patted Roy Orbison black hair, then fingered a gold and ruby necklace hanging between lumpy cleavage. Said, "Lord, yes, they fought all the time. She was such a tramp you know. Both of them. The pudgy brunette too. The walls here are thin. I could follow entire conversations."

I pictured Cleo Bell spending hours with empty glass at ear, full glass in hand leaning against the living room wall. I said, "You heard the fight Saturday morning?"

"No." She sounded sorry. "I was at the store. The Jewel on Thurston?" She grinned a sloppy grin and hiccuped sour liquor fumes in my face.

He right hand skimmed my knee, came to rest. I removed it discreetly. She giggled, said, "Whatever happened to your face, Mr. Kooger."

"Kruger."

"That's right, Kruger."

"It's not a pretty story. Let's skip it."

"You in a fight?"

"Kinda."

"You don't look too good."

"You should see the other guy."

She made the ditz grin again. She'd never heard the line. She screwed up her face like maybe I was flirting.

I said, "When Stone came at you in the hallway, was he actually running?"

"Well, trotting like. Walking very fast."

"And he said nothing."

"No."

"What kind of look was on his face? He look mad, scared, anxious, jubilant—what?"

"I couldn't say. The hallway is dark and everything happened so fast. I turned the corner from the entryway. I heard the door slam at the end of the hall and saw this impossibly tall person bearing down on me. I knew who it was right away. I tried to move aside, but all of a sudden I was on the floor with groceries all around me, cans rolling, bottles spinning. He never even stopped. He said, 'Dammit,' when we collided and that was all." She sounded angry at the end, but then the boozy grin snuck back. "You wouldn't do a thing like that, would you Mr. Kruger?"

"I ever knock you flat when you're carrying groceries you have my word I'll help you pick them up. Why'd you call Andrea Gale a tramp?"

She looked confused. "Well, because she had so many men." She spread her arms wide. "All ages from teenagers to grandfathers. Both of 'em did. I never knew their names. The men, I mean. Sometimes last summer, I'd step out on the balcony in the evening and Andrea or Lisa'd be sitting out there with one of the men. They'd say 'Hi,' but they'd never introduce—" She hooted a laugh, then clamped her hand over her mouth like something just occurred to her.

"What's the joke?"

"I believe they were afraid of the competition. You know, from a mature woman."

"I don't blame them."

She beamed and said, "Andrea did introduce one man to me. Oh, last fall, I believe it was. A very distinguished-looking gentleman."

"What was his name?"

"I don't remember the name. I saw him around here several times after that. He was *very* friendly to me. They had a real yeller once too. Right in the hallway."

"What about?"

"I imagine he strongly disapproved of the life she led."

Her hand rested on my knee again. I used the movement of lighting a new Kool and adjusting the ashtray on the table to slide away. I glanced at her. Watched her sway back and forth. I said, "Did you see her with other men after she started seeing David Stone?"

"Lord, yes. The men never stopped, honey. Like I said, older men, younger men, men in between. How do you think two young girls were able to live in an apartment complex like this? Don't get me wrong, this is not the most elegant place I've ever lived, but it's not cheap and it's nicer than most kids can afford. And the new sports cars they both drove? I mean, Andrea used to." She suddenly spread her arms wide again, sloshing gin on the couch. "Men, that's how." She burped loudly.

"That's how what?"

"How they could afford to live here."

"They received money from these men?"

"Of course." She leaned forward, pointed her finger at the coffee table and whispered without looking at me, "Mr. Kooger, some things you just—*perceive* are going on."

"You're not actually accusing them of prostitution?"

"Well—" She hiccuped. "If I found out that was true I would not be shocked."

"Tell me everything you know about David Stone."

"I don't know anything about David Stone. I didn't even know his name until the police talked to me Saturday afternoon. I called him Ponytail. I had nicknames for all of 'em. I saw him with the Farrell girl early on. Then one day in the hall, he was hand in hand with Andrea Gale and after that I saw those two together a lot. Must of got tired of the one, decided to take up with the other." She teetered forward then snapped herself erect. Then she whispered as I held my breath. "Andrea was much the better looking of the two. A tramp, but such a beautiful girl." She fumbled with a crinkled cigarette pack. When she got one out, I lit her up so she wouldn't start her face on fire. She said, "Where was I?"

"David Stone ditched the brunette for the blonde."

"Oh, him. Of all their men, I believed him to be the absolute bottom of the barrel. I never understood what either one saw in him. He's not attractive. He has that ponytail and he's so skinny. Was *very* sullen if you encountered him in the hallway or the parking lot. You'd say something to him and he'd walk past you like you weren't even there. Acted like he was some sort of superior being. Looking at him I couldn't understand what he thought he had the rest of us don't. The girls had some very attractive men visiting them. Pretty young girls can make older men jump through hoops. I remember when I was nineteen—"

"Ever listen to a fight when you knew it was Andrea Gale and David Stone?"

"Sure." She fidgeted with the top button on her blouse. It popped loose from the buttonhole. She looked down at it, giggled, looked at me and said, "Oops."

"What was said when they fought?"

She pretended to be embarrassed. "Swear words." She lowered her voice. "So many swear words. I wouldn't repeat what they said, but it was Ef this, ef that, motheref. She swore worse than he did. He'd call her a whore. She'd tell him what she did was her own business, he didn't like it, he could shove it. They'd go back and forth like that."

"Ever hear blows being struck? Punches, slapping, screaming?"

"Oh, sure. And she threw stuff. You could hear things breaking against the wall."

I said, "You seen Lisa Farrell since the murder?"

"Little while ago. I heard someone entering 101. I thought it was the police again so I peeked out to see if they needed to talk to me, but it was Lisa. I asked her was she okay. She's fine, but she's moving of course. Who could live in a place after that? She said she came for her clothes and things."

I thanked Cleo Bell for the talk. She said, "But you could stay and have another Pepsi, or even better, join me for a gin and tonic." Her glass was tilted forward between her knees. There was no liquid left in it.

I said, "I'll come back another time," and stood.

The glass slipped free and bounced on the carpet. I bent to pick it up.

Cleo Bell blindsided me like Dick Butkus putting a lick on a Green Bay Packer. The coffee table provided brief resistance and then it toppled over and we were on the floor. Me on my back, her straddling me like I needed mouth to mouth. She whispered, "Don't leave yet." I pushed her partially off, we rolled on the carpet like puppies in slow motion. She grew three more pairs of hands, made little moans and sighs. She said, "Those girls had too many men." Her wandering hands brushed my nose. Felt like a boxer's fist. I shouted in pain and that startled her. She stopped for a second and I was able to push myself away.

I stood, straightened my clothes. She sat on the floor, legs slightly spread in front of her. All the buttons on her blouse were undone and a white push-up bra peeped out. She looked coyly up at me from under a ledge of disheveled hair.

Like nothing had happened I said, "I'll see myself out,

Mrs. Bell. Thanks again."

She put a lock of hair in her mouth and chewed it. Then she belched loudly and started to giggle.

# EIGHT

I stood outside 101 for almost a minute before I knocked. I was reasonably sure I wouldn't get the same response as Saturday, but you never know.

When the door opened, I said, "Hi, Lisa." She looked at me warily. Her hair was pulled back off her face in a single braid. Her face was devoid of makeup. She looked very young and very vulnerable. She had on a snug black T-shirt and tight fitting stone-washed jeans. "Let's talk?"

She said, "If you want," and led me into the living room. I'd been in the room two days ago, but I didn't recognize anything in it except for the sofa I sat on. It took me a bit to cop to the fact that Andrea's body had been such a focal point of my attention that I couldn't have described one other object in this room after I left Saturday afternoon.

Lisa pulled a brown kitchen chair across the carpet and sat in front of me.

I said, "Police move fast out here. In Chicago, this apartment'd be locked up for a week with the police tape on the door."

"They told me this morning they were pretty much done. They had all weekend."

"I hear you're moving."

"Wouldn't you?"

"Suppose so. Where'd you stay the last two nights?"

"That's kind of a personal question, isn't it?"

"You don't have to answer it."

"It's no big deal. With my parents. Ever heard of Oswego?"

"No."

"It's a small town about forty-five minutes from here."
She pointed in the direction of the bedrooms. "I brought
two suitcases. I'm getting my clothes today." Her voice
trailed off a bit. "I'll get the other stuff later."

"You moving in with your parents?"

"No way."

"Couldn't handle that?"

She shrugged. "If I had to maybe I could. But I don't. My
father found me an apartment here in Johnson City. I'm
moving in this week. I took the week off to get everything
arranged. Get my head straight and move and stuff."

"Can you talk about Saturday morning?"

She looked down, picked at her fingernails. "David killed
her, didn't he? What's to talk about?"

"David says he didn't kill her."

"What else would he say?"

"He says I should ask you about two men. One named
Headon, one named Wylie. Stone suspects they were
involved with Andrea in some way."

Lisa rolled her eyes and turned her head to look out the
patio window. She said, almost under her breath, "God,
David Stone is such an arrogant, possessive, paranoid jerk."

"Seems to be the consensus."

Still looking away, Lisa said, "Ronald Headon owns the
factory where Andrea and I work. I mean, worked—well, I
still do."

"Past tense takes a while."

"He came on to Andrea real heavy a couple of times, but
he comes on to every female in the building who's under
fifty years and under two hundred pounds. You can imagine
what he was like around her. Still he's harmless. It's not like
you lose your job if you refuse him."

"Andrea refused him?"

"Yeah."

"You refused him?"

She curled her lip. Said, "Yeah."

"Does everybody refuse him?"

"I wouldn't know, but it's almost like a game. He does it
like he's half kidding so if he gets turned down it's no big
deal. Hardly anybody takes him seriously. I don't

understand why David would point a finger at him of all people. I mean, he knew we worked at Headon Engineering, and Ronald Headon is a big name in this town, but why would he suspect Headon and Andrea had a thing going?"

"Maybe she told him Headon was coming on to her. He says he heard the name a lot."

"What's that supposed to mean?"

"It might mean she was thinking of Headon all the time. You know how it is when you're attracted to somebody. The person dominates your thoughts, you seize any opportunity to talk about 'em. She never said anything to you about Headon?"

"Never."

"Ronald Headon never visited here?"

"Of course not."

I said, "Then I don't understand either. What about Wylie?"

"Wylie I never heard of. Or I don't remember, which means he couldn't of been too close to Andrea."

I said, "You know a bar called the Blue Palm?"

"I know where it is. I've never been in it."

"You know Buddy Baker or Eduardo Torres?"

"Baker, no. I think there was an Eddie Torres who wanted to go out with Andrea a long time ago."

"That right? Very short, very wide tough guy? Lots of muscles?"

"I don't remember how he looked. Just the name and that's vague. I could be wrong, it could of been a name close to that. There were a lot of men in Andrea's life and like I said, it was a long time ago."

I said, "Stone contends either this Wylie or Headon paid Torres and Baker to work him over last week. Purpose of the beating was to tell Stone to stay away from Andrea. I didn't know about this until today. Saturday, before you showed, I saw the Blue Palm and Torres' and Baker's names on a piece of paper in Andrea's bedroom. I went downtown to visit the boys, wanting to learn if or how they connected. They're connected all right." I pointed at my face. "They were waiting for somebody to show up. I'm thinking Andrea hired me to intimidate these guys. Like pull a gun on 'em or something."

"Would you of?"

"I don't even own a gun. And I don't hire for that kind of work for obvious reasons, but I guess PI's from Chicago have a certain rep."

"You mean like sleazy?"

"Sleazy seems a little extreme, but yeah, along those lines. Would Andrea have done something like that? Hire somebody to go after the goons who beat up Stone?"

Lisa didn't answer right away. She looked out the window, chewing her lower lip. Then she said, "Well, she did care for David. As much as she could care for any man. If he told her he'd been beat up to make him stay away from her, she might of got mad and wanted to take care of it."

"I heard she saw other men while she was going out with David."

"Sure, she saw other men, but they didn't matter to her. David couldn't understand that."

"Behavior like that's hard for most men to understand."

"Yeah, I know all about the 'you are *my* woman' bit. I mean, she cared for David, cared a lot, but she knew he'd never be able to give her anything. And boy, did she like things. So she saw him because she wanted to and she saw the other men because she needed to. She knew the way she felt about David would subside sooner or later. She'd been through it before."

"Sounds like Andrea didn't subscribe to the theory of one man for a lifetime."

"Hardly."

"Do you?"

"Get real."

I said, "Let's look at it from another angle. Would Andrea have hired Torres and Baker to beat Stone up? I mean if she wanted to break things off and he couldn't let go?"

"Of course not."

"Stone thinks it's possible."

"Maybe things between them were worse than I thought."

"How bad did you think things were?"

Lisa shrugged. "They fought a lot."

I said, "Were you and Andrea close friends or she just a roommate?"

"We knew each other since kindergarten. We were close, but we were closer when we were like in junior high and high school back in Oswego. Spent all our time together then, on the phone every night."

"Why'd you leave Oswego for Johnson City?"

She stared at a spot over my head. "I don't know. We were bored living in a small town, but Chicago's too big. Johnson City is like somewhere in between. It was Andrea's idea."

"What was Andrea like?"

Lisa's eyes met mine, then moved quickly to look out the window again. She shook her head slightly like she was thinking about something that had puzzled her for a long time. She said, "Andrea was very—superficial. That's the best word I can think of. She was so beautiful it spoiled her, made her arrogant sometimes. Not all the time, but some. Because of her looks everybody treated her different—even me. I think she got used to that. Started to rely on it to get her way. It almost always worked. She was dumb about book things. In high school I did most every research project she had assigned. She was smart about other things. Like how to use men, string 'em along till she extracted every last penny she could get." Lisa shook her head with amazement. "She was like a buzzsaw with men. She was so beautiful they'd change their entire life-style, some of 'em, to keep her. Specially the old boys. They loved being seen in public with Andrea. Show her off at restaurants and the club, you know?"

"Like she was a trophy."

"Exactly. Anyway, all this eventually caused her to act like she was supposed to be the center of attention everywhere she went. She came to accept it, like it was owed to her. Did David tell you he and I were a couple first?"

"Mrs. Bell did."

She made a dry laugh. "She would. Andrea and I called her Ma Bell because she spread rumors so fast, she was like a human telephone. Every time you saw her she'd have all these stories to tell about the other people who live here."

"She's a very lonely lady."

"She's very something. First time I brought David here and he got a load of Andrea I knew it was all over for this kid. I could see that look on his face—the desire in the eyes? About two weeks later, I came home from work on a Saturday morning and found them on the floor in the hallway. They were half undressed screwing right on the floor. D'you believe that?"

"What'd you do?"

"I refused to let either of them know it hurt. They started fumbling around, grabbing for clothes. I said, 'Thank God I finally got a reason to dump him.' I stepped over them and went to my room. Didn't even slam the door. They both apologized later. Said it just *happened* and they promised each other they were going to tell me."

"The old 'it just happened' excuse. I love that one."

Lisa made a bleak smile.

"But you stayed friends?"

"Yeah. That wasn't the first time. I mean, that was the most shocking, but other boyfriends of mine ended up chasing her."

"It didn't bother you?"

"Sometimes it did a little, but not a lot. We were friends such a long time and none of the men meant much to me. If any of 'em had it might of been different. Besides, it wasn't her fault. Each time the man initiated things. Why blame her because men are jerks."

"She couldn't say no?"

"Andrea viewed romance like she was a lioness and every man was wild prey. She loved the chase and all the little games that went with it. When that part was over she usually lost interest in the man and got practical, started to extract the money. She just couldn't resist the hunt part. But this was one time the joke was on her. I think she really fell for David."

"Why? It doesn't appear the man has a whole lot going for him."

"He's got brains. Least enough he can fake being an intellectual. Andrea was a sucker for brainy men. These model handsome jocks and the sleek rich men with their chains and

Porsches fawned all over her, but the three or four times she fell hard for somebody it was the brainy, nerd types. And one of 'em killed her."

"*Maybe* killed her. What's David Stone do for a living?"

"He claims he's a student at West Central College here in town. He pushes a little 'caine, does tutoring. He lives with his parents and they've got some money."

"Sounds like he'd of needed more than some if he was planning to keep Andrea."

"He was starting to find that out."

I stared at the floor, thinking. I knew there were other things to ask but the questions weren't coming. I said, "I'd like to talk to Ronald Headon."

Lisa stood and walked to the sliding glass window. Looking out, her back to me, she said in a barely audible voice, "So talk to him. It's not like you need my permission."

"Where's he live? Where's his factory?"

"Headon Engineering is on Fifth Avenue, in an industrial park the other side of town right before you hit the cornfields. I don't know where he lives."

"This place big?"

"Pretty big. They've automated a lot of jobs lately so there's not as many people as there used to be, but it's a big place."

The Saturday thing had hung over the entire conversation, making the talk awkward and strained. Seemed we were both afraid to bring it up, but I couldn't leave without saying something. I stood, said, "Listen, Lisa. Before I go I wanna apologize about Saturday—"

She turned around, put her hand out, said, "Forget it. I wanted to say something too. I wanna forget everything that happened Saturday. Let's pretend we just met thirty minutes ago when you knocked on the door."

We shook hands, both of us smiling a little. After a second she smiled wide and that made her very pretty. I had the feeling we were going to get along fine.

# NINE

Headon Engineering consisted of four enormous concrete and steel buildings connected with covered walkways. The buildings and the rolling picnic-tabled lawns and the parking lot at the south end took up three or four city blocks of space.

A steel-mesh fence ran around the whole thing. At the gate to the parking lot, I told my name to a turkey-necked senior citizen in a blue and gold security uniform. It took him forever to write it on his legal pad. He staggered to the front of the Skylark and wrote down my license plate number maybe in case the name I gave was a phony. As he did I leaned out and said, "What if I stole the car?" He ignored me.

Another ancient guard stopped me just inside the employees' entrance. He sat behind a desk with a big sign taped to it that said, ALL NON-EMPLOYEES *MUST* STOP HERE. He took longer than forever to write my name on another legal pad. Asked who I came to see and why. He stood up. I was hoping he'd say walk this way so I could do my old coot walk but he only said "Follow me," so I did. We went down a series of short halls, through one of the glass-enclosed building connectors, down some more halls. Ended up in an enormous blue-carpeted office full of desks and file cabinets and computer terminals and preppy-dressed men and women. The old boy pointed toward the front of the room and said, "Mr. Headon's office is behind that wooden door. One that says Mr. Headon, President."

I said, "Now there's a novel idea."

But of course Mr. Headon, President, had a secretary to get by first. Good thing I'm a determined detective. Miss Clara Tannehill had her own office and seemed proud of that even if her office was the size of a baby's closet. The woman was in her forties, skinny as a swizzle stick, with a long, thin face and limp brown-gray hair that hung like dying weeds. Bifocals straddled a very pointed nose. She wore a severe tan dress that matched her frown. I doubted if Headon came on to this one, but then you always need someone to get the work done.

Miss Tannehill asked my name and why was I here. I told her. She said, "You don't have an appointment."

I admitted that was true.

"You're not with the Johnson City police?"

True, too.

"Mr. Headon is a very busy man. He doesn't see people he doesn't know." She said "Mr. Headon" the way Jerry Falwell says "God." Her cheeks flushed and her eyes glowed.

I said, "All I need is ten minutes. And I'm sure he'd like to hear what it is I have to tell him."

"I'm afraid it's impossible."

I decided to warm her up by appealing to her pride of company. I said, "Headon Engineering is much larger than I anticipated. What're your main products?"

She said quickly, "We manufacture engines of all types, all sizes, engine related components, and power systems. Here." She reached into her desk and tossed a small pamphlet at me. "You read this you'll learn all about us. Now if you'll excuse me, I have work to do." She lifted a plastic tub full of rubber-banded packets of mail up from the floor to her desk, started to slit envelopes with a long metal opener.

I said, "I got all day," and sat in the only other chair in her office. Took out my fingernail clippers, started to manicure my nails. Clara Tannehill continued slicing envelopes, sneaking a peek at me every twenty seconds. I showed her my suavest smile each time.

After a few minutes, she erupted off the chair with a noisy sigh and punched open a wooden door to the right of her desk. A minute later, she stormed back. In poorly suppressed fury, she said, "Mr. Headon can spare five minutes. That's five." She smiled like she'd put one over on me by splitting my request in half.

"You mean like one less than six, right?"

Headon's office was dark wood walls, bucolic landscape paintings, and royal blue carpet so plush my shoes disappeared as I walked. He sat in an overstuffed executive chair behind a huge rosewood desk with leather inlay on top. A blown-up aerial photo of the Headon Engineering complex hung on the wall behind him.

He wanted to establish the pecking order immediately. Some men need to. I stood on the other side of the desk for a minute as unnoticed as yesterday's news while he worked through a stack of forms. He skimmed each paper, made a large X at the bottom, then placed the form on a second pile.

Like his secretary, Headon was long and lean. He had gray hair cropped short and a pink-cheeked baby face. He looked years younger than the early fifties Lisa had told me he was. The knot of his maroon tie hung away from his collar and his white sleeves were rolled halfway to the elbow. As he worked he made little squirms and jerks in the chair, like some kind of power source inside him was set on super high.

After a minute went by, I started to cop an attitude. Like most nobodies I resent arrogance and detest power plays. Besides, he'd just wasted twenty percent of my allotted time. I said, "An 'X', Headon? You should at least learn to write your own name. Can't conceal illiteracy forever."

He glanced up, eyes wide, pretending to just notice I stood there. He looked down at the papers, then at me. Said briskly, "Ah, a joke. Yes, very funny. The 'X' means it's been approved by me. Purchase orders, you know. Your name is?"

"Dan Kruger."

"Yes, right, Miss Tannehill said that. And you are?"

"A detective. Private."

"Right, right. You know, you don't look like a detective."

"Thank God for that. It's funny, you don't look like the kind of man who can't keep his hands off the female employees."

Headon's eyes narrowed. He leaned back in the chair, placed the eraser end of the pencil against his mouth, gave me a long mean look. Said, icily, "I'm not sure I understand what you just said."

"I didn't stutter. I used English."

"Miss Tannehill said you were here to speak about the

Andrea Gale matter. Mr. Kruger, I knew Andrea by sight.
She worked here for two years I believe. Her murder was a
shock and like the other employees I was deeply saddened.
Someone that pretty, that young. Her whole life ahead of
her." He leaned forward, put his elbows on the desk and
shook his head.

I said, "Oh, the humanity."

He reddened. Said, "That's what I know about Andrea
Gale and that's what I told the Johnson City police."

"I heard you might be a little sadder than some of the
other employees."

The pencil started to make a brisk bouncing on the desk.
"What do you mean? Listen you, the *real* police talked to
me and asked two or three general questions. I told them I
could hardly be expected to keep track of all my employees.
They saw the logic in that. They made no insinuations.
Where do you get off making a statement like that?"

"Because I have a fresh angle the *real* police don't know
about. Yet."

"Fresh angle? I was told there is a prime suspect, I was
told that suspect is already in custody, and I was told on the
QT who that suspect is."

"The suspect suspects someone else."

"Meaning?"

"The names Eduardo Torres and Buddy Baker ring a
bell?"

"They work here too? Am I expected to know the names
of over five hundred people?"

"They work for you but they don't work here."

"Dammit, Kruger, quit dancing around this thing and put
your cards on the table. I don't wish to be rude, but I've got
an important marketing meeting in fifteen minutes. I don't
have time to listen to riddles."

"Of course you wish to be rude. Men like you wouldn't
feel manly if they weren't rude to men like me." I kneaded
my eyebrows. This was not going well at all.

The pencil tapping stopped and I received what I assumed
was Headon's best glare. He said slowly, "Like I told you,
the real police talked to me at my home yesterday after they
learned Andrea Gale worked here. I presume they talked to

her co-workers and her supervisors. I was asked three rou-
tine questions. How long had she worked here? Did I know
her? Had I heard any rumors concerning her? I answered
their questions. I said, ask Miss Tannehill, no, and no. They
were satisfied and they left." He rose up off his chair a little,
leaned toward me. Said, "You're not the real police." He
pointed the pencil and raised his voice. "So fuck off!" He sat
back, smiling a little. He *loved* acting manly.

I said, "Then why does David Stone suspect you were
fooling around with her? Why does he suspect you hired two
goons to beat him up, warn him to stay away from Andrea?
He pick your name out of a hat?"

"This is getting to the point where you and David Stone
may end up in court, Kruger. If you repeat that story outside this room, I guarantee that's where you'll be. A panicky
kid, about to be arrested for murder, throws out something
like this from desperation and you fall for it like it's gospel."

"When people pay me, I check out what they want
checked out."

"So you're working for that slimeball? Okay, listen you. I
think I've bent over backward here. This is my factory. You
show up without an appointment, upset my secretary, stroll
into *my* office and proceed to make the foulest, the basest
insinuations."

I said, "I'm so ashamed."

Headon pressed a button and leaned toward a small box
on his desk. Said, "Miss Tannehill, call the police." A fuzzy,
"Yes, sir," emanated from the box.

"They coming for me?"

"They are."

"What's the crime? Casting foul, base insinuations?"

"No, that's for when I call my lawyer. I'm going to have
you thrown out."

"You got security guards."

"You've penetrated the security guard's area, I want the
police."

I said, "I never penetrated a security guard's area in my
life."

Headon said, "I'm not without influence in this town,
Kruger. Police'll be here directly. Count on it."

I said, "I heard you crave young girls, Ron."

He pointed the pencil at me and jabbed it several times like it was a TV remote control and maybe, just maybe, he could click me away. His pink cheeks turned to a bright, waxy red. He said, "I've been happily married for close to thirty years. You slimeball you. Who the hell are you? From under what rock did you crawl? Huh? What rock? I never met you before in my life, yet you barge into my office and do nothing but insult me. Get out of here *now!*" His eyes narrowed into what *had* to be his best glare. If he had a better one he could crack safes.

I said, "My, my, my."

But I left. I blew Clara a kiss on my way through her office, said, "He said to tell you he feels a little randy. Wants you should go right in." She did her best to ignore me.

I was angry at myself. I'd botched an entire interrogation because I let myself get ticked off over nothing. The schmuck wanted to play a power game up front and I had to cop an attitude. Things regressed from there and I ended up with a large, uncooperating enemy and no answers.

And Headon's reactions bothered me. He hadn't acted evasive or guilty or nervous about anything I said. Just mad.

I headed for the Johnson City cop shop. I needed to talk to David Stone some more. I wanted to know more about why he'd fingered Headon and this Wylie, whoever he was. I had a feeling I was climbing the wrong tree and I hated to climb the wrong tree in a strange town. Especially a wrong tree with a very rich man sitting on the top branch.

I parked a couple hundred feet south of the police building in front of a hardware store. In a vacant lot across the street, kids were playing softball, mudcaked from shoes to knees. Having a blast.

As I got out of the Skylark, a loud voice called my name from the direction of the station. It was McCoy.

He walked toward me. As he got closer, he said, "Can't you get along with anyone, Kruger?"

"I love my fellow man. Not my fault if they don't love back."

I walked to the rear bumper of the Skylark and waited for

him. When he got to me, he said, "I got a call couple minutes ago said you were harassing one of our most important citizens. As a consequence, Ronald Headon don't like you much. Lisa Farrell don't like you 'cause you scared the living shit out of her. I'm not too sure Dennison and Stone like you even if they did hire you. They got some serious reservations. I know I don't like you." He made a fist, then extended each finger one at a time. Said, "Lessee, Headon, Farrell, Stone, Dennison, me. That's just about everybody you met out here, ain't it?"

"Lisa Farrell likes me fine now."

He paused, chewed the inside of his mouth a bit. Said, "Look at your face."

"A thing I do as little as possible."

"I believe it. I just left a message with some guy name of Torkelson at your office. Sure didn't think you'd be stopping by here. Why didn't you tell me about you and Torres? Why do I find that out from the bleeding heart lawyer in there?"

"It was no biggie. He took offense at something I said."

"What'd you say?"

"I said you were a hell of a cop."

McCoy rubbed the bridge of his nose. I looked at the kids. They'd stopped playing ball and were watching us.

He said, "Well, don't tell the police anything, hot shot. Make yourself look even more guilty when Torres turns up dead with a knife handle sticking out his ribs."

My stomach took a long shivery dive. I said, "I'd never use a knife on a guy with muscles like iron."

"Thing is an hour ago I hear two guys got beat up by Eduardo Torres lately. Neither said diddly to the police. One was in custody last night, one wasn't. Last night Torres got dead."

"I was home."

"Of course you were."

"I imagine a man like Torres had made a couple more enemies than me and Stone."

"Oh sure, but you gotta admit that looks funny, right?" He gave me his croc smile. "Suspicious? We find you wandering around a murder scene. When you leave there, you go to a bar for no reason I can think of and get worked over. You don't tell a soul about it. Forty-odd hours later we find the man who did the workover dead. It's only a dead beaner, true. And a bad beaner at that, but still—looks kinda fishy."

"I was home. All night. Alone."

"Why did I know you'd say that? Come on inside so we can talk."

# TEN

McCoy led me into the building, then up a flight of stairs to a windowless, fluorescent-bright interrogation room on the second floor. The room had gray walls, a metal desk, a black swivel chair, and two wooden folding chairs. He told me to sit in one of the wooden chairs. He left, came back with an immense black lieutenant named Snow who carried himself like an African prince. He stood straight as a pole, crossed his arms and gave me his best badass stare for fifteen seconds, his eyes saying what the hell kind of junk we have here? Typical cop intimidation ploy. I never did it much when I was fuzz because I always started laughing, but most cops are macho enough they think strong men weep when they lay the laser stare on 'em. I smiled and winked.

Snow sat in the swivel chair, dismissed McCoy with a wave of his hand. He said in the basest of bass voices, "Tell me about your visit to the Blue Palm Saturday."

I told him. Most of it anyway. When I finished, Snow said, "Nobody here is broken up over this guy checkin' out, hear what I'm sayin'? After I listen to this, I suspect you aren't either."

"I always grieve when the good die young."

"McCoy suggested you for a suspect after we learned about your trip to the bar. But I think he was just throwing out theories. Baker's too obvious. I called Chicago. Your rating isn't A-1, my man, but the people I talked to said you'd never kill a man even in revenge. They *did* say you're a walking pharmacy and any given time I could shake you down for possession." He smiled. "You clean right now?"

I made a quick mental checklist. No pot, the Valium I have a scrip for. But I had five whites wrapped in tin foil in my wallet. God, I'd hate to go to jail for five lousy whites. I said, "I'm clean as Prince Charming."

"You're a bigger liar than Pinocchio, but not to worry. I got the whole history. I'll give a pass to any white Chicago cop who freaks out so bad over winging a black kid he has to quit the force. Some of those guys in there'd put a notch on their gun. I know, I worked in that city ten years before I came out here."

I said, "Understand, I'm not into any hard stuff. A pill now and then, the occasional joint. Booze, that's my biggest problem. I been on the wagon almost a month."

He said, "Booze is always the biggest problem, but nobody wants to know. I remember back in Nam. You there?"

"No."

"The generals shipped narcs over and put 'em in uniform to stop the enlisted men from smokin' pot. Poor grunts just wanted to get the hell out of the war for a few hours so they puffed a little grass. They got the stockade for that, but the very same officers issued us amphetamines before we hit the field. To keep us alert and provide that extra energy." He grinned. "Man, the dopers thought they'd died and gone to heaven. Free speed, courtesy of the U.S. Marines. And this stuff was heavy. Brown and clear Dexies. I'm sure you remember brown and clear Dexies. Two or three caps of that shit keep you humming for a week." Snow grinned again. "Man, there was some wired motherfuckers over there. Personally, I prefer scotch and soda, but to each his own. McCoy give you a hard time?"

"McCoy don't like me."

"McCoy don't like nobody. Don't take it personal."

"He gets this sour look on his face everytime he sees me."

Snow said, "I think he's got problems with his feet. Corns and such. He always has a look on his face like his feet hurt."

"Could be he's constipated. It's the same look people in those ads for Ex-Lax have before the chemicals unplug 'em."

Snow galloped thick brown fingers on the desk. He said, "Okay, here's how it is. As of now, Baker is our man. He was the only other person in the Blue Palm when we found Torres. Torres was in that little basement office where you went. Naked on the couch. Severe trauma to the back of the head, a blade in his chest. Clothes in a pile on the desk. Baker was passed out on the floor under the front window. The scuzzbag blew a thirty-five on the breathalyzer and this was at nine-thirty, so he must of been big time ripped around 3:00 or 4:00 A.M. I'd hate to see how much booze a monster that size'd have to drink to blow a thirty-five four hours after he stopped drinking."

"Who called the police?"

"Anonymous tip. Wasn't 911 so we can't trace it. Dispatcher said it sounded like a male. Call came a little after nine."

"What's Baker say?"

"Baker said rowser-bowse-dyah-dyah for about three hours. Sober, the man is not what you'd term articulate; condition he was in this morning he might as well of spoken Martian. This man is so dumb he wouldn't piss if his pants were on fire. I *think* he claims they threw a private party after closing time. Just a few friends getting drunk and naked."

"Any names?"

"He's havin' trouble remembering his own name, let alone others. He vaguely remembers having a shouting match with Torres over a girl. Course he lost. Baker was only the bouncer, Torres ran the place. Next thing he remembers after that is getting a bucket of ice water splashed on him and cops screaming in his face." He paused, still galloping his fingers. "I can see now where there could be a connection between this kill and the Gale one, and we might look into that, but as far as I'm concerned, right now Baker is the prime suspect. I wish we could of gotten some prints off the knife and I'd like to know who the other people at that party were, but—" He made a big shrug. "We got two bad guys off the street. If you catch my drift."

I did. Baker was one American considered guilty until proven innocent. I said, "I got a legitimate reason to be in Johnson City."

Snow started to doodle on a scratch pad in front of him. He sketched a pistol, shaded in the butt. Drew a bullet firing from the barrel. Eventually he said, "I know that. But McCoy tells me you got Ronald Headon good and angry at you today. Ronald Headon is not a good man to get on the wrong side of."

"I know, but he made me mad. I went to see him because I heard he had more than a passing interest in Andrea Gale."

"We just heard Stone's theory. We're hearing a lot of things a lot later than we'd like to."

I for sure caught his drift now.

He said, "We heard about Stone getting beat up by Torres and Baker and the supposed reason why. We found that mildly interesting. Then we heard about you going down there. Why'd you go to the Blue Palm anyway?"

"The only thing Andrea told me about the job was I had to go to a bar called the Blue Palm."

Snow stared for some seconds. He knew I was lying, but there wasn't much he could do. He couldn't ask Andrea or Torres about it and I wasn't about to admit to pocketing the scrap of paper with the names on it. He said, "Why would that be the only thing she told you?"

"Maybe my reputation preceded me."

"Meaning?"

"If a bar was involved, I'd do anything."

"Why'd she hire you?"

"Never found out." To get him off that line, I said, "You know, I can't believe Dennison told you this stuff. I work for his client and here he runs to you telling a story makes me look shady."

"Don't get bent out of shape, PI, but you *are* shady. I'm sure we'd never of heard any of it except you both got beat up by Torres last week and his man was in jail last night and you weren't. He was only trying to spring his man, not finger you. But if you *were* guilty, well, you're an outsider so he wouldn't lose much sleep. *If* the two murders were related it would make Stone look less guilty. Personally, I think they're not tied together. I gotta admit I'm not as positive about that since I talked to Dennison, but I still like Stone for Gale and Baker for Torres. Two people lost it and killed the person caused them to lose it."

"You're not gonna talk to Headon?"

"Not unless I hear something from somebody besides Stone. Stone's the type of puke who'd finger his mother if it'd get him back on the street. I think he's just flingin' out names."

Snow stood, bent forward, placed his palms flat on the top of the desk, stared me in the eye. He said, "Now I realize you been hired to do a job out here. I can't stop you and I wouldn't want to. A man has to earn a living. I don't know how things are done in Chicago, but you start being nice to us, hear what I'm sayin'? And you start being nice to our citizens. If you're gonna keep poking your nose in this affair, I don't wanna hear about things forty-eight hours after they happen, and I don't want the town's richest mahoney calling here again raisin' beaucoup hell because some Chicago pill-popper he's never seen before in his life just barged into his office and started accusing him of being a womanizer and a murderer. You got all that?"

"All of it," I said. "By the way, did Dennison mention a man named Wylie to you guys?"

"He did."

"Know who he is?"

"No."

"You care to find out?"

"No."

"Stone still here?"

"Of course."

"Can I talk to him?"

"No."

"Dennison still here?"

"No."

"Know where he is?"

"Office is at 434 Jackson Place. He might be there, he might not. I don't know where he lives. I don't care about finding that out either. Bye."

I decided Dennison and I needed to talk.

434 Jackson Place was in an upscale neighborhood full of upscale-type shops. It was a renovated three-story Victorian mansion painted gray with pale pink trim. Dennison's office was on the third floor. A card and gift shop was on the first floor, a gourmet food store on the second. I walked through the gift shop, which reeked of potpourri, then up a curving, carpeted staircase.

His office was as cluttered as a teenager's bedroom with files and papers and open books everywhere. Dennison sat behind a small oak desk piled high with more lawyer stuff. He was on the phone. Had his coat off, shirt collar open, loafers up on the edge of the desk. He massaged his eyes with his free hand and his boyish face had a worried look. When he saw me at the door, he instantly rearranged the face to a cheery expression and waved me in, pointing at a cane-backed chair at the side of the desk.

He said, "Gotta go," and hung up.

I was still hot. I said, "Police ain't crazy about the Gale-Torres relation theory you told 'em. I ain't crazy about you tellin' 'em."

He swung his feet to the floor, tugged his collar. Said, "I know. I told them about the fights—"

"It's not called a fight, Dennison, when one of the combatants has his hands held behind his back. Not that I would of done any better if they weren't."

"I thought it might help David Stone."

"By—" I pointed at my chest.

He raised a hand. "I in no way suggested you were guilty of Torres' murder. Just that if the murders were connected, David was innocent."

"You don't know how glad I am to hear that. I'd hate to think the people paying me suspected me of murder. Understand, I don't blame the police for refusing to buy the theory. I know you don't have a lot of felony crime out here and this way they get three undesirables off the street and two murders solved. Everything nice and neat. Police love nice and neat and police love solved murders. I'd be neat but a drunken psycho's a little neater. They really want me to fade away now. I get lots of hints."

"You want, you're still working for the Stones. They've said nothing to me to indicate otherwise."

"Also good to hear. Level Dennison, you think David Stone is innocent? Honest now."

"I really do."

"So who's this Wylie? Nobody's heard of the man."

"Stone doesn't know either. He opened up to me a little after you left. He says it was the return name on some envelopes he found in Andrea's bedroom. No letters, just envelopes."

"Any address?"

"No address, no first name. Just Wylie. Postmarked in Johnson City though."

"That's it? That could make it anybody. Her grandmother." Dennison shook his head. "No. Stone claims Andrea told him it was a rich, older man. They had a huge fight over it not long before she died. He confronted her about the envelopes, demanded to know who Wylie was and what was in the missing letters. She wouldn't say anything except to brag about him being a rich old bird and wouldn't David like to know what the letters were about."

"Just because she said all this doesn't make it so. He realize that?"

"He seems convinced she was telling the truth."

I scrunched down in the chair, looked up at the ivory painted ceiling. Said, "I talked to Ronald Headon. He got real indignant. Fact, he seemed so genuinely indignant it makes me suspect David is just throwing names out at random to try and save his neck. Any name he can think of."

"I think he's not."

"You think Stone is telling the truth about all of it, then?"

"I think Andrea was seeing Headon, or planning to see him, or had seen him. I don't know why she'd bring it up unless that was the case, but as to why David Stone believes Headon was the man who hired Baker and Torres? He seems convinced, but he doesn't offer much to corroborate it."

"So do I pursue the Headon angle? I don't like putting my neck on the chopping block in a town where I don't know my way around unless I got a support group."

Dennison frowned, ran shaky fingers around his mouth.

Said, "It's his old man's money and it's David's theory so I'd say go ahead. Just be a little more circumspect."

"You got Headon's home address?"

"Sure, somewhere." He slipped on a pair of tortoise-shelled glasses and sorted through the papers in front of him. "I got it from the police book of unlisted numbers. Here it is. He lives in that country club thing outside of town. Bunch of houses all worth about three quarter of a mil. Place has an eighteen-hole golf course, a huge lake stocked with trout, all kinds of fun stuff. It's called Blissful Estates and he lives on Blissful Road."

With a straight face I wrote 722 Blissful Road in my notebook and told Dennison thanks.

# ELEVEN

I drove downtown to the Blue Palm. Two black and white squad cars sat out front. A large yellow sticker on the door said CLOSED, POLICE INVESTIGATION.

I drove some more. Hardly any cars cruised the streets and very few pedestrians. I studied the buildings. Didn't see a one that was built after World War Two. They were primarily three-story stone structures with plate glass windows on the bottom floor and fancy trimwork lining the roof and doors. No doubt downtown Johnson City had been handsome and vibrant in its day, but that day was long gone. Now there was as much plywood as plate glass and "Building for Lease" signs were as plentiful as saloons. Including the Blue Palm I counted sixteen bars. All were small and had names like Carol's Cove and Tommy's Tap.

Next to one called Henry's Hideaway was a sandwich shop. At the top of its window MAURY'S BBQ was printed in red. Underneath, the menu and prices were listed and under that a bunch of slogans like "Try Maury's Hotdog—Hugest in Town." I dislike men who brag about such things, but I was starving so I parked and went inside.

I sat on a red-cushioned chrome stool in front of a formica counter laden with ketchup and mustard bottles and glass canisters of sugar. I ordered an egg salad sandwich and coffee and ate while half-listening to three retirees at the other end of the counter grouse about the Cubs' pennant chances and the governor's latest tax proposal. But mostly about the Cubs. Sometimes I think I'm the only White Sox fan left in the state.

Maury's face was dark and wrinkled and he was close to toothless. He wore a white paper sanitary cap and a filthy cook's apron. I said, "What in hell happened to your downtown, Maury? Looks like the Third World out there."

He leaned against a stainless steel cooler, folded his arms across his chest. Eyed me up while shifting a toothpick from one side of his mouth to the other. He wanted to ask about my face, but he said, "The usual. In '72, Eagle Mountain Mall opened up out on the east side. Did some damage, but I'd estimate 'bout half the stores down here stayed put. Next five, six years was dicey. Then in '78, the huge one, the Johnson City Mall, opened on the west side. Inside of six months this place was like a ghost town. Every anchor store we had closed up. Ain't nothin' left now but cheap hotels and dog ass bars. Only people downtown these days are retirees who didn't save enough and people down on their luck."

"You're still around."

"I'm too old to move, too poor to close." He nodded at the three men. "The resident hotels'll keep me goin' till I'm sixty-five. I'll make it. Just."

Through a mouthful of sandwich I said, "Same thing happened all over the Midwest. Hell, all over the country probably."

"Doesn't mean I have to like it. I remember when this downtown swarmed with people, every night of the week. To me those shopping malls are—immoral, wicked things. They're like symbols of unadulterated greed. Where's the character in places like that? Course the city has a planning commission studying things so they can change downtown back like it used to be. This is the third commission tackled it. I figure it'll only take about fifty years."

He moved away and I sipped a cup of coffee as thick and foul tasting as engine sludge. I thought long and hard. Which was a little easier to do in my current sober state.

I wished I knew what Snow really thought. Obviously something had gone on between Andrea Gale and the Blue Palm boys. They'd been waiting for someone to show up. But Snow preferred to believe in coincidence, or did he want me to think he believed in coincidence? And maybe it *was* coincidence. Stone freaked and killed Andrea, Baker freaked and killed Torres. It could be that.

But I was getting paid to act like it wasn't so I had to keep nosing around. Right now I had major doubts about Stone's Headon-Wylie theory, but it was all I had. I wanted to talk with the "happily married" Mrs. Headon, but it was five-thirty and Mr. Headon might be home now. I didn't want him opening the door at 722 Blissful Road and finding me with my finger on the doorbell. He might call the National Guard this time.

So I asked Maury how did I get to Oswego?

He gave me precise directions. Said, "Practically a straight shot from Johnson City."

Two miles out of Johnson City, I was hopelessly lost. City boys should never get off main roads and attempt to drive country ones. It was dusk and then the rain started again. Became a downpour, making an unrelenting splatter on the roof. When I came to crossroads, I peered through clopping wipers trying to decipher what was printed on the tiny green road signs that had names like Birnbaum Farm Road. I came upon subdivisions of bi-level ranch houses that were identical except for color. Journeyed through towns with names like Shabbona and Somonauk; smaller towns that maybe didn't even have names. It was spooky out here in the dark and the rain with endless open space all around me. I felt twinges of panic.

At ten to seven, I entered Oswego from the south end. Somehow I'd gotten on Route 71. The limit sign said 2,980 people.

From what I could tell in the dark, it was a pretty town. Lots of large Victorian houses, well kept. Lawns as big as parking lots.

I stopped at a restaurant in the block-long business district. Asked to see a phone directory. It was as skinny as *Time* magazine on a slow week. One Farrell. I asked the ponytailed blonde behind the counter where the address was. She said it was only three blocks away. I had the feeling everything in town was only three blocks away.

The Farrell house was in the middle of a neighborhood of ten or twelve small wooden houses. It was the only group of woebegone houses I'd seen since I entered town. Most other places this would be your basic working class block, but in comparison to what was around them these dwellings looked downright decrepit.

I pulled in the gravel drive and sat for a bit, smoking a Kool. I pushed Run-DMC's *King of Rock* into the deck, fast forwarded to "Rock Box" and cranked it to full volume. I waited for the rain to let up, wondered why in hell I was here.

The porch light winked on. Lisa came out. She wore an oversized blouse untucked over tight-fitting blue jeans. She peered at me under her palm like an Indian. I rolled the window down, turned on the overhead light. When she saw it was me, she made a puzzled face, but waved.

She ducked inside, came back with an umbrella. After some long splashy jumps she was in the car. She said, "What are you doing here?"

"Been asking myself that very question."

"You here to talk about Andrea some more?"

"Not really."

"I bet. How'd you find me?"

"Wasn't easy."

She smelled like violets and wet laundry. She made a small smile. Said, "So what are the options? Answer me serious, you here for business or pleasure?"

"I really don't know."

She looked in my eyes. Made a shrug. "So show me Chicago."

I said, "This is no night to cruise Chicago. You could show me Oswego, but I think I've just seen it."

She said, "Well, let's do something. Hang on." She ran

back inside, was gone ten minutes. Came back wearing
black jeans, a bulky white turtleneck sweater, black slouch
boots. She closed the car door, said, "Let's go to Johnson
City."

I groaned, but that's where I headed.

# TWELVE

We hopped the downtown bars for an hour. She slammed
down 7-7's and they soon washed away her distracted, halt-
ing manner. She became animated, vivacious. While drinking she had the habit of combing her fingers through her
hair, forehead to nape, and after an hour of that, the top of
her thick black hair was no longer carefully styled but
looked like the burning bush, sticking up and out all over,
knots of it twisting to the sides like miniature goat horns.
Between the bizarre 'do and changed personality, it was like
I was with a completely new Lisa Farrell.

The third bar was called the Red Star. She hit her stride
there. Started talking a mile a minute about the things that
young women in bars believe constitute fascinating conversation. Lisa loved Roseanne Barr and Eddie Murphy. She
described in detail the last three episodes of "Roseanne." I
told her I'd seen the *Beverly Hills Cop* movies even though I
hadn't because I could tell she was dying to launch into
scene-by-scene plot summaries. Then I heard how Andrea
had been on a jogging kick the last couple months so Lisa
started jogging too, but after she jogged she felt so hungry
she'd eat three sweet rolls so, like, what was the point? Then
she moved to the personal habits—mostly sexual—of her co-
workers at Headon Engineering. She went on to other
topics, but the interest level stayed constant. Most of what
she had to say was about as interesting and profound as the
information on a *Playmate* Data Sheet.

In the parking lot of the Red Star, Lisa said we should go

to the Crazy Alm. It had live bands every night of the week. Surprise! I thought of Gant and the skinhead girl. Said, sure.

On the way, Lisa bounced her palms against her thighs, keeping white person time to the reggae beat of a Burning Spear tape. Her sense of rhythm was as bad as her topics of conversation, so to distract her I said, "You and Andrea went to the Crazy Alm a lot?"

"All the time."

"Together?"

"Sometimes. But never on Wednesday night because they have wet T-shirt contests. Andrea thought they were sleazy."

"You don't?"

"I only got drunk enough to enter one time, but I think it's a fun night. Men sure get wild and crazy."

"Why weren't you there Friday night?"

"Had a date. He wasn't the rock bar type."

"You missed a hot band."

Lisa shrugged.

I said, "Remember I asked about Eduardo Torres this afternoon?"

"I knew this was coming. Yeah, I thought about it later, why?"

"He was murdered last night."

She didn't act surprised. Said, "Who killed him?"

"Police say his personal moron, Buddy Baker."

"It's weird, happening right after he beat up you and David."

"That occurred to other people too."

"Police talk to you?"

"Uh huh. You say you thought about Torres later. Remember any more?"

"It probably was him, but like I said, it was a while back."

"They meet at the Blue Palm?"

"I don't know if the Blue Palm was even around back then. Most of those bars change names every year or so when they change owners. I know I've never been in it. I couldn't say for sure about Andrea."

"But an Eddie Torres was interested in Andrea?"

"Think so. It would of been when we were juniors in high school. We came up here all the time. There was some guy here Andrea thought was a super stud. We met a lot of people. Most of the men we met, hell, *all* the men we met wanted to jump Andrea's bones. And I just remember an Eddie Torres was one of the men. I think he was dealing coke. We were small town girls, which meant real live coke dealers impressed the hell out of us."

"Did she ever go out with him?"

"I don't remember. Jesus, stop with the questions, will-ya?"

I grinned, said, "Questions are my job, girl, but I'll give it a rest."

The Crazy Alm was jammed and rowdy. I love rowdy when I'm on stage. I do not care for rowdy when I'm in the audience.

For three songs we stood at the back of the room. The noise was deafening, almost a barrier to moving. The band was strictly garage level Heavy Metal. Four guys with permed shoulder-length hair, black T-shirts, ripped-at-the-knee jeans, well-practiced blank expressions. The lead guitarist could play nine-million-notes-a-second solos, and did at every opportunity, but the only chords he seemed to know were the three-note bottom string ones. Like most kids these days. Nobody wants to be a guitar player anymore, everybody wants to be a guitar gun slinger. A shredder. Can't really blame them; Eddie Van Halen is their hero and he's richer than Rockefeller and he sleeps with Valerie Bertinelli. What most of them neglect to notice is, he's not only fast, he's good. The rest of the band's grasp of rhythm and dynamics was rudimentary at best. Singer was better looking than ours, though.

They went on break and we went to the bar. Some people there said, "Hey, Full Frontal Nudity" when I stepped up to order a Pepsi for me and a 7-7 for Lisa. Gant was behind the bar. He said, "When's FFN comin' back?"

Lisa looked at me with wide eyes. I said, "Told you you missed a hot band."

She said, "I'm mildly impressed."

I said to Gant, "Cop named McCoy visit you?"

"Came in Saturday night. Talked for awhile. Everything you told him was exactly like I remembered it. He was disappointed. The man doesn't like you, Dan." He set the drinks in front of me, put on a solemn face. Said, "They're comped. What a shame about Andrea, eh? Such a sweetheart. Lisa, I'm sorry as hell about it. You know how I felt about Andrea."

Lisa said, "I know." She turned away from Gant and said in my ear, "I know you wanted to pull her panties off every time you laid eyes on her."

I told Gant I needed to talk to him alone.

He said, "Give me ten minutes, then go to my office." He pointed to the other side of the room.

Lisa and I made our way through the dark and the din to a table halfway between the stage and the bar. The packed people and the noise had me tense and uncomfortable. My hands kept tapping and fidgeting. I said, "Every man in this town must of been madly in lust with Andrea Gale."

"You saw her. Weren't you?"

I sipped some Pepsi. Thought it best not to answer.

She said, "Why aren't you drinking?"

Good question. I was feeling so much anxiety my nerves were zapping constant orders to the brain and the orders were "calm us the fuck down. Alcohol needed NOW!" I held up my Pepsi and said, "I am."

"I mean alcohol. You've ordered Pepsi all night. You an alcoholic?"

"Ann Landers says I am. You know those quizzes she runs? The fifteen yes or no questions to see if your drinking's out of hand? Like, do you have blackouts? Do you drink before breakfast? Do you drink before you go out drinking? I took that quiz and I had thirteen yeses. Worried me so much I stayed drunk for a week."

She nodded like she knew it all along. "I didn't mean to pry, but nowadays when a person doesn't drink you usually find it's because they're alcoholic."

Two enormous bikers in chains and T-shirts two tables from us suddenly stood and stirred the stacked smoke with roundhouse rights. Neither connected, but their table wobbled, then fell over with a crash, spilling three pitchers of beer. One swung again and punched a passerby in the throat. That poor slob collapsed to the floor, clawing his neck. The fighters were quickly hustled out the door by a platoon of bouncers. Girlfriends trailed behind, shouting swear words.

Everybody but me applauded and hooted. My anxiety level rose another notch. Some purple and red neon signs that said DANCE DANCE DANCE started pulsing on the wall in front of me. Pulsing way too fast.

Lisa was laughing and clapping her hands. She said, "Place is full of some disorderly dudes."

I smiled weakly. Said, "Lisa, let's get out of here. I'll talk to Gant later."

"Not yet," she whined. "We just sat down. I wanna hear the band."

"These shredheads should be gonged."

She leaned forward, rested her hand on my arm. Said, "Relax, Dan. We'll leave real soon."

"Real soon is not soon enough."

Gant came to the table, said, "Follow," and we worked our way to his office. He shut the door behind us, muffling the club sounds. I sat in an upholstered burgundy chair. He sat behind a black desk, rubbed his very round belly and then fingered the knot of his ponytail. He said, "I loved that line you kept saying Friday night. You know, 'the drunker you all get the better we all sound, so keep the register ringin'.' I'm gonna get signs made up and hang 'em over the bar. Gonna say 'the drunker you get, the better they sound.'"

"You'll need a brewery in the basement next time this band gigs."

"Huh?"

I said, "Never mind. I'm just gettin' old. Tell me everything McCoy said to you."

"Didn't say much really. He called you a Chitown lowlife. Said he wasn't so sure you didn't kill Andrea Gale."

"He say why I'd do that?"

"Not for sure. I received the impression he figured you tried for sex, got rebuffed and it pissed you off."

I said, "If I murdered girls everytime I got rebuffed trying for sex I'd be in Joliet for my next two hundred incarnations. You set him straight about how I met her?"

"What he said you said was just how it happened, mister. I told him that."

"What'd you know about Andrea Gale?"

Gant smiled, raised his eyebrows. "A stone fox. God, I'd of *paid* to tap into that babe. She hung out here a lot. Her and Lisa. You got a thing goin' with Lisa tonight?"

I ignored him, said, "Andrea and Lisa come here with a lot of different men?"

"Sometimes. Sometimes they came by themselves. But mister, they left by themselves very seldom. I gave it my best shot with Andrea. Never made the connection."

I said, "You know a Ronald Headon?"

"Headon Engineering?"

I nodded.

"I know of him, don't know the man personally. Our paths don't cross much."

"Ever seen the man in here with Andrea?"

Gant whomped his belly a couple of times, threw his head back and made a barking laugh. "Headon in here? Dan, that is a good one. You're implying Headon had Andrea on the side. Well, maybe he did. Lots of men did. But he'd never of brought her here."

"Tell me more about Andrea."

He scratched ahis head. "She was a sexpot, but basically a good kid. Liked recreational drugs, but not a druggie. Average interests, but you couldn't call her average because of that face and bod. Really, that's all I know." He leaned back, tapped his belly again. "So when's Full Frontal comin' back, Dan? Band is hot. I dig that roadhouse rock, that honky tonk, Memphis blues thang. Like this band tonight is okay, but they're just kids. Hell, I'm fifty-two. I like that roots stuff. Girls get off on it too. One of the reasons I run the Crazy Alm is to get my hands inside the panties of young babes. At my age that ain't easy. You gotta have a gimmick. How about you? You like 'em young?"

I said, "I wouldn't if it meant I had to endure bands like this one to lure 'em."

Gant smiled ear to ear, his eyes becoming slits. It made him look like a hippie Buddha. He said, "Hell, you're in a band. You got nothing to worry about."

I said, "Did McCoy talk to the skinhead girl?"

"Heather? I dunno."

"Her name is Heather?"

Gant laughed. "Yeah, ain't that great? You think Heather you think penny loafers and cardigan sweaters and pleated corduroy slacks. This Heather wears chains and biker boots and shaves her head. Eats pills like they were sunflower seeds. Fucks like a rabbit too. Shoulda stuck with her, mister. You'd of gotten lucky easy." He giggled. "I did after you and your singer finally took off. That's why I let her stick around after hours. If there's nobody else—"

"The shaved head is cool, but for me it's not real alluring."

He waved his hand. "Like I said, I'm fifty-two. I ain't picky, mister."

"Know where Heather lives?"

"No. We do it downstairs. I got a small room with a bed in it. Used to be a janitor's room, but I fixed it up for fun. Mirrors, colored lights, a bong for the potheads. Lots of girls drunk on their ass at two A.M. need that emotional release." He giggled again. "Anyway, I never did her at her place."

"I wanna know what McCoy told her and what she told him." I gave Gant one of my PI cards. Said, "Next time she shows, have her call me."

Gant said, "Will do."

We left the room, entered the clamor. Lisa was gone from the table. She came back in five minutes. She was buzzed big time now. Under the tousled hair her face was lopsided, a ditzy grin stuck to it.

The band started again. So loud it hurt, but the rest of the room dug it. They whooped and cheered as the musicians crashed into a ponderous, roaring riff I was vaguely aware of. Eight bars in, the lead guitarist started two-handed tapping up and down the fretboard and then he leaned on the whammy bar for ten seconds, trying to cop a Hendrix lick. Except this cat was light years from me, let alone Hendrix, and he was creating a truly tasteless lead.

A Baby Huey type with a beginner's beard and a POISON ROCKS T-shirt was making a Budweiser waltz to the bar. He cradled three empty pitchers like they were newborn babies. He plowed into the side of my chair, straightened himself and glared down at me. He weaved like a cobra looking at a flute. By reading his lips I could tell he said, "Dude, what the fuck?"

I said, "Yo mama," knowing it didn't matter what I said.

He shouted, "You bastard." He set the pitchers on the table, made a fist and drew it back.

I'm not a violent man, but I'm not Gandhi either. You get beat up enough, you learn to avoid it any way possible. I shot my elbow up and into his balls as hard as I could.

He shouted into the bedlam and clamped both hands over his crotch. He gagged, then sat fast, started squirming furiously.

I looked around. Only the four people at the table next to ours had noticed. They thought it extremely humorous.

I leaned across the table and tapped Lisa's arm. Shouted in her ear, "Lisa, we *are* going."

"It's only ten."

I pointed at the floor. The lumberjack size Poison fan was still writhing in a puddle of beer. Through the gasps and the retches he tried to yell something at me. I was not curious to know what. I said, "This clown will be getting off the floor in about two minutes. I'm not going to be here when he does."

Lisa half stood so she could see the clown on the floor. She looked from him to me, made a face and pointed at me. Said, "You?"

"Come on."

The rain had stopped and now the air was clean and damp. Delicious after the polluted bar. I sucked a long lungful.

We walked along the side of the Crazy Alm. Lisa wrapped her arm around my waist and made little squeezes with her hand on my side. She said, "Why'd you put that dude on the floor?"

"Thought he'd look better down there than me."

"He was huge. How'd you do it?"

"I insulted his manhood."

She squeezed hard and said, "Where do you go in the City when you go out?"

"I don't go out much. I see enough nightlife when Full Frontal gigs."

"Where do you guys play?"

"In Chicago, Mulligans, Fitzgerald's, Cubby Bear Lounge, some other places. There's other clubs in northern Illinois like the Crazy Alm. Not many though."

"Take me with you sometime?"

"It's boring as hell, Lisa. The road with a bar band ain't like touring with the Rolling Stones."

We were at the Skylark. Me at the driver door, Lisa on the passenger side. A voice on the other side of the car next to me said quietly, "Hey, Slick."

I turned and squinted. Expected to see the lumberjack bearing down on me. But it wasn't him. It was a sawed-off man of thirty or so with shoulder-length dark hair. He limped around the front of the car toward me. I braced and then another voice behind me said, "Get the fuck outta this town."

Lisa shouted, "No!"

I turned away from the first man to see who owned the second voice, but not fast enough. The back of my head exploded like an M-80 had gone off in my brain. The stars and fireworks came back. I sat down in a cold puddle and felt the water soak my crotch. Then a boot rushed at my face from the direction of the first guy. I tried to roll away from it, but it moved too fast and thudded into my right bicep. I cradled my head with my arms and curled into a ball.

Lisa was screaming. I heard the second man run around the back of the car toward her. There were two hard slaps and the screaming stopped.

The first man kicked my ribs, then my back. I spun over, grabbed his ankle, twisted left. Off balance from the last kick he splashed on his ass. I tried to beat him to a standing position, but even with a bum leg he was quicker. He swore like a sailor's parrot. He punched the side of my head as I came up from the ground and put me down again.

Grunting, he took two measured steps and the boot collided with my bicep again, shooting an icy numbness up and down my arm. Then he said, "Let's go, Auggie." As they moved away, he said in a stage whisper, "Remember, Private *Dickhead*, stay outta this town. That's all you gotta do to avoid incidents like this."

I rolled to my hands and knees in the water, shook my head. Lisa ran around the front of the Skylark and kneeled next to me. She was whimpering. She said, "Dan, are you alright?"

"Yeah." I shook my head again. Immense pain. I said, "Maybe not." I got into a kneeling position, took a deep breath. The spots where he'd nailed my ribs and back burned like the bones there were made of dry ice. I said, "You okay?" I touched her lip. It was hot and swollen and sticky. I said, "He bloodied your lip, girl." Lisa started to cry hard.

I stood slowly, pulled Lisa to her feet. Put my arms around her. She sobbed into my chest.

If nothing else, Lisa and I had come a long way since Saturday.

# THIRTEEN

I didn't want Snow hearing about this later on so I drove to the Johnson City station, reported the assault to a desk man who had all the compassion of a Fortune 500 CEO who decides he can pretty up the bottom line by laying off fifteen hundred people. Then I drove Lisa back to Oswego. She kept a Kleenex pressed to her lip and didn't talk until we got to her parent's house, then she said she was sorry. I told her it wasn't her fault, somebody in Johnson City didn't like me. Hell, nobody in Johnson City liked me. I'd been in the damn town only three times and two times I got the tar beat out of me.

She said, "You got to be careful, Dan. Maybe you should just stay out of Johnson City like they said."

"Lisa, I need the money."

Before she closed the door she whispered, "Call me."

It was another long, hurting ride to Chicago. I stopped at Weiss Memorial again. The ER nurse was a hundred and fifty years old and weighed four hundred pounds, but she remembered my name and that made me feel better. She said, "You picking these fights, Mr. Kruger? Better you should drop down a class or two." She X-rayed me, said, "Nothing's broke, but your arms and ribs are gonna look like a spectacular sunset for a few days." She asked did I need more codeine pills for the pain. I said, damn straight.

So I spent Tuesday vegged on the couch. I was starting to spot a trend here. I worked in Johnson City for a day, got beat up at the end of it, then spent the next day at home, convalescing on 'deine's. Not a schedule I cared to follow for any length of time, although the 'deine days had their moments.

I called Priceman. Told him to cancel the week's practices because I had a job that was actually going to pay money. He said it was cool, Full Frontal had nothing going this week, but next weekend it was off to some burg in Iowa, the name of which escaped him, for a Friday through Sunday gig. Two hundred a night, which would just about cover gas and hotel rooms. I told him we had a Crazy Alm gig sewed up whenever we wanted it. We both agreed it was thrilling the way FFN's career was taking off. The cover of *Rolling Stone* was just around the corner. We talked about canning Justus Walker, then decided why bother. At the rate we were gigging, no doubt he'd quit soon and save us the trouble.

Wednesday morning I ate five whites and drank a pot of black coffee for breakfast. I carried Bugs to the Skylark and we headed for suburbia one more time. Just like Saturday, the pills kicked in about the time I hit the toll plaza and I started rapping a streak to Bugs about the case and my thoughts on it. The few I had. Bugs took it all in, decided to sleep on it. I muttered, "Thanks, wabbit."

I was wired tight as a snare drum when I pulled off the

highway into Blissful Estates. Just inside the entrance was an imposing stone and iron abstract sculpture, which was supposed to symbolically illustrate what a swanky place it was. I drove the length of Blissful Road, gawking like I was in a foreign country.

Blissful Estates was like if you picked up a small section of Kenilworth and dropped it in the middle of a cornfield. It consisted of about twenty mansions. All were set back from the winding street, half-hidden by many trees and huge shrubs. The lawns were large and meticulously landscaped and rolled down to the street. The golf course was at the end of the street, three miles from the highway. The clubhouse was dark glass and redwood and slightly smaller than the White House. Lake Road ran left and right in front of the course. A large sign said Blissful Lake was a mile west. I decided to pass on checking out the lake.

It was eight-thirty. I doubled back and found 722. A bronze Seville and a black BMW sat in a cul-de-sac halfway up the drive. Trees and shrubs made it hard to see much of the house. You could see just enough to know there was this massive *thing* up there. I parked the Skylark down the street just beyond a curve, wondered how long it'd take to get rousted. A place like this I might not last thirty seconds.

The speed had me jittery. I sucked on Kools, played "Wipe Out" on the steering wheel with my fingers, turned the radio on and started pressing the station buttons in four-four time just to be doing something.

At ten to nine, Headon backed the Seville onto Blissful Road, headed toward the highway.

When he was out of sight, I got out and walked briskly to and up the driveway. A canopy of budding branches arched above me. The closer I got to the house, the more of it I could see and the bigger it looked. Gray stone with dark brick trimming. The windows were fan-shaped and framed with cedar. A huge, two-story bay window curved out of a turret-like section on the right side. There was an attached garage bigger than the house I lived in. I wondered if I'd have to cross a moat.

The BMW was freshly waxed, so glossy you could shave by it. I asked myself why would someone wash and wax a car with all the rain we'd been having? Then I thought maybe the rich *are* different from you and me. They have their cars waxed even when they know it's going to rain. I told myself that was profound.

The door was fan-shaped too with a limestone arch. Floral designs were carved into the stone. It was about three times wider than any door I'd stood in front of before. I pressed the bell. Heard chimes inside the house. Almost immediately a woman with weepy blue eyes opened the door. She blinked rapidly and dabbed at the eyes with a crushed hanky. She wasn't dressed like a maid, didn't carry herself like one.

I said, "Mrs. Ronald Headon?" My voice was harsh and scratchy, like my larynx was caked with mud.

She didn't say yes, she didn't say no. The woman was mid-fortyish and tiny—barely five foot—with delicate features and plenty of freckles sprinkled on a pixie face. From beneath a curly strawberry blond wig that was slightly askew, wisps of gray hair peeked out. The woman wore a furry pink robe. The first two buttons were undone. The skin exposed there was grainy, like sand.

I played it confident. I said, "Mrs. Headon, I'd like to talk to you for a minute."

"I can't let you in."

"I only wanna talk. I've come a long way to see you."

"Did I ask you to?" She touched her eyes with the hankie again. Said, "I know who you are." She scratched her stomach absentmindedly, gazed past me for some seconds.

I said, "One short conversation can't hurt anything."

Her attention snapped back. She looked at me like I'd suddenly changed faces and she had to study this new one. Then she said, "Screw him, come in."

She led me right, down a parquet-floored hallway lined with lacquered, oriental-painted floor vases into the room behind the bay window. The room was two-stories high, had a beamed-ceiling and two oak-paneled, handcarved limestone fireplaces. There were long, tapestried sofas and heavy, leather-upholstered armchairs. Beautifully designed Tiffany lamps sat on tables and hung from the ceiling. Across the room was a fifty-inch TV screen and next to it, a compact stacked, state-of-the-art sound system connected to speakers as big as Yugos. Give me a room like this and I'd retire from real life and jam like a sumbitch.

I sat in one of the armchairs. Mrs. Headon went to an octagon-shaped, brass and oak coffee table in the corner of the room. She flicked a switch on the side of it and the top of the table rose. Liquor bottles slowly emerged. I watched, fascinated. I said, "Where do you get one of those?" She had her back to me and didn't answer. I heard the clink of ice into glass, the slosh of poured liquor.

I checked out the room, admiring the sheer opulence of it. I said, "Can I see the prisoners in the dungeon if I ask real nice?"

She ignored that too, said, "What're you drinking?"

"I don't drink these days."

"Why not?"

"Being drunk is not productive."

She made a bitter laugh. "What is it you wanna produce?"

I hate trick questions. I said, "A sober life I guess."

"What's a sober life get you? A gold star on your tombstone? Hundred years from now we'll all be dead and the sober people'll be just as dead as the drunk ones."

I was thinking please don't talk to me like this when I'm on ups. Ups make me say fuck it. I said, "I got this problem, Mrs. Headon. You are Mrs. Headon, right?" She didn't answer, so I went on, "See, one day when I was nineteen, somebody asked if they could buy me a drink. Next thing I knew I was thirty-eight and everything in between was kind of blurry."

She said, "You can't blame a person for wanting to leave this world for awhile."

"I don't blame anyone."

She said, "Life ain't shit."

"There's fun parts."

"Not in mine." She turned and faced me, holding a glass with a brown drink in it.

"Damn few in mine now that you mention it. But as I look around this room I gotta believe there's more potential for fun in your life than mine."

She sipped and said, "I read in a book that every culture
ever discovered fermented something. Even the most backward savages in the middle of some jungle in the mountains
of Borneo or somewhere. Corn, hops, grapes, potatoes, dan-
delions, sugar, grass, whatever. This book said the urge to
escape and get high is as natural as sex, hunger and thirst."

I said, "Medication for the human condition."

"Not just humans, even animals do it."

I said, "Not the Eskimos."

She made a puzzled face.

"Eskimos didn't know about alcohol until the white man
introduced 'em to it. You can't grow anything up there."

"But if you could ferment ice or fish they'd of done it."

I nodded. "No doubt."

She said, "Same book claimed civilization started when
ancient man stopped wandering so he could cultivate grain
to make beer."

"I been sober over four weeks. Hate to blow it."

"See, you can quit. If you've done it once you can do it
again. Have one little drink with me and then you can climb
back on the wagon. One little drink never hurt anyone."

Being a lush, I recognized what was going on here. Drinking drunks hate sober drunks. Misery loves company and
when a drunk sees another drunk sober up it's scary because
it's a reminder that the life they're leading will kill them
eventually. They have to stop or die and when they're confronted with somebody who's stopped, they're left with the
die part. Nobody likes having that shoved in their face.

But I was high and her logic seemed as sound as a 1950
dollar. She was right, one little drink was not a problem for
me; the problem was when I went months at a time with a
bottle in my hand. Besides, a drink now would be almost
like medicine, it would soften the speed. I said, "Brandy."

Mrs. Headon smiled like the devil putting one over on
God and turned to pour.

It slid down like toasted honey and then the lovely circle
of warmth grew in my belly. I closed my eyes and sighed. I
said, "This isn't Christian Brothers."

Mrs. Headon smiled wider. Said, "Conde de Osborne. It's
imported. From Spain."

I drained the snifter, said, "Again." My voice was back to normal.

When she came back with seconds, I said, "This house looks rich. You don't."

"How do rich women look?"

"Arrogant."

"So that was a compliment?"

"Yes."

"Then thanks." She sat in a chair on the other side of the room by the big screen TV. She said, "My husband is rich enough I can look like I want."

"Why were you crying?"

"You think I'm a lush, don't you?" She held her glass up. "Not even nine-thirty in the morning?"

"I don't make judgments about people I've known ten minutes. Besides, marriage to Ronald Headon must be an ordeal."

She grinned a quick, private grin. It was gone as fast as a mouse darting across a kitchen floor. She said, "Where you from?"

"Chicago."

"I thought so. You—" Her voice trailed away.

The speed and brandy aligned themselves in perfect harmony. The speed supplying alertness and mental clarity, the brandy providing mellow nerves. I felt very "aware" and in tune with what was going on. And one thing I was aware of here was that a lot of hostile vibes floated around this house. The vibes I was getting did not support the happy marriage contention of Ronald Headon. Happily married women do not cry and crave liquor so early in the day cartoons are the only thing on TV. I'd been wondering how to go about finding out what I needed to know. I sensed I wouldn't have to beat around the bush. I said, "Mrs. Headon, I want to ask some questions about your husband."

She smiled the quick smile again.

"They're of a personal nature, but I have a feeling you'll want to answer them. A man is in jail and he could be there unjustly. Your answers could help right that injustice. Also, it's important that your husband not know I was here asking."

She looked into her drink, no expression on her face.

I said, "You ever suspected maybe your husband was cheating on you?"

She came out of the chair. Shouted, "Of course not. What the hell kind of question is that?"

And maybe I'd misread the entire situation.

She sat back in the chair. Her voice still loud she said, "How dare you, a stranger, walk into my house, and ask a question like that? My husband is a lot of things, but he does not cheat on me."

"Good," I said. "I hoped you'd say that." I tried to smile a sincere, warm smile, but it probably looked like a sneer because of the speed freezing my face muscles. I mentally trashed the Andrea Gale questions.

Calmer, she said, "Why would you ask that question?"

I shook my head, sipped more brandy.

She pointed at me and said, "You're Dan Kruger, aren't you? I knew who you were the second I opened the door. You're the private detective who got Ronald so worked up. I should call him, tell him you're here."

"Why would you wanna do that?"

"That's what he told me to do if you showed up. I was to slam the door in your face and call him immediately. Then call the police." She leaned back and crossed her legs under the robe, lifting it slightly as she did. She said, "But fuck him."

We both laughed.

"I said, "He told me you two been happily married for thirty years. I'm thinking he lied."

She said, "Look at me," and grinned over her glass. Her eyes gleamed and seemed to widen, giving her a slightly demented look. I noticed her front teeth were unnaturally thin, like they'd been filed.

I tried to smile back.

She said, "Stay," got up and padded out of the room on bare feet. Five minutes later she was back. The wig was straight now and she had makeup on. She wore black jeans and a light blue oversized flannel shirt untucked. She went to the coffee table-concealed bar and picked up the bottle of brandy, a six-pack of Michelob, and a bottle of Bombay

Sapphire gin. She hit the switch, the top lowered down, and it was just a coffee table again.

She walked to me, her right arm pressing the two bottles against her side, the six-pack in her left hand. She said, "Take the booze," so I did. She said, "I gotta move. Vacate this place for a while. You ever feel like that? Where if you don't, like, go, you'll freak out? Fly apart or something? We'll go to my brother's house. We'll visit my brother." She knelt in front of me to tie shiny white running shoes. I caught a glimpse of orange-sized, sandy-skinned breasts.

I stood. She grabbed hold of my elbow and pulled herself up.

I wasn't wild about visiting anybody with this woman. From the look in her eyes and the way she talked and acted, I perceived Mrs. Headon had a shaky grip on her sanity this morning and people in that condition are not people I enjoy hanging out with. But I was involved with alcohol again and my body was urging me to get this high thing moving forward.

Plus there was the case to think about. If she got drunker perhaps she'd open up a bit.

So I didn't say a thing as I followed her back down the hallway, my right arm cradling the bottles. I stumbled to the BMW. As we got in I said, "What's your name?"

"Sandra Headon. You can call me Sandy. San. Whatever." There was an inflated velour cushion between us. She lifted off the seat and scooted it underneath her. When she sat on it, her head was even with mine.

"Name's appropriate."

"Why's that?"

"Never mind. Sandy, you know a man name of Wylie?"

She slammed her door, looked at me, eyes blazing. She said, "None of that now. Ask your questions another time. We're getting drunk today." The anger evaporated like spit in fire and she giggled. "I mean drunker. We're gonna finish what we started." She pulled on a pair of deerskin driving gloves.

We stopped at the Skylark so I could transfer Bugs to the BMW's backseat. She was as nonchalant about Bugs as Jimmy Stewart was about Harvey.

When Sandy got to the highway, she didn't slow down or look to see what was coming. She squealed a right turn at about fifty-five miles per hour. She held out her right hand, demanded "Beer."

I tore one from the plastic and gave it to her. Did the same for myself. I swigged it empty with three long swallows, then started in on the brandy. Judging from the early returns, this was not going to be a ride I wanted to make sober.

Sandy Headon mumbled to herself as the BMW winded out to ninety. We whizzed by bare farm fields like a hellhound was on our trail.

# FOURTEEN

We stayed on the state highway going west. Every ten miles or so, we passed through a dinky farm town with three blocks of frame houses on either side of a one-block business district. Take away the neon signs and the parked automobiles and these towns probably looked exactly like they looked in 1890. Each one had a hundred fewer inhabitants than the previous one. I figured about the time we hit Iowa, we'd pass through a town nobody lived in.

Sandy Headon was a graduate of the Chauffeur From Hell Driving School. She didn't slow the Beamer under seventy-five unless it was absolutely necessary. She loved stop signs. They were infrequent but when one loomed ahead she stomped the brakes at the last second, fishtailing to a halt, then squealed forward, revving out to warp speed. A couple she just blew.

A third of the way into the brandy I built enough courage to stop worrying whether this ride would be my last. I started to enjoy it. I studied huge red barns with a tourist's appreciation. Inspected immense puddled fields too wet to be plowed. At least I assumed that was the reason.

Agriculture is one of the numerous subjects I know absolutely nothing about.

Sandy kept up a steady muttering. Every few minutes
she'd say, "Look at me, Daniel." When I did, she didn't
look back or say a word. She'd stare at the road, smiling
that enigmatic, crazy smile.

I had speed and booze shooting through me and I needed
to talk. So I did. I gabbed about city life versus country. I
remarked on the respective life-styles. Slow lane, fast lane,
stuff like that. I wondered why would anybody wanna live
in a place where there was nothing to do after six o'clock.
Hell, I said, there's nothing to do out here before six o'clock.
Half these towns didn't even have a bar. Where did people
socialize? I told Sandy how traumatic it would be for a city
boy like me to live in a Shabbona or a Paw Paw. I blathered
on. I scored some telling arguments, but Sandy didn't appreciate any of them because she wasn't listening. We were a
fun ride, no mistake. Me chattering away like a shit-scared
spider monkey, Sandy murmuring darkly to herself about
God knows what, and Bugs fast asleep in his cage on the
backseat, ignoring both of us.

Thirty-five minutes after we left Blissful Estates, Sandy
slowed to a crawl and peered ahead, eyes narrow, face
against the steering wheel. "I always miss it," she
whispered. Another mile and she said, "Ah, ha," and made
a sharp right onto a sunken gravel road. The BMW bot-
tomed out as we left the highway, but that didn't faze her.
She lead footed back to seventy-five. The stones clanged and
spit off the car's undercarriage. I shut my eyes twice when
we approached sharp curves, but she made both, braking
and sliding and swerving.

Her brother lived in a two-story, dingy gray farmhouse
just off the gravel road five miles from the highway. It was
old and run-down. Two whitewashed buildings were behind
the house. They were too small to be barns, too big to be
outhouses. I didn't know what else farms had. Sandy parked
on a strip of grass next to a barbed wire fence that surrounded the house and yard. I said, "This place got a indoor
toilet?"

Sandy said, "Of course. This isn't Mississippi for

Chrissakes."

She rolled down her window, tapped two short honks on the horn. I heard a male voice from beyond the out buildings shout, "Backyard." We went through the gate and walked past the house, then between the two buildings. I asked Sandy what they were. She said, "I don't know. Guess they used to store stuff in 'em."

"Like what?"

"Stuff. Corn, maybe. How should I know?"

Behind the buildings two men stood twenty yards apart, playing catch with a baseball. There was a half empty four litre jug of Gallo Paisano next to each man.

Sandy said, "Hey, George," to the man closest to us. "This is Daniel. I met him this morning."

"Hey, babe," he answered. He stared my way, sizing me up. I nodded, said, "George," and he nodded back. His eyes returned to Sandy and he said, "How's the bastard?"

Sandy shook her head and said, "Samo samo."

George looked about thirty. He wore baggy khaki pants, a torn white T-shirt, and black warehouse boots. He was a little taller than Sandy and weighed maybe as much as a bag of wet leaves. He had a prominent Roman nose and feet the size of bread loaves. He looked at the other man, said, "Okay, the arm's warm."

The other man was a hulking, corpulent creature with blond Brillo pad hair. He'd barely glanced at us. Sandy said, "That's Dwayne." Dwayne squatted, balancing himself by placing his right hand on the ground next to him. As he hunkered down, his T-shirt rode up, exposing handfuls of pinkish belly fat. He stuck his left hand over a paper plate on the ground in front of him, making a target. He wore a child's catching mitt that on him looked like a mitten.

George went into a herky-jerky windup, his arms and legs flapping around like a flag in a windstorm, then threw the ball. It bounced twice in front of the paper plate and skidded along the grass. Dwayne lunged to his left, missed the ball, ended up face down eating lawn. He stood without a word, tracked the ball down, lumbered back and tossed it to George. George threw ten more pitches. Dwayne caught six, chased four. After the tenth pitch, both men refreshed themselves with long swallows from the jug.

Sandy said to me, "George is going to Florida next spring to catch on with a major league baseball team." She smiled tolerantly. "He plans to be a relief pitcher."

I said, "Ah," and nodded like it was the most sensible idea in the world.

George grinned self-consciously. He pushed an old navy White Sox cap down tight over springy black curls, then tugged at the visor, embarrassed.

I walked over and stood behind Dwayne. George said, "Call 'em?" I said, "Sure." George's face got firm. He threw more pitches. All started out straight as a taut rope and slower than slow, all died three-quarters of the way to the plate like a gunshot bird. Dwayne dived one way, then the other. Little League pitchers would be hard pressed to make a team with the stuff George had. I called six strikes and four balls, but I was tipsy and felt charitable. After the tenth pitch, the three of us tipped our bottles.

Dwayne had shouted, "Atta baby," each time I said "Strike!" He turned to me after his drink of wine and grinned a goofy smile. Said, "I'm gonna be his personal catcher. Like Tim McCarver used to be for Steve Carlton. You hearda' them, right? When they bring George in to pitch they'll hafta' bring me in to catch. He's gonna have it put in the contract."

I said, "Better put in a clause says I have to umpire."

Dwayne looked baffled.

I said, "Just a joke, Dwayne. This is really a great idea. I wish I'd thought of it. Relief pitchers make tons of money."

Dwayne said, "Oh, it's not the money so much." I waited, but he didn't say what "it" was.

After a bit it started to drizzle. Sandy and I went into the house, followed by George and Dwayne.

We went to the living room, sat on the wooden floor. I leaned against the front of a brown couch. A nineteen-inch black-and-white TV had been on when we walked in so I stared at it. George and Dwayne ignored their guests at first and discussed what pitches they'd throw Canseco and Puckett and Boggs. When they agreed on pitching strategy, George got up and put a heavy metal record on a 1950's hi-fit set.

Dwayne twisted two joints and we passed them around.

When the dope was smoked up, George scooted over to Sandy and the two whispered in each other's ear. Dwayne leaned close to me and said, "So you think George has a live arm? We watch baseball on TV all the time. I think George has as good a chance as anybody. Some of those guys ain't that good. I think we can make the Bigs after maybe one season in Triple A."

I said, "When'd you guys think of this?"

Dwayne said, "'Bout a month ago. See, George and me don't want no nine-to-five job. Can't live that way. We tried once. We used to live with my brother, Buster, in Johnson City and we did the day job bit. But that kind of life's too hectic so we moved out here. You can party loud as you want, nobody around to hassle you."

"There's a lot to be said for country life."

"Sure is. Anyway, we were sittin' here like this one day last month readin' about spring training and it just came to George. What's every manager complain about all the time?"

I shook my head.

"Lack of pitching, right? We both played a lot of ball when we was kids. It'd be a shame to waste all that practice. George said, that's it, that's what we'll do. You get big bucks, you travel for free, they pay you food money. It's not a bad way to live."

I said, "You guys'd have to clean up. They got drug tests now you know."

Dwayne's face fell. After a long second, he said, "No shit?" and shook his head slightly. He leaned back, face grave like this was something he had to ponder.

A part of my brain asked myself what in hell was I doing in the middle of a country full of washed-out cornfields getting high with three loonies—two of which loonies were so out of touch with reality they made the third loony look downright sane. But the rest of my brain told me to chill. Somedays I'm paid to get beat up. Today I was getting paid to get high and hang out. And I might learn something here. No doubt I was too trashed to recognize any pertinent information if it was presented to me now, but I could always work it loose later.

Then everybody got quiet. We watched "The Newlyweds" and it seemed serious and life-enhancing. I hung on every response. The commercials were abstract. And erudite. Then the TV sound started being filtered through cotton. People squawked like ducks. The show was on for ten minutes, then the station switched to an old movie. Twenty minutes into the movie, I realized I couldn't follow the plot. Or who was who. Or if Gable or Cooper was the star. Or remember a single thing that had happened during the first twenty minutes. Then the movie was over and I realized it'd been two hours not twenty minutes.

It was at this point I realized George and Dwayne smoked killer dope. If they copped smoke like this on a regular basis I understood how a retard idea like two potheads going to Florida and joining a major league baseball team seemed plausible.

At three o'clock, the two future Big Leaguers started to nod. Before he went under, George said to Sandy, "Remember, babe, I'd do anything for you. Anything."

Sandy looked quickly at him, then at me. She looked flustered. She said, "I know you would, hon. That's what keeps me goin'."

The boys snored. It was another half hour before Sandy said, "You still pretty high?"

I said, "Take my sunglasses off and tell me if my eyes are open."

"What?"

"Never mind. Old joke."

She said, "I can drive now." We got up. Sandy took a folded check from her shirt pocket and tucked it inside George's belt. He thanked her with a raspy snore. He scratched his chin like he was trying to remove skin and dribbled a glob of saliva onto his shirt. Sandy kissed the top of his cap and said, "Let's go."

# FIFTEEN

Going back, Sandy drove slow and careful. She observed speed limits and remembered what stop signs were for. The urge to "go" spent, her demeanor became almost tranquil. There was no "Look at me, Daniel," no mumbling.

I was glad. My nerves felt like jagged wires from the speed crash. I was nauseated and had a monster headache. I sipped brandy now just to stay on top of the sickness.

Ten miles onto the highway, she said, "It's rare when people who just met are as silent as we've been most of the time. People usually babble just to cover up their nervousness about being with a stranger."

I grunted. Thought, where in hell were you on the way out when I couldn't keep my mouth shut, but all I said was, "I'm too toasted to talk."

She said, "George and Dwayne smoke that stuff all day long. Have for years."

"That what the check was for?"

"I give him a check every week. What he spends it on is his business. He's an adult. In years anyway." She threw an empty beer can out the window and slipped the last can we had out of its plastic ring. She popped it, then stuck it between her thighs where the top peeked out like a metallic gold saddle pommel.

I said, "His business is turning his brain into Swiss cheese, he's puffin' smoke like that day in, day out."

Sandy didn't answer. She stared ahead for a bit, sipping sometimes from the Michelob can. Suddenly she said, "My husband grew up knowing he'd be rich someday. He was confident of it. He didn't care what he had to do, but one way or another he was going to make it. And he did. He's just about the richest man in Johnson City. Daniel, don't let anyone tell you different—a man can be ninety-five years old, weigh four hundred pounds, not have a tooth in his mouth or a hair on his head, but if he's got plenty of money, he'll attract women. A rich man gets all the bimbos he wants." Still staring ahead, she bummed a Kool from me, lit it with the dash lighter. There was a pause as she inhaled and blew out a deep lungful, then she said, "The honest answer to your question is, yes, Ronald cheats on his wife— on me. It's easier using the third person, to say 'wife' instead of 'me.' Know what I mean?"

"I do."

"Sometimes you need to say these things. Talk about it to get the anger out of your system. And you seem like a decent sort. Least you're not from town anyway, so hopefully this conversation will stay in the car. I mean most people've heard about it and if you're poking around you'll hear it over and over. I just don't want people feeling sorry for me."

"The man's a jerk. It's not your fault. Nobody should feel sorry for you."

"Ronald's committed adultery for years and I suspect he'll continue doing it so long as his equipment operates. You'll never know how low a woman's self-esteem falls when she finds out she's not enough for her man. That he's gotta have more."

"Works both ways. Men lose self-esteem when their women cheat."

"Do they?" she almost spat. "I tried that. Sent Ronald over the edge for awhile, but in the long run all it did was make him stay away from home more." She took a long drag on the Kool, blew out smoke. "Anyway, I quit that fast. Made me feel tawdry. My upbringing I guess. I just put up with the situation now, try to ignore it, try and deal with it. But it's tough to deal with rage."

I nodded. "It makes you drink and get nuts. The fight you had this morning about Andrea Gale?"

"Who's that?"

"Don't play dumb, Sandy. He told you about my visit to his office."

"No specifics, no names. He said you cast aspersions on his character."

The nausea got worse and I sipped a spot of brandy. Prayed I wouldn't go much lower. There's always a downside to street speed. You'd think one would learn.

We were silent again for a bit, then Sandy pointed at a farmhouse and barn. Said, "That's what I come from. Both sides of my family were farmers for generations. My mother was a diagnosed manic-depressive. There wasn't any money for hospitals or a shrink so she suffered, which meant the rest of the family suffered. Even when she was in an up mood she was impossible to live with. Just in a different way. She slit her wrists when I was sixteen, George was just a baby. I came home from school and found her in the bathtub, cold water running so it would wash all the blood down the drain. She was white as a clean sheet. George was in the next room crying his lungs out in the crib. I picked him up and ran to the nearest house. They went and found my father, called the sheriff. I sat in their kitchen, hugging George and crying the rest of the day."

I looked at her. She was watching the road, no expression on her face.

"My father ran off a week after the funeral. I never saw him again. I heard he ended up in Nebraska and died about five years later."

"He never contacted you?"

"Never. He wasn't close to me. Just my mother. My mother was his whole life. He was a very high strung, overly sensitive man. Not strong emotionally. You can imagine what my mother's death did to him. Folks explained he couldn't handle the trauma. His wife a suicide, leaving two kids to raise. Two kids he really didn't care about. He just didn't have the right makeup to deal with all that so he split. I don't know why people assumed I had the right makeup to raise a baby while I was still in high school right after my mother killed herself and my father ran off. That's what I did—I raised George, even though we moved in with my maternal grandmother in Johnson City. Old woman loved that, let me tell you. Don't think she didn't remind me every chance she got how grateful we should be that she saved us from an orphans' home."

I kept looking at her. Thought about the psychological damage a teenage girl would suffer from both parents abandoning ship within a week's time.

Sandy flicked the cigarette out the window and was silent for some seconds. I didn't speak for fear of distracting her. She said, "Now that I'm getting close to her age, I don't blame her really. She was old, she'd raised a family. Done her bit. At that age who wants a teenage girl and a baby in diapers dumped on their doorstep? If somebody was to do that to me now I'd raise some hell I guarantee it." She made a hollow laugh. "I was pretty as a picture then. Didn't drink or go to parties or swear or anything. Never even heard of marijuana. I was a cheerleader and back then there was like a code of conduct for cheerleaders. Like when you get older there's rules about aging." She looked at me. "You know the rules about aging?"

"Never heard of 'em."

"I'm not surprised. They're very important. Another five or six years you'll learn all about it."

She got quiet again and I wondered about the last statement a bit. I was tempted to ask, but I wanted her to keep with the story.

Sandy said, "When I was eighteen, Ronald Headon strutted into my life. He was tall, thin, handsome, glib. And older. Six years doesn't seem like much of a difference now, but at the time I thought he was the last word in sophistication. The man could of talked a nun out of her habit back then. He's lost that talent for sweet-talk, doesn't need it now. He just orders people around and things get done. He had a little money then. Inheritance or something. First time we ever talked serious, he told me how rich he's gonna be. And he made me believe it. I *knew* it would happen. Imagine how that sounded to a penniless farm girl with no mother or father who didn't know what to do with her future. He swept me right off my feet smack on my back. Grandma liked to broke my spine in two pushing me at him. I got pregnant, we got married. That's what you did back then. I lost the baby and there we were—two kids pressed together with no glue to keep us stuck. And inside a couple years, when he started to make something of himself, I started to see the real Ronald Headon. Driven, obsessed, cold-hearted, moody as hell. We got a new circle of friends and around them sometimes he acted like I was something he picked up at a garage sale." She stopped again. Looked out the side window and sighed, looked back at the road. "Thirty years later, I wake up every day and first thing I want is a drink. My husband spends all his time making money or screwing sluts or chairing charity groups to promote his image as an esteemed businessman. I got a simpleminded brother, all he wants to do is fry his brain and throw baseballs. That sound like a life to you?"

"Divorce him. Start over."

She nodded her head. Said, "I used to talk about divorce. Ronald always got upset. He doesn't think he's such a bad sort. He likes to pretend I know nothing about the other women. Appearances are very important to him. He's a fucking *pillar of the community*. He actually calls himself that. We're Catholic and he's active in the church, so there's another reason."

"Always amazes me how churchgoers rationalize sin."

"You just ask for forgiveness. It's easy really. Anyway, he wouldn't stand for a divorce. How would it look? He all the time tells me how lucky I am to have the things he can provide."

"Just like your grandmother."

"You got it. She saved me from the orphans' home, he took me from destitute farm girl to fur coats and BMW's." She laughed humorlessly. "But that was seven, eight years ago I talked like that. Now I don't have the courage or the energy to leave and start over. I'm getting old, Daniel. And who's to say I'd be any happier? It's not horrible *every* day. So I put up with it. The lies, the fights, him spending all his time chasing money like he still needs more, him screwing anything that'll lie still for a few minutes."

"Why's he think you know nothing about that?"

"He denies everything, everytime. I never actually caught him in the act. But I hear so many stories and there's so much circumstantial evidence. I mean, lipstick on his underwear? I found that once. I shoved those shorts right in his face. You know what the bastard said? 'I don't see a thing.' And there's a mouth print bright as one of those wax lips you used to get at the candy store on there. Ah, hell, I don't care anymore anyway."

She started to cry. I asked if she wanted me to drive. She shook her head. After a bit she said, "You blame me?"

I said, "Of course not."

Through the tears she said in a choked voice, "Because I'm afraid back there is where I'd end up sure as hell if I walked out. I don't have any self-discipline anymore. I don't think I can take care of myself. I'm used to having laundry ladies and cleaning ladies and Ronald handing me money whenever I need it. And my drinking is out of hand. If I feel like drinking I drink and when I start I can't stop. And I feel like drinking all the time. And I'd end up back there, I just know it, drinking myself sick everyday, taking care of a child in an adult's body and discussing how to pitch to major league baseball players. Is *that* a life? Is that any better than what I got now?"

I said, "Sandy, give yourself some credit. If you left, you wouldn't end up there. Your self-esteem is so low you got yourself convinced you can't hack the real world. That's the problem. World's a lot bigger than Johnson City and that farmhouse."

She sniffed loudly and said, "I shouldn't say things against George. He really would do anything for me."

I wanted to say, "Like killing your husband's mistress?" but this surely wasn't the time or place. I gave her one of my cards, told her to call me whenever she needed to talk. She put the card in her shirt pocket without looking at it.

I said, "Get into a rehab. Dry out. Then you'd have the energy and the confidence to start over."

She started to cry harder. "But I don't want to quit drinking. I just wanna get a handle on it."

Which made this a dead end conversation. I recalled the many times Marvin and I had had this very same talk. Only difference was Marvin said what I just said and I said what Sandy just said. Do as I say not as I do.

Both of us were silent the rest of the way. I was depressed. Rich people are just as scared of life and confused about the future as the rest of us? What in hell does it take to feel secure in this world?

# SIXTEEN

It was five-thirty when we got back to Blissful Estates. The
heavy gray clouds made dusk start early and lights were
winking on in rich men's homes all around us.

She braked at the entrance to the drive. I got out and
opened the back door, slid Bug's cage out. Sandy said, "Your
rabbit has good manners. It's like he was never there."

I leaned my arm on the open back door, looked inside and
said, "Remember, you call me if something comes up. Or if
you just need to talk."

Sandy rubbed her breastbone and made a forlorn smile.
"We'll see," she said.

She looked toward the house then at me and said in a
scared voice, "Hurry up, Daniel, go. Jesus, what's he doing
home now?"

Ronald Headon was halfway down the drive, charging
like an enraged Grizzly. I shut the door, set Bugs's cage on
the ground and walked around the front of the BMW, passing through the headlight beams. I leaned against the side
by the front tire.

"Go, Daniel, please," Sandy said out the window. "Get
out of here."

I'm not the bravest man in Illinois and I wasn't in peak
condition at the moment, but Ronald Headon was not a
man I'd run from on my most cowardly day.

As he got closer he started yelling. To his wife he said,
"You pathetic drunken slut! What did I tell you about this
piece of scum?"

He was going to pretend I wasn't there. He wanted to act
like it was just the two of them. Maybe he thought he could
get away with screaming at her and calling me scum if he
pretended I wasn't there. Or maybe I was supposed to feel
honored he bothered to call me anything at all.

He rushed past me, without so much as a glance. He
yanked the car door open, reached in and clamped both

hands around Sandy's neck, started to squeeze and shake. She twisted away, saying, "Please, Ronald," in a choked whisper.

He shouted, "I told you not to even talk to this scumbag and you spend the fucking *day* with him?"

I disliked this man on GP and now he was calling me names while pretending I was beneath notice. He was manhandling a woman half his size, a woman who at the moment I felt very sorry for. Plus I was on the losing side of several substances severely abused. My nerves were on a hair trigger. The trigger pulled, and something inside me exploded. I wanted Ronald Headon's blood.

I moved behind him, grabbed his shirt collar and a handful of hair and slammed his face against the edge of the car roof. He made a nipped scream and let go of Sandy. She shouted, "Daniel, don't!" I pulled his head back and positioned it like I was aiming to shove it through a small hole. He tried to squirm loose so I removed my right hand from the collar and wrapped it around his throat, pressing my thumb and index finger against either side of his larynx. He stopped moving. I kept a fistful of hair in my left hand, twisting it so it would feel to him like I could yank it out by its roots if I wanted.

He pressed his palms against his mouth, one on top of the other to hold the pain and blood in. He made muffled sounds that were either words or moans.

The rage still roared in me. I said in a hard voice, "Tell me something, Ronald. If this is happily married, what the fuck is your definition of unhappy?"

Sandy scrambled out the passenger door and ran clumsily toward the house, tripping and tottering, her sobs fading as she disappeared up the drive.

Headon took his hands away from his mouth, set them against the top of the car to brace himself. Through clenched teeth, his voice like a munchkin's because of the pressure from my fingers, he said, "You've had it, man. You have done it up royal now. You are through, creep." Removing his hands had let the blood flow and I felt sticky drops as it dribbled off his chin onto my hand.

"Right, Ronald. Whatever you say. You own this hunk of

shit metropolis in the middle of fucking nowhere. Soon I will sleep with the fishes."

He said, "I will make your life a misery."

He refused to submit an inch. Refused to let me know he was hurting. That was a mistake because what I wanted more than anything in the world at that moment was an acknowledgment of some kind from Ronald Headon. That he was in pain, that he was sorry, that he was afraid. Something. Anything. I was outraged by his pride. Soon as I felt his arms go slack I bounced his face off the roof again. Not as hard as the first time and his hands on the edge of the roof absorbed most of the blow, but he made a high-pitched, womanly scream.

Which made my rage dissipate as suddenly as it exploded and I stood there feeling sick and ashamed and remorseful. Headon moaned but didn't speak.

"Tell me again how I've had it, Ronald," I said wearily. "Maybe I deserve it. But afterward tell me about your girls. Tell me how one of 'em happened to get murdered Saturday morning. I've just seen up close and personal how you react when women tick you off. You get violent, Ronald. You choked your wife, didn't care I was watching you do it. Whatta you do when you're alone with her? What'd you do when you were alone with Andrea Gale?"

"I told you about Andrea Gale," he said. "What did my wife tell you? That no good drunken bitch—" I pulled his head back. He said, "Okay, okay, I'm no saint, but Sandy sure as hell is no angel. I'm telling you I didn't know Andrea Gale except that she worked on the floor at the plant."

"Come on," I said. "You got a rap at that place for hitting on the help. Andrea Gale was close to the best looking babe in this whole burg and you tell me you never noticed her? You are insulting my intelligence, Ronald."

"You got no business here, creep. You are going to regret this incident. You got my wife drunk and God knows what else went on. You think you can crawl out here from that cesspool of a city you live in and insult me in my office, rough me up in front of my home, you got it wrong. I'm *known* in this town."

"Your wife doesn't need encouragement from me to get

drunk. You're all the inspiration she'll ever need."

"I almost pity you for what's gonna happen after this. You better get out of here. Now."

"You in a hurry to finish the job on Sandy? Pity Torres isn't around anymore. Maybe he could do it for you."

"I'm not beating anybody. But if I did, she's my wife. What is she to you?"

Suddenly I felt like a horse's ass. Blundering into a situation I knew nothing about, acting like a damn white knight on a divine mission to protect damsels in distress. Who the hell did I think I was anyway?

I pulled his head below the roof, kneed his back, sending him sprawling into the front seat. I retrieved Bugs's cage and walked slowly to the Skylark.

I checked the glove compartment for the Valium bottle. Not there. How in hell did that happen? I rested my forehead on the steering wheel and started trembling from the afterclap of my violence. My heart was flip-flopping around my chest like a dying fish. My armpits were soaked and icy sweat flooded my ribcage. I started the car and kept my head on the wheel for some seconds, letting the soft vibrations from the engine soothe.

I put it in "D" and rolled slow past the Headon's drive. He'd pulled the BMW a third of the way up. He yelled at me out the window. I flipped him off. The sound of his shouting diminished as I moved away and I couldn't make out what he was saying, but I was pretty sure I wasn't being invited back for dinner.

When I got to the end of Blissful Road, I twisted the steering wheel savagely, gunning the Skylark onto the highway, just like Sandy Headon had done in the morning.

# SEVENTEEN

On the drive back to Chicago, I barely noticed the endless procession of doubled white lights sailing towards me. I felt sick as a dog from the drugs and the booze and my state of mind was a shambles. I became deeply depressed thinking about what I did to Ronald Headon. Don't like what somebody's doing, Dan? Shove their face into a car roof a few times. When it got down to the nit grit, I was no different than Eddie Torres or Buddy Baker. Three things invariably happen when I let rage push me over the edge into violence: I do something I regret; nothing gets solved, things usually get worse; and I suffer tremendous guilt afterward.

And my job performance sure wasn't lifting my spirits. As I reassessed the last five days, I realized I knew not much more than I did Saturday morning. I was not winning friends or influencing the people of Johnson City. Almost nobody I'd met cared for me a hell of a lot, and I'm like the next Joe, I wanna be liked. And everybody I'd met seemed to have at least a small reason to wanna see Andrea Gale dead. And this was only the people I'd talked to so far. There were other men in Andrea Gale's life. What about them? If married, what about *their* wives? Maybe their wives had dim bulb brothers who'd do anything for Sis too.

I was making the swerve on Lake Shore Drive where the old S-curve used to be when my brain finally exited the Johnson City fog and I became aware of what was going on around me. I was in the midst of a tightly packed bunch of late rush hour cars. To the left, the high rise office and apartment buildings were lit up to the clouds, twinkling and shining against the night. On my right, Lake Michigan blended into the night sky making a vertical blanket of blackness. A few tankers and cargo ships were out there, and the black blanket made their red and orange lights seem to bob in some kind of bottomless pit.

I exited at Irving Park, stopped at the red light underneath Lake Shore Drive. Ahead, the streets were crowded.
The pedestrians started to walk in jerky doubletime like a
Charlie Chaplin movie. I wondered what did all these people do? Where in hell were they going in such a rush? They
were like ants in the brown part of summer. Motion,
motion, motion. I thought of what Sandy Headon said. I
wanted to shout out the window, "In a hundred years we're
all gonna be dead. None of it matters."

Sounds intensified. Car horn honks, squealing brakes,
people's shouts. All turned to ten on some monstrous stereo.
The eye-wounding bright lights on the fronts of the stores
started marching up and down the block. For twenty
seconds, the sounds got even louder, the colors brighter,
until I had to shut my eyes. My neighborhood was ugly,
foreign and totally unfamiliar. Waves of nightmare-like
panic washed over me. My heart hammered high in my
chest, making it impossible to keep air in my lungs.

An A-1 anxiety attack. I hadn't had one in a while. A long
while. I said out loud, "Relax, Dan. All in your head. Too
much stress today. You fell off the wagon, you smoked too
much heavy dope, you feel guilt because you got violent.
You'll be fine in a few minutes. You've had these before.
They go away." My fingers thumped the steering wheel.

My apartment is a mile from the light. When the green
showed I drove there like Batman. I leaped the steps. The
Mexican couple who rent the second floor were screaming
Spanish at each other. That didn't help. I slammed the front
door, moved fast to the kitchen. I twisted open the sugar
tin, ran my hand through the granules, brought up the zip-
loc baggy with my stash of Valium and speed, ate two of the
tranks. Underneath the sink was a pint bottle of blackberry
brandy. Only booze in the house. I slid to the floor, leaned
my back against the cabinet, took a long swallow. I did the
giant diaphragm breaths the groupie at the bar in Madison
taught me one night last winter. The girl'd told me she'd
been in therapy for six years because of panic attacks and
excessive anxiety and she swore the deep breaths worked
because of some physiological reason or other. I told myself,
"You're home now. Home."

A few minutes later, I started to shiver and yawn and I knew the attack was going away. The hot bubbling in my stomach subsided. My heart ebbed from eight/four to two/four and slid down to my chest. Bottle in hand I walked back to the Skylark to get Bugs. The couple upstairs still fought. I turned and shouted, "Shut the fuck up, dammit!" and that made me feel better. But I knew draining the bottle would make me feel better yet.

The television hissed gray noise. The floor lamp at the end of the sofa seared my eyes. My clothes were soaked with sweat. I moved a dead arm and rolled over, fell from the couch to the floor. Far away the phone was ringing. I was dimly aware it had been ringing off and on for a long time. It sounded like it wouldn't stop this time until I answered it.

I crawled across the floor to the bedroom, switching the TV off on the way. I picked up the receiver, dropped it twice, put the wrong end to my ear, then the correct end and said, "Hello." Or something close.

"Daniel?" It was a woman. She was whispering.

I said loudly, "Who is this? Speak up."

"Daniel, it's Sandy Headon." Still whispering.

I moaned, placed my left palm on my forehead. "What do you want?" I was jamming the receiver into my ear to hear her. "What time is it?"

"Never mind the time. You asked me if I know somebody named Wylie."

"I remember."

"Well, I do."

"Why didn't you tell me today?"

"It was yesterday, hon. Because I have to think things out. Decide who I can trust. I decided I trust you."

"You mean I get a reward for popping your husband's face off a car roof."

She made a quick giggle. "Maybe that's it. You still wanna talk to Wylie?"

"Still do. Can you talk louder?"

"No."

"Hang on then."

I slid my Sony boom box across the rug, inserted a blank

TDK C-60. I pressed the REC button and put the micro-
phone next to my ear so it would hear what I heard. And
what I missed. "Start talking," I said.

In a fast whisper she said, "Man named Wylie worked
with Ronald long time ago. They were friends and business
partners till Ronald squeezed him out. Fact, Headon
Engineering was mostly Wylie's ideas and smarts in the
early stages. I don't know all the details, but the buyout was
messy and underhanded and it resulted in bad blood.
They've hated each other's guts ever since."

"You still talk to Wylie?"

"No. We kept in touch for a while. He hated Ronald so
bad he felt sorry for me. But we drifted apart. This happened like twenty years ago. I didn't know he was back in
the area. Last I'd heard he was on the West Coast. I know
he lost his shirt in another business deal in California maybe
ten years ago. He's no businessman. He's too nice a guy. You
gotta be a bastard to succeed in business. Like Ronald."

"What's his first name?"

"James. James Anthony Wylie. Why you wanna see him
so bad?"

"The people who hired me want him checked out. Is
Wylie back in Johnson City?"

"He's at the Jones Hotel. A dump, downtown on the south
edge. Don't know the room number. Listen, I gotta get off
here. He'll do a search and destroy he wakes up and I'm not
in bed."

"He work you over after I left?"

"I'm used to it."

"Where you at?"

"Room we were in this morning."

"Top up on the coffee table?"

"You really like that table, don't you? It's called The
Hydraulic Hideaway Bar Table."

"Every home should have one."

She clicked something against the receiver. Said, "Hear
the ice? I don't even pretend I'm gonna get on the wagon."

"You don't sound as depressed about things now."

"Ah, you know. Fuck it."

"Yeah, I know about fuck it. How's Ronald's face?"

"Ronald's face is sore. Got a lip like Louis Armstrong. Nose bled for an hour. He's not gonna press charges because of it being partly domestic. Doesn't want any publicity like that. Plans to tell people he fell down some stairs."

"I'm free and clear?"

"Not so fast, hon. A detective named McCoy came over and they talked for an hour in the library with the door locked. Those two been friends since high school. I don't know what they were cooking up in there, but watch yourself when you're in Johnson City."

I didn't want to think about what she just said.

Sandy whispered, "Gotta go," and hung up.

So did I. I leaned forward into a genuflecting position. With nothing else to concentrate on I started to comprehend just how Godawful I felt. I looked into the living room. The brandy bottle was empty on the floor by the couch, on its side in a puddle of dark gummy liquid. Next to it a green ashtray was full of squashed cigarette butts. Nauseating to look at. Depressing to think about. Four sober weeks down the drain.

A photograph of me now would certainly inspire trust and confidence in a potential client. Such a diligent, vigorous, dynamic man. No wonder I went twelve months between cases. I wanted to laugh, but something closer to a whimper came out. I croaked, "Kruger, get a life."

I stood and stumbled to the bed, fell on it like a sawed tree. I plunged into coma-like sleep.

# EIGHTEEN

This was odd.

McCoy and I faced each other in the tiny cell where I'd talked to David Stone and Dennison. It was so cold my teeth chattered like jiggled dice, but McCoy wore only baggy boxer underwear. With little red hearts sewn on. His hairy gut slopped over the waistband of his drawers. He ambled toward me in his apelike gait, a sneer on his face, grabbed both my shoulders and threw me face down on the floor. The floor was like ice. He said, "Know why? Because now we know who killed Andrea Gale." He cuffed my hands behind my neck, then stepped on my back and started jumping up and down.

"Wake up, Dan." A new voice. Not McCoy's. A woman's. "Come on, wake up Dan," it said. And it wasn't feet stomping my back, it was a small fist making gentle taps up and down my spine.

The new voice laughed. Said, "Dan, get up. Get up, Dan," three times in a sing-song tone like a mother waking a child. "Up and at 'em, Dan. It's noon."

I was trying dammit, but someone had clamped a vise around my skull and tightened it as far as it would go. That someone had also drained every last ounce of fluid from my body. I was parched. I slid my tongue around my teeth and the sides of my mouth. It was like rubbing a cotton swab against wool. I needed to drink a bathtub full of ice water. Water so cold it would glaciate my teeth. For good measure that someone had ignited a napalm bomb somewhere in my gut and the jelly-like burning raged up into my chest and throat.

Unfortunately that someone had been me, falling off the wagon with a resounding thud.

I tried to open my eyes. Only the left one worked. It saw Lisa Farrell.

She said, "Hi," brightly, waggled her fingers.

I groaned and rolled on my back. Stomach capsized. I shut my eyes tight so I wouldn't vomit, which I felt would be a rude way to say hello. I rested my forearm on my eyes to make more darkness. I said, "What do you want?" My chest and legs stung. My clothes were dry now but in drying they'd become stiff and rough as burlap. I breathed deep. I smelled like a dead goat that's been pissed on by an alley cat.

Lisa said, "I thought you didn't drink."

"Now you know why."

"You do have a problem, don't you?"

"Told you Dear Abby said so."

"I thought you were dead at first."

"I might of been. How's your lip?"

"Swelling's way down. Shoulda seen it yesterday. Look."

"In a minute."

"How do you feel?"

"Very dumb question."

"You're right. But get up. We're going to the Cubs game. I didn't know it but it's Opening Day. Streets around here are crawling with people. It's like a block party out there."

"How'd you get in?"

"Front door was unlocked. I thought you didn't do that in Chicago."

"I was overserved last night and when that happens I forget stuff like locking doors."

"I banged for five minutes. Hard. Wasn't for your car parked out front I'd of thought you weren't home."

"How'd you get tickets to Opening Day?"

"Some guy at a bar across from the ballfield."

"It's a ballpark."

"In a beer garden in a bar across the street from the ball*park*. Ferret-faced man in a long coat kept walking around the tables muttering 'Tickets, I got tickets,' real sly like."

"Murphy's Bleachers?"

"That's the place. I came to Chicago to see you. You weren't at your office and that insurance man gave me your home address and told me how to get here. So I drive here and have to park like a mile away and I'm walking here in the middle of this mob of people and I'm wondering what in hell is going on. When you didn't answer the first time, I walked over by the ballwhatever to check it out. I got us tickets, came back and found the door was unlocked."

I didn't ask what the tickets cost. She never asked me if I wanted to go so I didn't feel obligated to pay. I said, "Why'd you wanna see me?"

"Our first date didn't end so well. I still feel bad about that."

"That what that was? A date?"

"Well, kinda."

"I haven't had a date in ten years."

"I thought you could show me around Chicago."

"You never been to Chicago before?"

"Sure, lots of times. But I never know where I am."

I said, "I can't go to the Cub game. I don't think I'm getting out of bed today."

"Course you can." She tapped a bottle against my shoulder. Said, "Drink. I sipped on this on the way in. I got a friend says you can kill any size hangover with enough booze."

"I'm familiar with the theory." I opened my eyes to see what she was giving me. A bottle of Heublein Manhattan swayed in front of me. I said, "God, you mean people actually drink this stuff?" I half sat up, rested on my elbow, and took a short sip. Gagged, swallowed more right away to kill the retch. My stomach stabilized a bit. I said, "I got work to do today."

"You can take a few hours off to go to a baseball game. Johnson City's not goin' anywhere."

I made it to the shower. Stripped and stood under cold as I could stand water, bottle in hand, until I felt like a snowman. At first my internal organs did a pogo dance, but after a bit they calmed down. Out loud I said, "Kruger, go to the damn baseball game. It'll give you the illusion you got a social life."

In the bedroom, I pulled on two pair of wool socks, got into and buttoned a suit of thermal long underwear. I found my best pair of black Levi's, tucked in a red and black checked flannel shirt. Slipped my feet into a pair of fleece-lined tan chukka boots. I decided on my knee-length charcoal winter coat to wear over it all. Wasn't much of a fashion statement, but Wrigley in April has an Alaska zip code.

Lisa shouted from the living room, "Who are these people? Howling Wolf? The Neville Brothers?" She pronounced it Nev-vile. "Black Uhuru?" She pronounced that Uh-huh-ruh.

"Roots, rock and reggae," I said. "And it's Nev-ill and Ooo-hoo-roo."

"You listen to some really off-the-wall tunes, know that? I

never heard of these people. And that tape you played the other night? Never heard that music before let alone the band."

"They don't play the good stuff on the radio. It's a law I think."

I went to the kitchen, mixed Bunny Chow and chopped celery together in a bowl, took it to the living room and placed it inside the cage. Bugs twitched his nose, appreciating the bouquet, then started chomping. I couldn't remember if I'd fed him last night or not.

Lisa, watching, said, "You need a housekeeper. This apartment is fucked up. Clothes all over, there's an inch of dust on everything, all the ashtrays are full. That bottle over there is *stuck* in some gooey junk. It's filthy in here."

"I like a home looks lived in."

"Yeah, well this home looks like somebody died in it. Long time ago. And there's nothing in the refrigerator 'cept a bottle of dill pickles."

"I gotta eat something." I turned to her. "This why you drove all the way to Chicago? Badmouth my housekeeping?"

"What housekeeping? The place is a sty. Rabbit's cute though. What's his name?"

"Bugs."

"That's original."

"It was either Bugs or Long Eared Varmint and Bugs is easier to say when you're drunk. I was drunk all the time back when I got him. I can even fake Bugs out with Buzz." I lowered my voice to a whisper. "He can't tell the difference. Watch." I placed my head over where Bugs was devouring his chow. I said, "Bugs."

Bugs kept chewing.

I said, "Buzz."

Bugs kept chewing.

"See? Same reaction both times. I tell you he can't tell the difference."

Lisa rolled her eyes.

She wore pink jeans and a white polo shirt with a tiny red something on the pocket. She carried a thin white sweater. I said she better take one of my coats, but she said no, it was gorgeous out. I would've insisted, but after listening to her trash my crib, I shut up.

We walked the two blocks to Wrigley. Lisa jabbered the whole way, excited by the noise and the activity. I sucked on a Rolaid tablet, walked defensively, and half-listened to her chatter. I stared at her hair a lot. It shined and sparkled like rinsed coal, not done up in any kind of 'do, just hanging loose, coming to rest on her shoulders in a gracefully tangled mass. I hoped she wouldn't start with the compulsive finger grooming and ruin it.

The scalper had unloaded SRO tickets, which is all John Q. Public is gonna get for Opening Day unless he knows somebody. Especially against the Mets. Since 1969, Cub fans hate the Mets. They passionately love the '69 Cubs, who pulled one of the great chokes of all time, and absolutely detest the team that took advantage of it like somehow the whole thing was the Mets' fault. Go figure.

Ushers sent us here and there and here again. We ended up on the concrete walkway first base side under the upper deck, our backs against the chain link fence, crammed in with the rest of the sardines.

We stood next to a Mutt and Jeff pair of students from De Paul. Short one thought he was the next Sam Kinison and made a running, profane commentary on everything he saw, ballgame and otherwise, in a braying voice. Frequent pauses for the laughs no one but his buddy made.

Evidently his buddy who was about seven foot tall was there just so he could shout obscenities at Strawberry. Strawberry, of course, couldn't hear a word of it, but the act of yelling was enough to make the guy happy. The Strawberry hater had a Canon 35 with an attached lens the size of a siege howitzer.

I couldn't tell what he planned to shoot because where we stood you could only see brief pieces of the field—the right half of the infield and a portion of right and center fields. If the sea of people parted just right, I caught a glimpse of the batter and pitcher, but that was only a couple of times.

So I followed the game by the stomach-shaking roars and groans of the crowd. The only action I saw were ground balls to second. Depending on who was in the field and what sound the fans made I could determine hit or out. It was a surreal way to watch a baseball game.

But I had to admit it was good to be there. Wrigley is a magical green oasis in the middle of a concrete desert. Walking up the steps from the dark, noisy bowels of the park and encountering this shimmering emerald and tan land lying in front of you is always a trip. The sights and sounds of the park are among the few things in life that still delight me. The shouts and scurries of the vendors, the smell of beer and red hots, the excitement that buzzes the stands, the elegance and beauty of the park itself. I love Wrigley. I just hate the Cubs.

The wind was winter sharp off the Lake and a barely there sun conducted a game-long battle with the April grayness. Sometimes the clouds thinned enough so the players' shadows showed and the fans would cheer.

I was warm as toast but Lisa was freezing. I smiled to myself. She drank five beers in the first hour, saying it might warm her up. All it did was make her talk more, especially between innings. She told me about her new apartment, how she'd talked to Ronald Headon and he personally told her to take the week off with pay to "get my head straight." She talked about her constant war with her father. Least it sounded constant. Kept saying how neat it was to be in Chicago on Opening Day at Wrigley Field, watching a game that was on TV sets all over the country. I told her people in Waco, Texas, had cable knew more about what was going on in this game than we did. She said she didn't care about that. She just wanted to tell her friends she'd been there. And that's all Opening Day is now. People attend it so they can brag about it next day like they'd brag about being at the newest, trendiest nightclub.

Lisa leaned into me and used my arms for a jacket. She squealed and smacked her hands together and jumped up and down whenever the rest of the crowd did. Didn't keep her very warm though because Doc Gooden was hurling midsummer heat and the Cubs couldn't do a thing to him. Doc shut down the hometown two-zip. Cubs had five hits. I think.

Being the loyal White Sox partisan I am, I was happy, but the rest of the crowd was subdued and pouty as we filed slowly down the ramps, crunching peanut shells and skidding empty beer cups.

Lisa borrowed the crowd's mood. She stayed silent as she shuffled in front of me. It took thirty minutes to get on Addison. We were crossing Wilton Ave a block from my apartment, still in the middle of a mob, when she quietly said, "So who killed Andrea?"

"To be precise, I don't know."

"I think about her all the time."

"I would imagine so."

"You must suspect someone other than David, else you wouldn't keep nosing around."

"Who I suspect or don't suspect's got nothing to do with it. I nose around because I'm paid to nose around. And I nose where my employers tell me to nose, even if I don't always agree with 'em. When the money stops I stop."

"Who beat us up?"

"Two punks."

"Who hired the punks."

"Don't know that either."

"Is all this related?"

"Maybe. Yes. No. Probably. Lisa, I don't know."

"You gonna find out?"

"Gonna try."

"If it's not David, you don't care one way or the other who it might be?"

"Not even a little bit. Outside of you and one other person, nobody in Johnson City has been so nice to me that I'd hate to see them sent up for murder. While we're on the subject, I pushed Ronald Headon's face into the roof of his car yesterday. That and some other things messed me up last night. That's why I got so wasted."

"You're gonna hear about that."

"No doubt."

"Why'd it mess *you* up so bad?"

"I got this thing about needing to be in control. I *have* to show people I'm in control all the time. Even when I overdrink in public I rarely show it. With Headon I lost it completely, got violent. Felt like a thug when the rage left. I always hate myself after I do that."

"Lighten up, everybody loses control once in a while. Does things they regret. It's natural."

"I hate it anyway."

"Headon can make it rough for you out there."

"You got proof he screws the help?"

"I don't have video tape of it, but it's common knowledge. Everybody talks about it."

"He gets sincerely indignant when I mention it."

"He's got a reputation to protect. He likes to think he's discreet, you know? He's not gonna start reading off his conquests to a stranger. You should be able to figure that out."

"You know any of the women personally he's had affairs with?"

"No."

"Ones that do, what about *their* discretion?"

"A job at Headon Engineering is as good as it gets in Johnson City. Keep your mouth shut, keep your job. That's all the incentive for discretion they'd need. You can work at Headon Engineering for ten bucks an hour or you can work at a plastics factory or something for four-fifty."

"And the ones who say no, there's no reprisals?"

"No, I give the man credit for that. It's never do it or else. I never heard anybody got pinkslipped for saying no. Like I said, he starts out joking around so if you wanna say no he doesn't look like an idiot."

It was four o'clock. I reminded her I had work to do. She made a face, but said okay. We walked down Addison, then Halsted to her car.

It was a snow white Camaro with royal blue interior. I said, "Nice ride. Maybe I oughta get a job at Headon Engineering."

She didn't hear that, she was staring ahead, a bewildered look on her face. She said, "Couldn't it be David after all?"

"Sure. For Andrea. But what about Torres? If the two are linked then it's not David because he was in jail when Torres was killed."

"You think they are linked?"

I smiled. "Don't know that either."

She smiled back. "Are you any good at this?"

"Ask myself that all the time."

"You haven't learned *anything?*"

"Enough to make me totally confused."

She gave me a folded piece of paper. "My new apartment. Address and phone number. I'm all moved in. Phone's the same as before, I didn't know if Andrea gave you the number or not." She looked away from me. Said, "Dan, Andrea wasn't a very *nice* person. I mean—"

I made a laugh. Lisa looked back at me quick, red-faced. "No, really, she was my best friend, but she was awfully— well—immoral. I mean she was—"

"I said, "She was what?"

"Unprincipled."

"I thought we'd already established that." I leaned in and kissed her quick on the cheek. "I even heard a story or two about you."

She did the fingers through the hair bit. She smiled without wanting to, then decided she should be mad. She took off without saying goodbye.

I walked back to Fremont wondering just why in hell had Lisa Farrell come all the way to Chicago to see me.


# NINETEEN


The heels of Marvin's burgundy loafers rested on the edge of his desk, the new *Playboy* lay open in his lap, and he was muttering "Oh, my God" as I walked through the door. Marvin spends a lot of time with his feet on his desk, leafing through girlie magazines, saying "Oh, my God."

My mail was stacked neatly on the corner of my desk. Six envelopes. I sailed each, one after the other, into the circular file soon as I read that I might've already won two hundred fifty grand. What in hell did I want with two hundred fifty grand? I sat where the mail had been. Said, "Any calls?"

"Few. I let it ring."

"Attaway."

Eyes still in the magazine, he said, "I'm not an answering service. Get a machine, I keep telling you."

"Marvin, I'm sure you've noticed my career in private investigation has hit a bit of a lull. To the point where it's more like a hobby. I don't need no answering machine for a hobby."

"Girl here looking for you this morning."

"She found me. We went to Wrigley."

Marvin is a rabid Cub fan. He frowned.

"They lost," I said. I waited, but he said nothing. I said, "Trade cars tonight?"

"No way. I like my car without bullet holes in it."

"I never returned your car with bullet holes in it."

"I've seen 'em in yours."

"Only the wheels. Remember that crazy Floridge kid? Shot out all the tires? But you replace tires that have holes in 'em, Marvin, and the car is good as new. 'Sides, you got insurance, right?"

He flipped a page, smiled. Said, "Midwestern Insurance Group. You can't find lower rates in upper Illinois." That was their TV and radio slogan. He waited a minute, pretended to debate the issue in his mind. But I am Marvin's cross to bear, so like I knew he would he said, "Okay. But only tonight and only because I got nothin' goin' on."

Marvin went through a painful divorce three years ago and he was still gun shy. I said, "Marvin, you always got nothin' goin' on. You gotta get out more. Hit the bars. Live it up. Meet the girl of your dreams instead of looking at them pictures all the time. Real girls don't look like that. That's why you think real girls are so bland and plain."

He said, "Listen to Warren Beatty. The girl this morning. She involved in your case?"

"Roommate of the dead girl."

"What's her status?"

"Don't know."

"What do you know?"

"I'm pretty sure Stone—the guy who hired me—is innocent because I think the second murder is tied to the first and he couldn't of done the second. But as to who is guilty?"

I shrugged. "Everybody I meet has a reason."

"Maybe they all did it. Like that Christie book where the detective finds out all the suspects stabbed the victim once each."

It was getting dark. Another drizzle started. Water drops like clear marbles slipped slowly down the pane of glass that is the front of the office. I looked out at the flow of cars going down Lincoln Ave. Because of dusk and the sodium streetlights, all the cars were the same color, a washed out, ghastly orange. I said, "No wonder I'm so confused and depressed. It's rained for two solid weeks."

Marvin said, "The price we gotta pay for May flowers. And listen, don't even think about having a drink when you're driving my car."

"I'm on the wagon, you know that." I didn't tell him about the day before. Didn't need the lecture. Marvin enjoyed getting smashed once or twice a month, but it wasn't a lifestyle for him. He couldn't understand the constant craving. Me, I can never understand how a person can drink to excess two times a month and not touch the stuff the rest of the time.

Half an hour out of Chicago, the drizzle became a downpour. The windshield wipers ticked double time like metronomes on crank, pushing the rain to the corners of the glass. I'd picked Bugs up and he was in his cage on the passenger side of the seat. I said, "Hell of a ride, eh Bugs?"

Marvin buys a new Cadillac Seville every January 2nd. Always white, always fully loaded. After the rattletrap Skylark, the Seville seemed to float on air. The engine was whisper quiet. I turned the radio down every time I stopped to see if it had died. A brand new Caddy Seville was the last thing McCoy would expect to see me in.

An hour later, I marveled again at how ugly downtown Johnson City was. Even the rain didn't help. Most towns look like they're getting a bath when it rains. Johnson City just looked soggy and sad and forlorn.

The Jones was six blocks south of the Blue Palm. A four-story, white-painted wooden box that had probably been the talk of the town about the time Abe Lincoln split rails. The o's in Jones and Hotel were burned out of the sign attached to the corner of the building. In the muddy swatch of lawn between the sidewalk and the street, a small neon sign announced V c ncies.

I parked at the curb directly in front of the glass door. Told Bugs to chill for awhile. I got out and stood for a second, enjoying the contrast. Brand new Caddy in front of older-than-dirt fleabag hotel.

Six stairs up from the street was a small, underlit lobby. Ten stuffed vinyl armchairs each with an old man sitting in it. A few folding chairs, empty. The room was steamy with the smell of cigars and moist clothes. Some of the men read newspapers, some watched "Wheel of Fortune" on a sixteen-inch TV that sat on a card table at one end of the room. Signs on the wall above the TV said NO GUESTS AFTER 10 O'CLOCK and ONLY RESIDENTS AND THEIR GUESTS ALLOWED IN THE LOUNGE AREA.

The lady behind the counter shied against the wall as I approached. She was skinny and solemn-faced, and with her eyes bulging like eggs from anxiety, she looked like a praying mantis. She had a helmet of short gray hair and wore a three-sizes-too-big flower print dress.

She whispered, "Sir, I'm very worry, but you can't park in front." Her voice cracked on "front." "On account of a Fire Department law. There's a parking lot in back. It's a big fine, you get a ticket for it."

I said, "I'm on an expense account. Damn the Fire Department. I need to talk to James Wylie." I didn't have any gum so I offered a Kool.

She shook her head at the cigarette. Said, "I'm very sorry, but Mr. Wylie skipped Saturday morning owing two weeks rent."

"I'm very sorry too. You sure it was Saturday?"

"Yes."

"How long'd he live here?"

"Just a few months I think. See, my husband owns this hotel. He took sick with pneumonia so I been running the desk the last three weeks. I hardly ever set foot in the place before that. But we can't afford to hire a desk clerk except for weekends." She eyed the old boys in the room, leaned forward and whispered, "I hate this place. It's so depressing."

"Ma'am, it's depressing all over. 'Cept maybe Kenilworth."

She kept whispering, "But these men. They're just waiting to die. And truth is, I'm scared to death of most of 'em."

"They look like a docile lot."

"But you should hear them talk. Anyone uses the language these men do is bound to be evil. Mr. Wylie wasn't like that at all. He behaved as a gentleman at all times."

"You talked with him?"

"All the time. We became friends. He always stopped to chat on his way in or out. Sometimes we talked for an hour at a time. The other men barely say a word to me. And when they do they aren't civil. But James was so nice. Always courteous. That's why it hurt that he skipped."

"He give any sign something was wrong?"

She ran her tongue around her mouth. I hadn't muscled her, or raised my voice, and she looked a little more at ease. She said, "You aren't the police, right? Not looking like you do. What do you want him for? You don't want to hurt him, do you? Mr. Wylie is old and frail and gentle."

"Course not. I just need to ask him a question or two. He ever have visitors?"

"None. He was embarrassed that he lived here. He never came out and said so, but I could tell he was used to finer accommodations. He always dressed like a gentleman. The clothes were old, but nice. Wouldn't give the time of day to the bums over there. He implied on several occasions that he used to live a more prosperous lifestyle."

"He ever mention the name Andrea Gale?"

"No, I don't believe so."

"David Stone?"

"No."

"Ronald Headon?"

"That one I heard all the time. The big shot who owns the engineering plant, right? James disliked that man intensely. Said if it hadn't been for Ronald Headon, his life would of been entirely different."

"Any other names you remember?"

"No."

"Notify the police he left?"

"I called them Sunday night to see if there was a John Doe corpse or an accident. There wasn't. I didn't file a missing person. He must of had his reasons."

"So Wylie used to have money, but he didn't anymore?"

"He was living *here* wasn't he? I think he got by on some kind of government check. It wasn't very much. He implied a couple times he was gonna come into some money soon, but he didn't elaborate. I think he just said it because he thought I felt sorry for him. He was such a nice man. But he was as broke as everybody else who lives here. That's another reason this place is so depressing. Everybody's old and broke and waiting to die."

"Rent his room out yet?"

"No. His stuff's still up there. I'll wait until I need the room before I take it out. I'm hoping he'll come back. I miss him. He was my only friend here and I hate to lose touch with friends. You don't get many in life."

I said, "No you don't."

"Why do you ask about his room?"

"Let me take a quick look at it."

She looked past me, eyes nervous again. "Sir, I couldn't do that. Mr. Wylie is my friend and I don't know your intentions."

"Intentions are strictly honorable." I pulled a five from my wallet, curved it a bit and fanned myself. Said, "Just wanna take a quick look."

Timidly she said, "You got another one of those?"

I chuckled. "Your husband would be proud," I said.

# TWENTY

She placed a sign that said "Back in 10 Minutes" on the counter. She led me through the lobby and down a short corridor of doors with single digit numbers on them. At the end of the corridor was a flight of wooden stairs illuminated by a naked bulb. I followed her up the stairs. Twice she jerked her head back, eyes alarmed, like maybe I was sneaking peeks at her ankles.

The second floor was gloomier than the first. It smelled like all the residents did up here was spill beer and pee.

She stopped in front of 21. She stooped, but before she inserted the key she said, "You promise you do not intend to harm Mr. Wylie."

"I promise."

The room was smothering. The only window was directly across from the door. I moved quickly to open it. Took a long breath of rain-soggy air. The window overlooked a tiny patch of backyard and a tree taller than the hotel. Leaveless branches scraped the glass. Behind the yard was an alley. On the other side of the alley was the rear end of a liquor store. An electric sign at the side of the store said PACKAGED LIQUORS. A real estate agent would call that prime location.

The room was decorated in Early Dipsomaniac. Empty bottles were everywhere. Some Jack Daniels, probably purchased the day the government check came, but mostly it was wine; Night Train, Pink Lady, and the Angry Canine. The furnishings were a swaybacked bed, a three-drawer dresser with no knob handles, and a lime green easy chair with fringe skirt.

The lady tiptoed to the chair and sat down, started smoothing out her dress with nervous flicks of her hand.

I stood for some seconds, taking the room in. The lady said softly, "What exactly are you looking for?"

"I don't know."

I lifted the mattress, kneeled and peered under the bed.

Nothing there but dustballs the size of Idaho spuds. Each drawer of the dresser was slightly open so it could be slid out by pulling the top. I said, "How does a guy who had money end up in a place like this?" I rifled threadbare white shirts and black socks. Quickly added, "No offense meant."

"Sir," she said, "look at the bottles. No man intends to end up in a place like this. It's bad luck, bad breaks, and primarily addiction to alcohol. You look like a drinking man."

"How's a drinking man look?"

"Your hands shake, you're puffy in the face, you got dull eyes."

"Should of seen me six weeks ago."

"So you do drink?"

"I've been overserved on a few occasions. The 1970s and '80s come to mind."

"It's not funny."

"Funny worked for W.C. Fields."

"Have any family?"

"None I speak to."

"Married?"

"No."

"Girlfriend?"

I shook my head. "Got a rabbit. That count?"

"Well, sir, you might end up in a place like this yourself." She waited a beat. Said quietly, "No offense meant."

"Touché," I said. "Don't think it doesn't cross my mind."

She said, "I am addicted to alcohol myself."

"You?"

"Yes. But by the grace of God I've been sober for twelve years come June 14th. Are you familiar with the twelve steps?"

Mentally I groaned. I said, "I'm familiar with the program." But if I wanted a temperance lecture, I'd get trashed in front of Marvin, so I said, "Back to Wylie, he ever say what kind of money he had? He stinking rich? Just comfortable?"

The lady coughed delicately. Said, "Excuse me." Then, "To be honest, I don't think Mr. Wylie ever had any money. Not like wealthy amounts. It made a good story. An excuse

to be bitter, a reason to stay drunk. We discussed the program many times. I felt I was making real progress. If he'd
stayed just a week longer, I think I could of gotten him to a
four-day detox and then start to attend meetings."

No wonder the poor bastard skipped.

She said, "But I have to admit that even when intoxicated
he was extremely well behaved. Not like the rest of these
men."

I moved to the closet, untacked the orange blanket that
served as a door and tossed it on the bed. The smell of moth-
balls made my eyes tear. Several out-of-style dark suits hung
on paper-wrapped hangers. Also old pastel and tan dress
shirts with huge collars. Nineteen-seventies-type wide ties
were draped over a wooden hanger.

I said, "This isn't your usual alkie wardrobe."

The lady said, "Mr. Wylie was not a bum. He was a good
man who had a severe problem. He dressed nice, he spoke
nice. He was a man down on his luck."

"I'd say so."

"Sir, are you a private detective?"

"Says so in the yellow pages, but I'm having some
doubts."

"At first I couldn't determine what you might be, but then
it dawned on me. You're the first one I ever met. You don't
look like a private eye. Well, my conception of one."

"I look like a drunk, but not a private eye. Maybe that's
my problem right there."

"What's it like? Bein' a private eye. What's the most
important thing you do?"

"Ask questions instead of answer 'em. Did Wylie tell you a
story about Ronald Headon and himself? Like how they fell
out?"

"Sure he did."

I turned. Said, "He did? What was it?"

"Well, he told it two ways. One way he was rich and got
betrayed. The other he was poor but woulda become rich
except he got betrayed. Being intoxicated both times he
probably forgot the other version."

"Tell me the betrayed part."

"Way he tells it, him and Ronald Headon started up the

engineering firm more'n twenty-five years ago. Fifty-fifty partners. For a long time there was only like three employees and the two of them. They did a lot of the manual labor, all the sales, most of the office work, the shipping— everything. As time went by they expanded some, but it was always touch and go. That's the second version. In the first version, they expanded a lot and both had made a lot of money. I tend to believe the second one, the poor one."

"Me too."

"What transpired was Mr. Headon bid on and won some kind of important government contract or subcontract, or had an inside contact who helped him win it—Mr. Wylie was a little vague on the details, it was so long ago. Anyway, Mr. Headon never told a soul. Then he offered to buy Mr. Wylie's half at an inflated price. They weren't getting along and they were just keeping chins above water. Mr. Wylie said he wondered would they ever make any decent money so he accepted the offer. A month later he learned about the contract. Mr. Wylie claims Mr. Headon had family money to fall back on and he didn't. He thought that was why Mr. Headon offered to buy him out. He sold his half fast, because Mr. Headon offered more than it was worth. 'Course, after that contract was announced, half of the firm was worth a lot more than Mr. Wylie got. I never said nothin' to Mr. Wylie because I truly care for the man, but it's like they say, you can't cheat an honest man. He thought he was putting one over on Mr. Headon, but it was him got rooked."

I shook my head. Said, "So he got screwed twenty years ago. He's had plenty of time to get over it."

"Maybe he'd of ended up here no matter what happened twenty years ago. Some men just do."

On the floor of the closet under a drift of dirty clothes was a taped-together cardboard box. I shoved the laundry off and scooted the box across the floor, hoisted it on to the bed. It jiggled softly on the brown blanket.

Inside the box was the tattered residue of James Wylie's life.

On top was a 10 × 13 manila envelope. Inside the envelope were ten letters written in a feminine hand. They were dated 1944 and 1945. Each was one page long. They started "Dear James" and ended "Much Love, Your Pen Pal Marge." I scanned a couple. Marge had lived in Denton, Iowa. On a farm. Was a member of the Future Wives of America. The ink was faded and the stationery brittle and yellowing. The contents of the letters were boring as hell.

Also in that envelope were pictures of a husky, baby-faced sailor with a full head of brilliantined dark hair. I showed one to the lady.

"That's him," she said. "Was him. He looks plenty different from that now. Lost his hair and a lot of his weight for starters. He was a handsome man in his day, wasn't he?"

I put the contents of the envelope back inside and set the envelope on the blanket. In the box were more letters, lots of envelopes full of faded newspaper clippings describing decades-old sports events, Navy news, wedding engagements and the like. Wylie's name was mentioned in some. Some had ink lines drawn under other names. There was a small snap-shut case with two military medals inside, pinned to burgundy felt lining. There were several photos of plain-faced girls, wearing sweaters and too much lipstick, their hair done up in the styles of World War Two. There were packets of letters tied together with twine. I didn't go through the packets, I placed them on the blanket with the rest of the stuff.

"He ever get married?" I asked.

"He never said."

So far nothing here made James Wylie more than a broken down old rummy who kept the highlights of his life in a grocery box.

But at the very bottom of the box of memories lay an executive-size blue envelope. The only blue envelope in the box. A color snapshot was inside. It was a portrait of the young sailor as an old man. He was stoop-shouldered, shriveled in size and nearly bald. His smile exposed few teeth. But he was neatly dressed in stiff khaki pants, white shirt, and black parka, the hood bunched behind his neck. He looked content, happy even. He stood in a park or field. The horizon was far behind him and there were only piles of dirty snow in the background, no houses or buildings.

Andrea Gale stood next to him. Wylie's arm rested awkwardly on her shoulders. She wore a knee-length white leather coat and a red and blue striped scarf. Threads of hair lifted around her face from a winter wind and her cheeks were pink from the cold. She looked gorgeous. She stared directly into the camera, smiling like she knew something I'd give anything to know.

I put the picture back in the envelope and shoved it in my jacket pocket. I sat on the bed for a bit and thought about the photograph. Thought about Andrea being killed on Saturday, the same day James Wylie vanished. Thought about them standing in a field to have their picture taken not so long ago, friendly and smiling, Wylie's arm around Andrea.

"Anything?" the lady asked.

"Yeah, but I don't know what."

"Should I be expecting to see Mr. Wylie again?"

"I don't know," I said. I should have that printed on a T-shirt. I could just point to it instead of saying it seven hundred times a day. I said, "Thanks."

"My husband wouldn't want me to turn down ten dollars. Listen, should you run into Mr. Wylie, tell him to come back and visit Cora, okay? Tell him I won't even mention the rent due."

I said, "I'll do that if you ask around, see if your residents know where he is."

"Oh, I don't speak to most of 'em. They'd think I was askin' because I miss him."

"You do."

"It wouldn't be right. Me married and all. There'd be talk."

"Tell 'em it's for me."

She looked unsure, but said, "Maybe I'll do that."

# TWENTY-ONE

I sat in the Caddy in front of the Jones Hotel. One of the lobby sitters, a bewhiskered beanpole, lurched out the door and crouched on the sidewalk, staring at a puddle, pelted by rain. He leaned forward onto his hands, started to gag.

I lit a Kool, watched the cloud of exhaled smoke fill the car. Looked back at the guy with the dry heaves. I thought about what Cora said. I held my cigarette hand in front of me. It *did* shake. Not as bad as a month ago, but it was quivering. I flashed to the scene of me on the floor the morning Sandy Headon called. Similiar scenes pepper my adult life. I looked at the man on the sidewalk again. Out loud I said, "Cora, save me a room."

I put it in "D" and poked down Washington, pulled into a 7-Eleven. Underneath an overhang, three pay phones graffitied with gang logos were bolted to the front wall.

I dropped a quarter into the only one that worked, dialed the number Lisa had given me. Let it ring fifteen times. No answer.

The rain spattered heavy and it was dark and me and my rabbit were alone in a strange town. I leaned against the sandstone wall, shivering. Reflected on the glamorous life us PI's live. I thought about the photograph again. Wondered who'd taken it. There were lots of things to wonder about when I thought about that photograph.

Sandy answered when I dialed the Headon number. She was alone, but said I couldn't stop by, Ronald would be home any minute. She slurred words like both sides of her jaw were novocained. She said if I could find a Bobby's Tap, downtown Johnson City, I could talk to her in half an hour.

Fine, more progress. I didn't know exactly what kind, but finding a photograph of James Wylie hugging Andrea Gale and then setting up a meeting with Sandy Headon to talk about it was definitely progress of some sort.

Somewhere in my wallet I had Dennison's home and office

numbers on a scrap of paper. It took a while to find.

Dennison was at the office. He was not happy with me.

"Where you at, Kruger?" he said instead of hello. "You got half this fucking town pissed at you. And pissed at me for hiring you."

"I know of only two."

"One's the richest big-timer in town and the other's the big-timer's personal bodyguard."

"This the same Charles Dennison who hired me? Said don't worry about McCoy and his delusions of grandeur?"

"I erroneously assumed I was hiring a professional private investigator. Not a goddamn goon."

"You cut me to the quick."

"Your conduct has been inexcusable."

"You hired Dan Kruger, not Miss Manners. I assume you talked recently to either McCoy or Ronald Headon."

"You might say that. I tried to phone you all day. Why don't you get an answering machine?"

Five years ago no one owned one of the damn things, now nobody can live without one. I said, "I'm waiting for the price to come down," while thinking, I got your answering machine hangin', dork.

Dennison said, "Where in hell you been?"

"Wrigley Field. I never miss Opening Day. Cubs lost, but it was a heck of a game, Dennison, you shoulda—"

"Have you bothered to work on this case at all?"

"I squeeze it in here and there. Get off it, it's only been five days. I poked around enough to strongly suspect your man is innocent."

"You got proof? I need proof."

"No proof. I don't know who killed Andrea Gale. I don't know who killed Torres either, but I'm certain the two are connected." He didn't say anything. I added, "It's a hunch."

Dennison said, "This is great. I'll show up in court and tell the judge and jury my client is innocent. Why? Because a boozed-up sadist has a hunch. Maybe you jam the judge's face into the bench a couple of times, he'll agree."

A black Chevy Blazer pulled into the lot, parked next to Marv's Caddy. Nobody got out and because of the dark and the rain splashing the windows I couldn't see who was inside. I could only see the orange tip of a cigarette glow bright, then soft. Some seconds went by and still nobody got out. My heart kicked a little. Paranoia does indeed strike deep.

I said to Dennison, "What did McCoy say to you?"

"It wasn't McCoy."

"What do you care what Headon says to you? You're a lawyer for Chrissakes. He gives you a rough time, sue him."

"It's not your business what was discussed. Your business was to determine if my client was innocent of a felony charge of murder and providing me with proof of same. Your business was keeping me informed of your progress."

"Dennison, I'm not liking this past tense you've slipped into here."

"I use the past tense because that's what you are, pal. You are fired, discharged, terminated as of this phone call. Send me a bill. Itemized."

"You talk to Stone about this?"

The phone went dead. I slammed the receiver. It tried to jump back at me. I wrapped both hands around it and pulled, trying to detach the metal cord from the phone base. After some seconds, I realized I was making an ass of myself in front of a spectator. I laid the receiver gently on the hook while silently damning all chickenshit lawyers.

I felt like a spy behind enemy lines. Vulnerable, alone, and now with my support group gone, possessing decidedly dim prospects. I felt angry and scared.

I felt like I should get my butt out of Johnson City and back to Chicago where it belonged.

Then the window of the Blazer slid down. McCoy's face appeared. He said, "Attempted Vandalism of Ma Bell's property. That's a hefty fine, my man. We better talk about it."

# TWENTY-TWO

McCoy stepped down from the Blazer, got into the passenger side of the Caddy. I leaned against the wall for another second or two shaking my head, knowing how he'd found me. I lit a Kool, walked through the rain with it cupped in my hand.

He'd shoved Bugs's cage to my side of the car. I took it out, set it on the back seat. I got behind the wheel. Said, "So you're gonna lock me up and throw away the key for pulling on a telephone cord?" McCoy didn't respond. I said, "Your boss still sore about me denting his face?"

"My boss? The fuck you talkin' 'bout my boss?"

"Forget it."

He sat facing me, his back against the door panel. His left arm dangled behind the seat. A steady clicking sounded from the end of the hanging arm. The 7-Eleven provided just enough light to see his face. He was sneering like in the dream.

At first I wondered why he changed cars. He could've stayed dry in the Blazer. But I figured it out quick enough. His legs were crossed and he patted a huge black wingtip against the dashboard, leaving swipes of mud. The way he was twisted in the seat bunched his trenchcoat and water dribbled off the curls and wrinkles of the coat onto the seat. He knew the car wasn't mine and he was wanting to dirty it up best he could.

He exhaled cigarette smoke like he was trying to blow out a hundred candles. He grinned, smoked and clicked the pen for another thirty seconds. The only noise was the clicking and the rain that peppered the roof.

When McCoy spoke, it was slow and deliberate with frustration bubbling beneath the surface, like a teacher explaining a simple math problem for the tenth time to a particularly dense student. He said, "If I called you shit-for-brains, I'd be insulting shit. You been beat up twice. You been asked, advised and ordered by cops and civilians to stay out of Johnson City. Why you keep comin' back, Kruger?"

"It's such a beautiful town I can't stay away. And I got friends here."

He shook his head slowly, held his cigarette hand up in a "halt" gesture. "My, man," he said, "you got no friends here. I bet that fucking rabbit is the only friend you got in the whole world. And now you ain't even got a job. Nobody wants to see you, you got no reason to be here."

"It's a free country. In a free country you can visit any town you want."

"If all you did was visit we'd have no problem, but it ain't." He put his cigarette hand out like he was pointing, patted the cigarette with his index finger. A long ash dropped into the puddle of water forming around his knees.

I said, "This ain't my boat, McCoy. I'd appreciate if you didn't go out of your way to trash it."

McCoy stared at me like he couldn't believe what he heard. He held the cigarette out again, tapped it rapidly. The tip of fire fell off the end. McCoy said, "Oops. Ever so sorry."

I said, "Why do cops think police and PI's got to play dog and cat all the time?"

"Because we're the dogs, Kruger. It's a fun game if you're the dog." He smiled. "You talked to Dennison?"

"Just did."

"He fire you?"

"He fired me."

The smile got wider. He said, "See, Kruger, this is something Dennison and I now agree on. Know why? Because you're so lousy at what you do nobody wants you doing it anymore. His client is tired of throwing his money down an outhouse hole. You've had a week, you ain't done a thing except tick people off. David Stone killed the broad, Baker killed the spic. Open and shut. But you're running around, got conspiracy plots on the brain. You been buggin' a lot of fine people. Ronald Headon and Sandy Headon and George Howell and Lisa Farrell and the sweet little old lady at the Jones Hotel. Okay, maybe some of 'em ain't such fine people, but you understand what I'm sayin'. You're askin' all over 'bout some frail old wino used to work with Mr. Headon many, many years ago. Mr. Headon don't even remember this guy. What're you tryin' to stir up anyway?"

"I hope the sweet little old lady at the Jones made some dough out of this or did you just bully her?"

"Listen to Mr. Big Spender. A lousy ten bucks buys you a peek at a rummy's room. You expected loyalty and a zipped lip too? I heard Stone's BS theory. I tracked down Wylie's last known location. The sweet little old lady's been waiting for you. She called me before you pulled away from the curb."

I said, "Doesn't the fact Wylie took off Saturday, same day Andrea got killed, pique your curiosity?"

"Why should it? I told you Stone's theory is bull."

The pen clicked like a time bomb. He dropped his cigarette on the floor. He worked a pack of smokes from inside his coat, flicked it so a couple slid out, put the pack to his mouth, then snatched it away, leaving a cigarette between his lips. He put the pack back and lit up with a Bic lighter. He inhaled long and deep, then held his breath, letting lines of smoke seep from his nostrils.

I said, "You pretending you got some pot, McCoy?"

He sighed audibly, so I could hear it.

I said, "This silence and the cigarette thing supposed to be some kind of intimidating procedure? Should I be scared?"

"Kruger, you shouldn't of pushed Mr. Headon's face into the roof of his car."

"Fuck him," I said, "and fuck you."

He dropped the cigarette, grabbed my wrist and pulled me toward him. I tossed my arm in the air, his hand flew up and hit the ceiling.

McCoy was fast for an overweight man. Next thing I felt was pain in my ear and the side of my head. A short chop. He couldn't get any weight behind the punch, sitting like he was, but a clanging started in my ear so loud I couldn't hear much else. He pressed up against me, pinning me to the door. Bugs was going crazy in his cage, rustling the papers and banging off the sides.

His mouth next to my ear, McCoy said, "You really messed up in that driveway, man. All this runnin' around, askin' your questions—okay, but bangin' Mr. Headon's face in his own driveway. That was a big mistake."

"Sorry I hurt your boss."

"I told you, he ain't my fucking boss." His voice sank to a whisper, "I got a badge in this town, you ain't got diddly fucking squat. Not even a job now." He squeezed the back of my neck with his left hand. The pen pressed into my skin.

"Fuck you," I said again. Not brilliant repartee, true, but it got my point across.

"How can a man be so stupid?" He shoved me hard against the door, moved away. He opened the passenger door, got out and stood, bent over, watching me rub my ear. He squinted against the rain. Said, "Stay out of this town, Kruger. I'm so sick of telling you that. If I have to do it again, I don't know what I might do."

He slammed the door, immediately yanked it back open. "Get your stinking rock and roll band back together and make a living that way. I see you out here again without a guitar in your hand, PI, we're for sure gonna play some dog and cat." The door slammed again.

# TWENTY-THREE

Bobby's Tap was a gnat's butt classier than the rest of the taverns in downtown Johnson City, which meant it was still a joint. At the bar six men and two women sat hunched over drinks like lions guarding a kill, saying nothing.

I ordered Diet Pepsi for me, two gin and tonics and a Michelob tap for Sandy. The bartender had slicked-back hair, a long nose, and no chin. He walked behind a glass cabinet full of brightly labeled bottles. I heard the familiar, lovely sound of drinks being poured, the cool crunch of a scoop in a bucket of shaved ice. I told him I was expecting a friend and pointed to the last booth of ten that ran against the wall. I described Sandy. As I did, he ran slender fingers through his vaselined hair and his smile became a smirk. He knew my friend.

On the wall above the booth, an Olympia Beer advertisement rolled around providing silvery flickers of light. I took a drink of Pepsi, removed the envelope from my pocket and looked at the photo of Andrea Gale and James Wylie.

Sometimes when nothing's been happening and suddenly something does, you tend to lend it greater importance than it deserves. I told myself not to put too much emphasis on this photo or on James Wylie. Only thing this photo did was confirm what I'd been told by David Stone. Andrea Gale knew an old man named Wylie.

But looking at the photo, it felt better than that. This didn't fit the usual Andrea Gale-older man relationship. Wylie was no rich suitor—he wasn't getting sex, she wasn't getting money—but they seemed happy as hell about something. I hoped I could find out what.

It had been a rough evening and it might get rougher if I didn't leave Johnson City. My stomach was a mass of frayed electric cords. I eyed the gin and tonics, told myself no. As a reward for my willpower, I decided to eat two Valium. After all, my stomach was queasy, my nerves overloaded.

Sandy showed as I was lighting a third Kool. She wore a dark colored jumpsuit under an unbuttoned white raincoat. She peered through the dark until she found me, then joked with the ferret behind the bar. She wobbled toward me carrying a tall brown beverage in each hand.

I said, "Why do you drink in a dump like this?"

"You said I wasn't like other rich people. I'll drink anywhere."

I said, "I already got drinks."

She wrinkled her pug nose. "Then this'll save me a trip. What're you drinking?"

"Pepsi. Diet."

"Sheesh. On the wagon again."

"Kinda."

She tossed a gin tonic with one gulp, then emptied one of her glasses with three swallows. Said, "Ahhh," and slipped out of the raincoat. "Now, what's so important I had to get soaked?" She giggled, reached underneath the table and caressed the inside of my thigh with the tip of a finger. She sat back in the booth, made a mock surprised face.

Most of me ignored her. I said, "How's Ronald?"

"Lip's still swollen. Tomorrow he sees the dentist. A tooth is loose." She smiled.

"I got fired tonight."

Sandy hiccuped.

I said, "Everybody wants me out of Johnson City. Forget it's even on the map. I was planning to do that, but after Dennison canned me, McCoy belted me around, then threatened me. I'm stubborn, I got a little pride. I can't let a man like that tell me what to do. I decided to stay and keep working."

She twisted a curl in her wig and gave me a "Why in hell should I care about any of this?" look. She picked up the mug of beer, took a long sip. She licked away a foam mustache after she set the mug down.

"So what do you think?" I finally asked.

"You mean like what's my opinion?"

"Yeah, what's your opinion?"

"I think you should stay out of Johnson City too. I don't even know what you're after."

I watched her face. Said, "I think you do. Why'd you call me the other night, tell me where Wylie was?"

"I was angry at Ronald. I wish I hadn't, okay? I made a mistake."

"Wylie left the Jones Hotel Saturday morning. Hasn't been seen since."

"Same day the Gale slut was murdered."

"Slut?"

"I say it like I see it."

"Thought you didn't know her."

"I didn't, but because of all this stuff I asked around. She was a low rent slut."

"If Andrea Gale was your idea of low rent, you and I got enormously different definitions of low rent."

Sandy's exuberance had slowly evaporated and now she glared at me. Said, "That he left Saturday morning mean he had something to do with all this?"

"Might."

"And you think Ronald has something to do with it?"

"Why'd you use past tense with Wylie, present tense with your husband?"

"Huh?"

"Wylie 'had,' Ronald 'has.' "

"Just the words I used."

"I know. Why'd you use those?"

Her brain was too fogged to argue the subtleties of semantics. She shook her head, took a long swallow of beer, said, "Oh shut up, Daniel."

I said, "To answer the questions, it doesn't seem ludicrous to me that either one could be involved."

She drank more beer. "Well, it's ludicrous to me."

"I heard a few details about how your husband shafted Wylie."

"That was a long time ago. James forgot about it."

"Did he?"

More silence. She tried to stare me down, but her eyes were not fixing well. Like she was answering a question I never asked she said, "Besides, Ronald may play around on me, but he could do lots better than some brainless factory slut."

"Who looked like Miss America."

She shrugged.

I said, "Ronald got any other interests besides that factory? He gets people to jump like Dudley Moore in that movie where he walks on the hot sand. McCoy can't do enough for the guy. The lawyer who hired me talked tough as nails, cops didn't faze him, but he bailed out fast when Ronald put the squeeze on."

She looked at me, eyes wide, started to smile, but stopped and stared into her drink. Said, "Other interests? Land. Lots and lots of land. He worships real estate. Been buying it since he could afford to. And that was a long time ago."

"Like where?"

"Like where the shopping mall is. The new one? He owns that land. He's got a lot of plots downtown."

I whistled. "No wonder Dennison decided to fade away."

"Hey, listen. Ronald's not always a prick, okay? I know I make it sound like that, but there's good times." She chewed the corner of her mouth, stared at her drink. "Don't get mad, but I convinced him you'd leave all this alone if Dennison fired you. I sort of told him you gave me the impression you only worked if you got paid. So he arranged it."

"I never told you that. Why would you say something like that?"

"Maybe I'm afraid of what you'd find. I got a nice lifestyle. I don't wanna see it wrecked."

"You make even less sense than most rummies. Other day you had nothing good to say about your lifestyle. You wanted out if you only had the guts."

"Don't call me a rummy."

"You're afraid I might uncover something'll end your lifestyle."

"I don't know what you'll uncover. Just leave everything like it is. You're an outsider, you don't belong here. You might end up inconveniencing a lot of people, you keep poking around. What right do you have to do that in a place you didn't even know existed ten days ago?"

"It's a shame somebody had to inconvenience Andrea Gale. God forbid anybody else might suffer a little annoyance because she got murdered."

"The hell with that whore."

The Valium started to tingle and calm and I was grateful. I needed it. My conversations tonight were running pell mell downhill, and considering what had taken place during the first one, that was saying something. I said, "What I'm hearin' is just fantastic. You knew Andrea Gale, right? You knew your husband was having an affair with her. Come on, Sandy, if you got me fired, least you can do is answer some questions."

"I didn't know her, I swear it. It's an insulting question. And so what if I got you fired? If you stay away, it'll mean I saved your damn neck. You're not dealing with a bunch of English gentlemen here. Nothing personal, but people from your class don't count for much to men like my husband."

"Great, now we're gonna drag class into it. This is America, lady, where any man can grow up to be President. No matter how poor, no matter how stupid. Especially the latter." I spun the photo so the right side faced her, pushed it across the table.

She put her face down to the table to look at it, jerked her head back like a jack-in-the-box had jacked. She looked away, didn't ask who it was.

She'd known Andrea Gale.

She said, "That's James Wylie."

"Shoulda asked, who's the blonde?"

"You'll tell me. I don't know who it is."

"You're lying." I rubbed my forehead.

"I think you better go back to Chicago and stay there."

"Why? Brother George and buddy Dwayne be paying me a visit if I don't? Maybe like the one they paid Andrea Gale? They'll have to stand in line, babe."

She flipped her wrist and a raft of brown liquid flew at me. It splashed my face, burned my eyes. Dribbled down to my shirt and lap. Sandy ran unsteadily down the aisle and out the door.

I sat there, blinking, blotting my face with a bar napkin, impressed as hell with my social skills. I bet I could transform anybody I know into an enemy in ten minutes flat. If I don't know 'em, five.

# TWENTY-FOUR

I carried my Pepsi to the bar, sat on a stool. Jerked it in quarter circles with my butt. I was angry at myself and at Sandy and the V's weren't helping with that. I knew I hadn't been fired because Sandy told her husband I'd quit if the money stopped. McCoy and Headon had planned the squeeze on Dennison in the library the night I banged Headon's face. But it disturbed me that she wanted me out of town too. Who was she covering for? Herself? Her brother? Or her husband and, by extension, her lifestyle?

I looked at the glass in front of me, told myself it was absurd to drink Pepsi in a bar. Pepsi is what teenagers drink at a Pizza Hut. When men go to a bar, they drink liquor. Especially men with no job and big problems. That's why bars were invented. So men with big problems had a place to go where they could meet other men with big problems and they could all drink booze, get high, and say fuck it about big problems. Besides, moderation was the key word. If I moderated my intake, everything was cool. And I'd just gone four weeks with no booze. If I could do that I surely could keep the daily number of glasses at a reasonable number. Four sounded like a reasonable number.

The bartender was sponging the counter. I motioned, said, "Send this Pepsi to the nearest Pizza Hut and tell 'em to stick it up some kid's ass. Get me a double brandy."

When he set it in front of me, he said, "Don't feel bad, guy. Nobody's picked that piece up yet. And somebody almost always tries."

"It wasn't—"

"Hey, it's okay. You figured 'cause she agreed to meet you for a drink in a bar like this, you were gonna get lucky. They all think that."

"That right?" I took a long sip. The warm feeling came to my belly, the anger started to retreat.

He nodded. "She comes in here couple times a week, gets drunk as a skunk. Good looker for her age. Drives that BMW, God only knows why the thing ain't dinged all to hell, condition she's in most of the time. Men peg her for one of those rich bitches, bored silly, got nothin' better to do than get fried to the gills every night and pick up some young dick. I mean sometimes she can barely walk when she *gets* here. But they always strike out. Like you did." He winked. "Her 'n' me get along great though. And one of these nights I might give it a try."

"No doubt what she's waiting for." I sipped again. Felt warmer and calmer. "Know anything about her?"

"Sandy Headon? I told you, we're like this." He wrapped his middle finger around his index finger. "Know she's rich. Drinks like a sailor on shore leave."

"I known her two days, I know that much."

"She's got a baby brother no bigger than she is who ain't quite all there." He tapped the side of his head. "He barged in here one night 'bout a year ago lookin' for some wetback who got a little too insistent with Sandy. Brought a Baby Huey type along, who I suspect was supposed to inflict the damage. The shrimp sure wasn't going to. Had to call the cops to toss 'em out."

"They beat the guy up?"

"Nah, he wasn't here. They just stomped around, the brother kept yelling stuff like 'Nobody messes with my sister.' Both were high as the sky. Sandy apologized next time she came in. Said her brother goes bonkers when he thinks she's been insulted."

"What else you know about her?"

"Hates her husband, loves his money. Couldn't get a divorce even if she wanted 'cause they're Catholic and hubby is a big man in this town. Plus hubby knows how much he'd have to fork over if they split up and she suspects he'd pull strings left and right to where by the time they got to court he'd have nothing to his name. Some nights when she's really plastered, she tells me how rotten her life is and how she dreams about starting over."

"When she gonna do that?"

"Never will. Just talk. I mean, wouldn't you put up with a bunch of garbage to live in a mansion and drive a BMW? Have all the money you need? Let's see, both parents committed suicide when she was a kid. She raised the brother. Probably why he's so protective. She's more like his mother than his sister. Guess you might say I know a few things about her."

"Might say you're a discreet son-of-a-bitch too."

His upper lip curled. "Screw you. Finish your drink and hit the door." He swaggered down the bar, flipping the bar rag like he was killing flies.

A high-pitched, breathy voice said, "You needin' company?"

I turned and looked into a pair of empty brown eyes. They were stuck like raisins in a doughy, powder-caked face. The woman was maybe thirty-five with teased, bottle-blond hair. She wore a white gauze blouse over a delicate black bra. She'd bathed in perfume so cheap it was probably sold in gas stations. She said, "I saw what happened over there. That lady is cold, man. Like ice." She giggled, stopped abruptly.

I lit a Kool to kill the perfume smell.

She climbed on the next stool. Said, "Where you from? Never seen you here before."

"Chicago."

"Wow, Chi-town." She nodded, started to shudder. "I dig The City."

I said nothing.

She said, "If I go to jail, would you come visit me?"

I said, "Now that's an opening line I don't hear everyday."

"Just in case I do."

"You been there before?"

"Yeah. But I never *do* anything. Least nothing I remember later." She paused, then said, "But this time I'm gonna put that slut on the ground."

"You probably should."

"She said she came home and found me fucking on the floor. I don't fuck on the floor. I fuck in private. Sluts fuck on the floor."

I smiled at my drink, dragged on the Kool.

She said, "Is this funny?"

"Not to you."

"I'm not a slut."

"I know that."

"This makes me so mad. We were just talking."

"We?"

"Me 'n' Bobbie's ex. I'm so mad, but—" She finished her drink, held the glass in the air to get the ferret's attention.

"But what?"

"I'm a lot of things, but I'm not—I don't fuck on the floor."

"I'm glad to know that. Police will be too."

"Think so?"

"Know so. Used to be one. We were always glad to find out people didn't fuck on the floor."

Glass still in the air, she stared at me, face suspicious. She said, "Anyway, I'm sick of this."

"Of what?"

"Everything. I'm sick of everything. I'm always in trouble and I don't *do* anything. And the bitch called the cops on me after she found us talking. I got out of there fast, but she screamed after me that they'll find me. So if I go to jail, will you come visit me?"

"Nobody goes to jail for talking to a friend's ex-husband."

"Well, I mighta' done some other stuff. But—"

I stood, said, "I'll be there the fifth Saturday night of every month. Seven o'clock. Count on it." I moved for the door.

Her Betty Boop voice called after me, "Well, you don't have to take it out on me 'cause that cold-hearted old woman threw her drink on you."

It wasn't raining as hard now, but gusts of cold wind slapped needles of water against my face as I walked to the Caddy.

I drove around beautiful downtown Johnson City, got directions from a passerby, got lost, got fresh directions, and finally found Lisa's new apartment building.

It was a two-story, concrete and greenwood, octagon-shaped building. The sign on the street proclaimed it BIRCH-WOOD IN THE ROUND. I've always wanted to meet the people who dream up the names for these places, although this did sound better than BIRCHWOOD IN THE OCTAGON.

The Camaro was in the lot. The apartment number was 1210. I walked around five of the eight corners on a cement sidewalk surrounded by shrubbery. The floodlights made the raindrops on the branches sparkle like draped diamonds.

I found 1210, pounded hard on the door. Thought I heard talking sounds within, but a minute passed. I knocked again. The door opened a sliver and Lisa peeked out over a doorchain.

I said, "Hi."

She clasped the lapels of a blue terrycloth robe to her chest. Her face and hair were sweaty, her bangs plastered in drenched curls on her forehead. Her eyes were fever shiny and she blinked rapidly like she needed to do that to focus. Behind her it was dark except for the bluish glare of a TV set. Tobacco and marijuana smells seeped out the door.

She said, "Hi, Dan."

I said, "I was out and thought I'd stop by, but it looks like a bad time. I tried to call first."

"Oh, that was you."

"That was me."

She said, "If I'd known I'd of answered. I'm sorry, I got a killer headache. I wouldn't be very good company."

I said, "No problem."

"I had a good time at the game. Call me," she whispered. She closed the door.

To the door I said, "I did. If you'd answered you'd of saved me the trip."

I walked back to the Caddy, feeling strange emotions. I sat for some seconds smoking a Kool. I said, "Bugs, why in hell did I expect her to be alone? And why does it bother me she isn't?"

Bugs didn't answer. It's quite possible he didn't care.

# TWENTY-FIVE

I needed a place where I felt welcome. I headed for the Crazy Alm, the only place in town I could think of where that might happen.

Packed again. Same band. I winced, made my way to the bar. Gant smiled. I looked over both shoulders, but it was meant for me. I leaned to his ear and yelled, "A longnecked Miller and a double brandy."

"On the house. So long as Full Frontal comes back soon."

"If you can pack the house with these kids, why you need us? This place must be a gold mine."

The smile went ear to ear, closing his eyes again. "It's like I told you, I dig you guys."

I drank some beer, tossed back the brandy. Another one appeared like magic.

Unlike the rest of the stool sitters, I kept my back to the band. I alternated sips of brandy and beer. The warm spot in my stomach expanded. I love to feel warm. I held my hand in front of me. The shivering was gone, my hand was steady as an iron bar.

But forty-five minutes later, my head was thick as a brick. Part alcohol, part noise pollution. Finally, the band went on break. Someone was yelling, "Hey, Dan!" in my ear.

I turned, saw Heather the skinhead. She said, "You stone deaf?"

"Close."

"I been screaming in your ear for almost a minute. You never even flinched." Her eyes bored into mine, her tongue made snake-like flashes to moisten black lips.

I said, "It's the noise."

"The band stopped playing."

"For good?"

"For now."

"Damn."

"Yeah, I know they suck, but they're good for out here. Gant said you wanted to talk to me."

Another double and a fresh beer replaced my empties. I was pretty sure I was past four, but I could double up tonight, stay sober tomorrow. I said, "Lookit this. Free booze."

Heather said, "You're a star here. You guys are his favorite band."

"He means what he tells me?"

"Yep. Talks about you all the time." She skimmed her sandpaper head with her hand. I wanted to.

I lit a Kool, said, "Tell me, Heather, you hate blacks and Jews and Hispanics?"

"Why would you ask a question like that?"

"Lots of skinheads are skinheads because they hate everybody ain't a skinhead. Or at least white."

"Lots, but not all, right?"

"Right."

"I just dig the look. Shocks hell out of people in Johnson City. Specially my parents. I don't know from philosophies. Don't care. I take people case by case. Assholes are assholes regardless of color or creed."

"Amen."

She fidgeted and squirmed on the stool. She removed a cube of bubblegum from her leather coat, popped it in her mouth, started mashing it.

I said, "Really, Heather, cool on the crank. Stuff rots your insides, takes the enamel right off your teeth, fries the brain circuitry."

"You use it."

"How do you know?"

"I never met a rocker who didn't. You guys are as bad as truck drivers and they live on the stuff."

"Makes me an expert. You should listen to experts."

"You made mistakes so I wouldn't have to, right?"

"You're only, what, twenty-one?"

"Almost twenty-two."

"Body's young and strong now, but down the line—"

"You take a Nancy Reagan pill today?"

"Two of 'em. It'll wear off soon."

"You sound like my father."

"What's your father do?"

"Business executive by day, steady imbiber of scotch and soda by night. That's the part makes it kind of hard to take anything he says about this serious." She smiled. "Like you right now."

I smiled back. "So what he tells you he read somewhere. What I'm telling you is first hand knowledge. Advice from a man who's been there. Besides, I don't use it like you do."

"What about when you were young?"

"When I was young, it was the Sixties. Nothing anybody did or said from 1967 to 1970 should count. Should be like a grace period."

Heather made a face. "Yeah, yeah, yeah." She removed a Kool from my pack on the bar, lit it. Said, "I *love* being wired. Find me something better, I'll quit crank."

I said, "What's your father think about the shaved head and the leather jacket and the chains and biker boots?"

She grinned while blowing out smoke. "Hates it to hell. See, I adopted punk *and* skinhead. Either one'd be bad enough, both sends him right over the top. I was wearing the boots and leather and black. Had my hair dyed jet black. Played thrash at top volume all day. He considered me lowlife personified, right? All I ever heard was 'How could a daughter of mine end up like this?' Then I shaved my head. It was like my supreme moment to see the look on his face when I walked in the door. I thought he was gonna have a coronary."

"Why you so intent on freaking him out?"

She clapped her hands. "Sometime when we got a few hours we'll go into that. But it's not just him, I love shocking anybody shockable. I hate this whole white-collar, yuppie, money-grubbing career trip. Makes me wanna puke. They're trying to create an Ozzie and Harriet world out there. Well, I ain't fuckin' buying it."

"Heather, you were born twenty years too late. You would of loved the Sixties."

She said, "So what'd you wanna talk to me about? The cop who asked me questions?"

"Yeah, McCoy."

"An asshole."

"Taken case by case a good call. What'd he ask you?"

"First he looked at me like I was something the cat threw up. I love getting those looks, but that screwed it for him right there. Really put me on your side. He recited your version of what happened Friday night while the four of us waited around for your singer to get his ego slapped, then he kept trying to get me to say it was a lie."

"Like how?"

"Like did you really leave with Andrea Gale? Did you keep talking about her, saying what a super hot chick she was and how bad you wanted to jump her bones? Stuff like that."

"Anything else?"

"I'm supposed to call him whenever, if ever, I talk to you again."

"Gonna?"

"No way. You're all right, he's an asshole. I wouldn't of told him a thing if I'd watched you kill her."

Take that, sweet little old lady at the Jones Hotel. One person in this town was on my side. I said, "Did you know Andrea Gale?"

"Kind of."

"From here?"

"Here and parties around town. Mutual friends. We didn't hang out, but our paths crossed."

"What was she like?"

"An asshole." I grinned and so did she. She said, "Thing about her drove me nuts, she was constantly obsessing about her face and hair."

"What do you obsess about?"

"Not my face and hair."

"So what then?"

"Rock 'n' roll. Getting high."

"Heather, you're one of those bad influences parents always worry about."

"Thank you." She looked at me, then away. Said, "And fish."

"Fish?"

"I love fish. Tropical? I have a huge tank in my room. Forty gallons. I watch 'em for hours. They like hypnotize me."

"Yeah?" I grinned.

Heather got embarrassed. Said, "Anyway, Andrea Gale was a fluff who thought just because she was born with perfect bone structure she rated a free ride through life. We got along though."

"That surprises me."

"Well, God only knows what she said behind my back, right?"

"Right." I took the photo from my pocket, gave it to Heather. Said, "Ever see her with this guy?"

She put the photograph to her face, said, "It's too dark in here. I can't tell who either one of these people are."

The crowd started to whoop. We turned toward the stage. The band was slinging on their guitars. Heather said, "In ten seconds we aren't gonna hear ourselves think." She stood on the footrest at the bottom of the bar, leaned over the top of it and yelled, "Gant!" until she got his attention, then "The key!" He hurried to us, handed Heather a single gold key. Gave each of us a beer. He looked at me and winked. I blushed.

Heather took my hand and we walked the length of the

bar, pushed open a door marked EMPLOYEES ONLY. Went down a flight of stairs. At the bottom was a short hallway going left and right, a black-painted door on either end. She led me to the door on the right.

It was Gant's "fun" room. A king-size bed took up three-quarters of the space. Full-length mirrors were attached to two of the walls and the ceiling. Black lights and neon lights were on the other two walls, making the room a smoggy blend of red and purple. Heather turned a dimmer switch next to the door and the hard colors faded to a kind of soft rose.

The band kicked in above us. It sounded like an incoming jet passing overhead, except this jet stayed overhead.

We sat next to each other on the edge of the bed. I gave Heather the picture.

Next to the bed was a table with an Earth Look lamp on it. She flicked the lamp on and bent into its light, studying the photo. Said, "Andrea and James."

"You know James Wylie?"

"That's his last name?"

"Yeah, Wylie."

"I don't know him. I saw him talking to Andrea in the parking lot back of here twice."

"Why'd you happen to remember him?"

"He's kind of old for this place."

"He ever come inside?"

She shook her head.

"They just talking?"

"Yeah."

"Friendly talking or arguing?"

"Seemed friendly. But both times they shut up when I got close and started talking again as I moved away. When I went past 'em they smiled and Andrea'd go 'Hi, Heather.' Second time, just before I got out of earshot she said, 'But, James,' and then something I couldn't hear. That's how I knew his name."

"They in a car?"

"Standing by a car. Not hers though. I don't know if it was his."

"Remember what kind of car?"

"Nope."

"Could he be her father?"

"No way."

"Positive?"

"Yeah. I asked her later if he was one of her rich boy-friends. She was famous for that. Always had these rich old geezers chasing her around. She laughed and said he was an old family friend. I think her father died long time ago."

"Wylie lived at the Jones Hotel. Has a severe alcohol problem."

"The Jones? Guess he wasn't no rich boyfriend, was he?"

I said, "You curious why he was here?"

"Not as much as you."

"I mean, didn't it strike you as odd, an old man and this young girl talking in a parking lot?"

"No. People're always standing around in the lot, scoring dope, smoking a doobie, tryin' to cop a quickie in the back-seat, stuff like that. If he was an old friend down on his luck, maybe he was looking for a handout."

"When'd you see him here?"

"Couple weeks ago."

"And only twice."

"Only twice. What's this all about? He kill her?"

"So many people could of killed Andrea Gale it's like a black comedy."

"McCoy implied you might of."

"He'd love it to be me. He say why I'd kill someone I just met?"

"You became enraged when she wouldn't screw."

"So you afraid to be alone with me?"

Heather made a laugh, then stared into my eyes. Her eyelids got narrow. She chomped the gum double time.

I tried to envision her with long black hair and minus the black lipstick and eyeshadow. Her lips were full, her brown eyes large and round like a puppy's. Her cheeks sunk in a lit-tle, making her face too gaunt without hair to frame it. But it wasn't a bad face and she could've been a very pretty girl if she wanted. But like she said the first time we talked, there's other effects to strive for.

She said, "You know, I was hacked at you the other night.

We had a fresh conversation going, but soon as Andrea piped up, it was like I wasn't there anymore."

"As I remember we had a pretty one-sided conversation going."

"I was overamped and you were just sittin' there, bein' a grouch. I *had* to make most of the talk."

"I agreed with your theory by the way."

"Andrea Gale wouldn't of known what the hell I was talking about. She probably listened to Rick Astley records."

I said, "She hired me for a job. Jobs are so rare, when I get one it's like an event. It was nothing personal."

"Well, you and I got more in common than you'd ever have with a fluff like her. We're street people. Misfits." She drank some beer. "And we're proud of it."

"One of us is proud of it, the other is more like resigned to it."

"Gant told me you said I wasn't too—alluring. Was that the word?"

I finished the beer, smoked the end of the Kool, dropped the butt down the neck of the bottle and set the bottle on the floor. "I mighta said that, Heather, but I'm getting old. I also said you looked cool. I figure you'd prefer cool to alluring." I smiled. "Why'd you bring it up? You wanna fight?"

She laughed again. This was a nice laugh. Soft and natural.

I said, "You smell nice for a speedfreak skinhead."

She said, "I bet you're an animal with the ladies."

"Why's that?"

"You say incredibly romantic things."

"Aw, shucks," I said.

"Lay down," she said.

In the mirror on the ceiling, I watched as she unbuckled my belt, slid my zipper down, pulled off my boots and then my jeans. I listened to the bombast above us and pondered what it was going to be like, having sex with a skinhead punk girl. They slam dance, do they slam fuck? I guess at a certain point we all do, but I wondered if this was going to be some kind of freaky, painful affair.

Then I said the hell with it. I'd been treated like a mangy

dog all night and now I was going to have physical interaction with a female human being. I didn't care if she intended to pierce my torso with an entire box of safety pins so long as I got a kiss afterward.

She completely undressed me, then stood and took her clothes off, slowly, an article at a time. We watched each other while she did. Everything was black, down to her tiny bra and panties. Then she crawled onto the bed and straddled my thighs, sitting straight up so I could admire her. Where our bodies met was warm, like a steamy shower.

Like her face, her body was too thin because of the drugs, but her breasts were high and firm and her stomach and thighs taut and solid. No flab, no sag, none of the damned marks of age that plague all of us eventually.

She pointed and said, "I think you're starting to find me alluring, Dan." She bent forward, covering me. We kissed slow and sloppy. She tasted like bubblegum and beer.

And she was as tender and gentle and sensitive as the rest of us when we're naked with someone for the first time.

# TWENTY-SIX

When everything, including the whispering was done, I nodded out. When I woke up, Heather was gone. I didn't know what time it was, but the band still made noise above me so it wasn't 2:00 A.M. yet.

I found my clothes, dug out and lit a Kool. I stretched on the bed and smoked it, thinking.

There was so much to think about. Too much. Too many people. Headon and McCoy, best of buddies. A rich man and his private cop. Sandy Headon. Hated her marriage, but deathly afraid of the world beyond it. Her brother George. A manchild who'd do "anything" for his sister. George's buddy, Dwayne, who could back up whatever "anything" George dreamed up.

And then there was the oddest set of buddies. James Wylie and Andrea Gale. Meeting in a rock club parking lot, smiling like happy kids into a camera. And then on the same day, one was murdered and the other vanished.

When I finished the cigarette, I got dressed, made my way upstairs. Gant leered and gave me a thumbs up. I ignored him. I stood at the bar, scanned the place. Gant shouted, "You lookin' for Heather?"

I nodded.

He leaned toward me. "She left. Temporarily. She's always in and out of this place. But you know that, right?" He laughed like a dirty old man and I realized I didn't like the guy very much. He said, "You wanna see her again? She worships guitar players."

"Tell her I'll be back."

Bugs was awake when I got behind the wheel of the Seville. I said, "Forget it, wabbit. A gentleman never tells."

I went back to the Jones Hotel. Three men still sat in the lobby. Either dead or asleep. One made a sudden snore that sounded like canvas ripping. The TV was on, its silver glare the only light in the room.

I pressed a black button. The sweet little old lady shuffled, yawning, from a room behind the desk. When she saw me, she jerked awake and stood there like a deer in headlights.

I said, "Relax, Cora, I know you tipped McCoy off, but all I want is a room. Wylie's."

She hesitated. I glowered. She said, "Okay. You sure you ain't sore?"

"I'm sure. I'll pay you five bucks more than the rate if you don't call him this time."

She handed me the key, said, "Keep your money, mister. He only wanted to know if you came looking for Mr. Wylie. I never even told him you went to the room and looked around."

"He knew I had."

"Honest, I just told him what you were driving and what direction you went. He didn't say nothin' about if you needed a room. My husband would have a fit, I was to get a paying customer in trouble with the law. Less they caused

problems of course." She frowned, looked like she was about
to cry. "I hate bein' put in the middle of things like this, but
he wears a badge and he's such a—"

"Bully?"

She nodded. "What'm I suppose to do? He didn't hurt
you, did he?"

"No. He helped get me fired, but by sheer stupidity on his
part, he convinced me to stay on the job anyway. Running
back and forth to Chicago is getting old. I'm gonna relocate
for the time being. Unless you tell him, I figure this is the
last place McCoy'd expect me to be."

"I'm surprised, I 'spect he'd be."

"Did he ask to look at Wylie's room?"

"No. Only wanted to know if you came looking for him or
if Mr. Wylie came back."

"Would you of told him about Wylie?"

"After I warned Mr. Wylie maybe. I hadn't decided
that."

I paid her, called Marvin from the pay phone by the
sign-in desk. He went from groggy to irate in a milli-second
when I told him the Seville was fine but I'd be using it a few
more days. I held the phone at arm's length until the
squawking ceased. When I put it back to my ear, I heard
the dial tone.

Cora said, "You know the way," and shuffled back to her
closet.

I went to the car, removed Bugs and we went upstairs. In
the room, I cracked the window to let the cool night air in,
then opened the cage. Bugs hopped out, looked around ten-
tatively, then started to sniff and explore and chew.

I lay on the bed, my head on a pillow at the bottom. I
took off my boots, rested my feet on the tubular steel head-
board. Wylie's box sat next to me. I removed the contents,
stacked everything on the blanket. I went through the things
I'd looked at earlier, one by one, carefully this time.

Many of the faces in the old photos matched up now that
I studied them. Just changing hair styles and colors. One girl
had changed the color and style many times and gone
through three styles of glasses. In one photo, no glasses.
Judging from the styles of clothes and hair, James Wylie

pretty much gave up on the female race after the mid-Sixties. Or they'd given up on him.

Eventually I put these letters and photos back in the box. Nothing of interest here to anybody but James Wylie.

That left the three packets of faded envelopes tied with twine that I hadn't looked through the first time. Using the file on my fingernail clippers, I sawed through the string tying the first one. As the older envelopes slid apart, I saw that between them there were more photos and new white envelopes with photos inside.

The first photo I picked up was a 5 × 7 shot of a twenty-ish Sandy Headon standing between an equally young look-ing Ronald Headon and an early middle-aged James Wylie. Sandy smiled like a little pixie, her arms wrapped around the men's waists. The top of her head came to their shoulders.

She had on a pleated skirt that flared out like a Christmas tree. Her hair was curled short like the wig she wore now. The men wore baggy suits and were laughing hard at something off camera. They leaned forward, weak from their merriment.

The pose was eerily similar to the photograph of Andrea Gale and James Wylie. I took that one out and held the two together, comparing one to the other. The photos were like before and after shots of a man who'd undergone months of chemo. Teeth were missing, the hair was bleached of color and mostly gone. So much of the body was wasted away that in the second shot he resembled a child's drawing of a stick man.

I looked at the back of the photo. In faint pencil was writ-ten ME & THE H'S—SPRING '60. Underneath that, in red fine line marker, the same hand, but more spidery, had scribbled STICK A SWORD UP YOUR ASS RONALD SHIT-HEADON.

Sure Sandy, James Wylie had forgotten all about the dirty trick his friend had pulled on him so long ago.

There were more photos, mainly of the girls I'd seen ear-lier. The backs of all of these pictures had obscene and abusive remarks written in red under the original captions that told who, where and when. There were more photos of Ronald Headon. The vilest ranting was saved for him.

I tried to envision Wylie on the "red ink" night, or more likely morning. I pictured something like this happening at two or three A.M. I know the moods an alcoholic falls prey to and I could see Wylie in the middle of a bender, enraged at life, consumed by self-loathing and self-pity. I watched him drag his cardboard box of memories from the closet. JAMES WYLIE, THIS IS YOUR LIFE would seem like a cruel joke on such a night. I've been there many times. I understood exactly why James Wylie needed to let fly at all the people who'd used and abused him, who'd left him and let him down; who'd caused his life to be one long pointless parade of betrayal and pain and futility. To a bitter old drunk, bone weary of wearing a gentle, nice-guy facade for people like Cora, that would mean everybody he ever knew, although Ronald Headon obviously occupied the number one spot on his list.

I wondered what the sweet little old lady downstairs would say about dear Mr. Wylie if she could read the backs of these photos. I sympathized with him now; she never could.

He had even reviled and defaced himself. A goatee and devil horns were scratched onto a photo of him as a young navy man. A short, yellowed newspaper clipping told of a promotion to office manager at D.F. Steele. It was dated July 9, 1955. Across the top and down the sides he'd scrawled JAMES WYLIE MAKES HIS FIRST MOVE UP THE CORPORATE LADDER—WHAT A BRIGHT FUTURE FOR THIS SODOMITE! There was a photograph taken in a nightclub booth of himself and a pretty young woman. On the back it said, A DEGENERATE SODOMITE AND THE CHEAPEST SLUT HE COULD FIND. LIFE CAN ONLY GET BETTER FOR THESE TWO. FUCK THEM.

I opened the second packet. More photos between the letters. Everything dated from late '40s to mid-'60s. A lot were Wylie and Headon or just Headon. In the photos they were always smiling at the camera and they looked comfortable together, like close friends. On the back of every one, Headon was vilified in that spindly red writing as the foulest human being who ever drew a breath. Wylie showed marvelous creativity for a rummy; he never repeated himself.

The last bundle was tied tighter than the rest and was

circled with thick yellow twine instead of white. I had to use my teeth and the file to break the string. As the letters showered my chest, I looked for the photos. There was only one envelope, new and starkly white in contrast to the older corn-colored ones. I opened it, came off the bed slowly, like the Frankenstein monster waking up for the first time. I said, "Holy shit, Bugs."

The white envelope contained five Polaroid color snapshots. The lighting had been poor; they were grainy and wavy. But you could tell who the subjects were.

There were two. Three if you counted the bed. Ronald Headon and Andrea Gale. Naked as Adam and Eve before the serpent. They were on the sofa doing things men and women do when they get naked and assume they're all alone. Things nobody'd do if they thought somebody with a camera was on the other side of a window. They were doing these things with imagination and flair.

My first thought was exhilarating. My ship had come in, my six numbers had come up on Saturday night. I had five pictures of a murdered blonde frolicking in the buff with a very vulnerable, very married, very rich Catholic community pillar.

Then I made a bleak laugh. Said out loud, "Who'm I trying to kid, Bugs?" I could dream about blackmail, but I couldn't do it. Then I thought about how dead Andrea Gale was and how James Wylie was nowhere to be found and how Ronald Headon owned his own cop. I wasn't smiling while I thought about these things.

I scooped up the stack of letters and photos that had been in the packets, dumped it all back in the box except the five Polaroids. I lay back, lit a Kool and blew smoke at a water stain on the ceiling. I looked at the Polaroids again one at a time, then laid them on my stomach and thought some more.

I would've given Marvin's Cadillac to see James Wylie open the door and walk into the room. But I was pretty sure now that he never would.

# TWENTY-SEVEN

I didn't sleep much the rest of the night. When I did, I dreamt about the Polaroids, and in the dreams everybody and their brother knew I had 'em and there were chases and beatings and sometimes people took time out to have sex with Andrea Gale while the rest of us took pictures.

I spent the awake time reviewing things, deciding what to do next. I could go straight to Headon Engineering, dash past Miss Clara Tannehill, pitch the Polaroids on Headon's desk and say, "Explain these, Ronald." But I didn't think it would be in my best interest to do that. Not now. I doubted if many people knew about the Polaroids and those that knew about them obviously hadn't known where they were. It wouldn't hurt to keep it that way for awhile.

But as usual I couldn't come up with a detailed plan, which meant I'd have to wing it. What a unique experience that would be.

But I definitely needed a kinder, gentler town to work in. So at 9:00 A.M. I barreled through the doors of the Johnson City Police Department like an indignant indicted alderman. I strode the corridor like I was everyone's boss. Got directions from a redheaded lady cop who looked bemused, went up a flight of stairs two at a time, found Snow's cubicle. I rapped on the frosted window, opened the door and walked in. I plopped my butt in the chair at the side of his desk.

Snow rolled his chair back, put his feet up on the desk, legs crossed, and sipped coffee from a white mug. He didn't talk. He stared at me over the mug.

I began to feel somewhat less imperious. I said, "Got a minute?"

"Might."

"McCoy get a major promotion yesterday?"

Snow frowned.

"Like to God. Or at least mayor."

Snow looked into his mug. Said, "Damn."

"He able to dictate who can and cannot visit Johnson City?"

" 'Course not."

"While we're on the subject of McCoy, it S.O.P. in this town for detectives to run interference for your wealthier citizens? They encouraged to moonlight as personal body-guards for these people?"

"He tell you to stay out?"

"With 'or else' at the end."

"And I told that redneck."

"He didn't listen to you."

"You breakin' any laws?"

"Just stumblin' around, askin' questions."

"He told me you were fired and left. Didn't say a thing about he ordered you out."

"I got a right to check on things if I think things are screwy and I think things are plenty screwy."

"Only to the point where you don't annoy people."

"Me? Annoy? I ask questions because I'm a searcher for truth."

Snow said, "You're a bargain basement private eye, Kruger, and bargain basement private eyes could give a fuck about the truth. Truth to a PI means 'what's in it for me.' "

I said, "There's not much for me in this mess. So little in fact that I'd be home in bed right now if McCoy hadn't decided to run his macho act by me after I got fired."

Snow said, "He gave you a rough time after you got canned, now you're staying on the job. Means you're stubborn."

"As a mule. And twice as smart."

"Remember who said that." He swallowed more coffee, made horse galloping sounds with thick brown fingers on the side of the mug. "The Gale murder and the Torres murder are both his. He's bound to get teed off you keep poking around, acting like they're unsolved when he's got two dudes sittin' in jail for 'em. You're trying to show him up."

"Way he's actin' there's more to it than that."

"How about the way you're actin'? You holding back on us? I played straight with you, Kruger."

"You did, you're the first cop ever has."

The coffee aroma was strong and enticing. I asked if he had more. He nodded at a steel pot on a hot plate on top of a filing cabinet.

I got up and walked to it, removed the top styrofoam cup from an upside down stack. Snow watched me attentively. I said, "Doesn't matter how teed he gets, he can't order people to stay out of town."

"I realize that."

"I mean, if I break a law, throw my butt in jail, but you can't tell me to leave town if I'm minding my P's and Q's."

"I ain't arguing with you. You're really enjoying this, aren't you?"

"I'm hinting that maybe you should talk to McCoy."

"Maybe I will. But remember what I said. I ever find you dug up evidence germane to these cases and didn't share, I'll bust your monkey ass myself, you hear what I'm sayin'?"

I said, "Ooh, germane. I love it when cops talk shop. Or was that dirty?"

Snow grinned without wanting to.

I pondered how germane five Polaroid snapshots of Ronald Headon and Andrea Gale naked and frolicking were to Andrea Gale's murder. Decided at this point, not very. Snow appeared to be a good cop and a decent man, but I didn't trust him a hundred percent yet. McCoy had adversely colored my opinion of the Johnson City police force. I said, "Say I do, I'm not sure I'd care to share with McCoy."

"Then come to me."

"I guess I could do that. But why is it PI's always have to share with cops, but cops never share with us?"

Snow shrugged. "I didn't make the rules."

Report sheets and requisition forms were scattered under and around the hot plate. I said, "You might wanna clean this up should the Fire Marshall drop by."

"Fuck the Fire Marshall."

I poured some coffee, took a swallow. It was thicker than mud and as bitter as battery acid. My stomach reacted like I'd drunk Drano. I gagged, spit up on myself.

Snow laughed like hell. He pounded the armrest of the

chair, tears rolled from his eyes. He said, "Man, I was sittin' here *waitin'* for you to swallow that stuff."

I choked, "What is this?"

"Special Afro-Cajun coffee."

"What's in it?"

"You don't wanna know."

He chuckled and wiped his eyes with his fingers while I coughed. When I could see and swallow again, I said, "You ever get a coroner's report on Andrea?"

Snow was still grinning. "Just had the tar beat out of her. In coroner lingo 'Cranial trauma caused by multiple blunt instrument injuries.' Usual catchall. Means he used anything from a pistol butt to a frozen leg of lamb." Both hands holding the mug, he gently sloshed the coffee. His face got serious. "You know, ever since you walked in here, you got a look on your face, a way about you, says you're way ahead of somebody, Kruger, and I'm feeling it's us. I don't like that feeling."

"I'm offended you don't take me at my word."

"The day I take a private at his word they'll be shoving me to pension on a mental disability. I told you I ain't like the rest of these hicks out here. I dealt with your kind in the city for ten years."

I slurped a tiny sip of the coffee. Immediately felt a surge. I said, "This ain't half bad at that, Snow, you get used to it. Stuff's like liquid speed."

Snow didn't answer. He stared at my face like he was reading an eye chart. Like a dolt, I shoved my hand in my pocket and fingered the envelope with the Polaroids to make sure it was there. Attaboy Dan, why don't you just pull 'em out and hand 'em to the man?

Snow suddenly shook his head, made a face like he smelled bad cheese and said, "You're ugly as a four-eyed bulldog, Kruger."

I fluttered my eyes, Scarlett O'Hara-style.

He said, "Okay, I can tell McCoy to lay off, but I can't make the man like you."

"McCoy ever likes me, I'll want a personality transplant." I headed for the door.

"And you share," Snow shouted as I shut it.

# TWENTY-EIGHT

I dialed Lisa Farrell from a pay phone in the Cop Shop lobby. PIGS SUCK was written in fine line marker by the coin release lever. Lisa didn't answer. I didn't know if that meant she wasn't home or was too occupied to pick up the phone. I said, "Get a damn answering machine, Lisa."

Ronald Headon answered after the second ring when I tried to reach Sandy. I set the receiver back on the hook.

I stood there a bit. Caught myself fingering the envelope with the Polaroids again reassuring myself it was still there. I felt like a ten-year-old kid with a fifty dollar bill in his pocket.

For lack of a better plan, I decided to make the farm town drive to see George and Dwayne.

Ten miles out, I stopped at the Kountry Kitchen in a town called Richardville for coffee and eggs. I eavesdropped on a truck driver and two farmers wearing John Deere caps and overalls. They told corny jokes, complained how the rain was messing up their planting schedules, told more corny jokes. I felt like I was on "Hee Haw."

Then, like they were reading my mind, they started talking state politics. The waitress, a skinny old girl named Bernice, even piped in on this subject. I quickly learned the consensus sentiment in the sticks regarding Chicagoans was on a par with my opinion of child abusers. City slickers was the kindest term they used. They were sick as hell of watching their tax dollars keep that "sewercity" of dope addicts and welfare cheats above water. I winced a few times, but tossed the eggs down in silence. They grow some big boys in the boonies.

Half an hour later, I slowed the Seville to a crawl at each farm road just like Sandy did. I said, "Bugs, we may die out here if I get lost. Just go round and round forever." That didn't scare Bugs. If I set him loose out here, he'd live like a king. Eventually I came to the road I wanted. I turned onto it and listened to the roar of the stones underneath as I crept toward the farmhouse. This time the noise upset Bugs so I talked nonsense to him in a soft voice.

George's battered Chevy was parked on the front lawn. Next to it, a rusted out VW van, brush painted aqua green, sank half a foot into swampy, chewed-up grass.

I went through the gate, pounded on the front door. No one answered. I followed the cement walk to the backyard, gave a yell. Nothing. George and his personal catcher weren't preparing for the American League today. Wherever he was, Jose Canseco was resting a little easier.

I walked around the corner to the other side of the house. The back door was wide open.

Empty beer cans and wine bottles littered the kitchen countertops. On the table, large glass ashtrays were jammed with squashed cigarette butts. Wadded potato chip and pretzel bags dotted the floor like sagebrush.

I walked down the short hallway into the living room. It was full of empties too. I kicked a Gilbey's gin bottle. It whirlybirded across the floor, scattered a pyramid of Old Style cans. Made a hell of a racket. I stood for a bit, waiting, but still nobody stirred.

The two windows facing north were open and must've been all night. It was chilly in here. Lacy, white curtains billowed with the breeze. I eased the frames down. The sky was grayer than an hour ago and lower than an attic ceiling.

There was a door off the living room. I knocked softly, pushed it open and peeked in. My heart took a leap off a high dive. A pimply-faced, black-haired girl with long, bony legs lay on her back on the floor at the end of a child-sized bed. She wore only a dingy white T-shirt.

I wasn't paranoid or anything; I just assumed she was dead. As I started walking to her to feel for a pulse, she snorted like a horse, rolled onto her stomach and started to snore. She was so skinny her butt looked like two dinner rolls.

I closed the door, leaned against it. Took a deep breath.

Something's wrong when you automatically assume sleeping people are dead.

I went back to the hallway where a flight of stairs started.

The staircase was narrow. I had to turn slightly to navigate it. The steps groaned under my feet. After six steps there was a small landing, then six more steps doubling back.

At the top, a boy and girl, naked and insensible, lay tangled together like octopi tentacles. The girl was blonde, chubby and pretty. The boy had spiked orange hair and the kind of buck teeth parents point at to scare their kids off sucking their thumb. Personal hygiene did not seem to be a priority with either one. I held my breath and stepped over them.

To the left was a narrow hallway with four open doorways. This area was above the living room. The first two doorways, left and right, opened to empty rooms. No furniture, no people. Also no windows. You could probably roast meat in these rooms in August.

In the second room on the left, Dwayne snoozed contentedly, scratching his crotch and mumbling to himself. He was fully dressed and alone.

George was in the room across from him. He was alone too, except for an almost empty jug of dago red that leaned against his ribs. His pitching arm curled around it.

I shook him awake. It took some time. I said, "George, I'm guessing you boys broke training last night. Bet you blew curfew too."

He stared at me with listless eyes. After twenty seconds, they focused. He sat up fast and started to talk. Nothing intelligible came out. Then he sagged back and laid his arm on top of his eyes. I felt genuine empathy for George at that moment. Red wine hangovers are killers.

I patted his arm. Said, "It's the tannins George. You aspire to be a wino, better switch to white. The high's not as cozy but your head's always the same size next day."

He groaned.

I said, "Grab some hair of the dog. I'll be in the living room. We gotta talk."

He nodded and waved me away.

# TWENTY-NINE

I sat on the sofa, smoked a Kool. I was two drags from the filter when I heard sounds of movement upstairs. Someone said something that ended with "Now, dammit!" There was a slap and the blonde shrieked. A minute later, she and the bucktooth punk were in the downstairs hallway buttoning and adjusting clothes. The punk went to the bedroom, stuck his head in and yelled, "Jeanie get up, we been evicted." He went into the room.

The upstairs blonde looked me over. She said, "You here last night?" She slowly tucked a lemon colored blouse into faded jeans, then zipped up.

"Missed this one."

"Too bad." She puffed hair out of eyes that were big and bloodshot and wet.

The punk stumbled from the bedroom leading the skinny girl by the hand. He'd gotten a pair of pants on her. Lime green thongs made a gentle, rhythmic slap as she walked away. She was moaning and her free hand was clamped on her forehead.

The blonde said, "I'm Rhonda. See you around maybe." She winked.

I winked back. Lit another Kool and thought, Dan, you dog you.

Five minutes later, George came down. He moved as slow as Uncle Joe. His index finger was curled through the ring on the neck of the wine jug and the jug jiggled against his thigh as he walked into the room. He dragged a three-legged milking stool away from the wall and sat on it.

"You wanna talk to Dwayne too?" he asked, staring at the floor in front of him. "He don't wanna get up."

"That bottle follows you around like a puppy."

He looked at it, then me. "Had a rough night."

"So'd I."

"I usually don't drink this early, but you know how it is, some mornings you gotta have help." His voice was hoarse and loopy.

"I know how it is."

He said, "How early is it?"

"Not very. 'Bout eleven."

"Oh." He shifted his feet and accidentally booted a couple of empties in front of the stool, wincing at the noise. "Major party here last night."

"I deduced that, George." I flipped my cigarette into the hubcap ashtray. It tumbled down the hill of butts to the floor. George watched as it scorched a brown spot in the wood.

I said, "You care a lot for Sandy, don't you?"

"She's the only person in the world I care about. Rest of the world can go fuck itself."

"I care about her too. I'd like to help her."

"Who are you?"

I told him my name. Said, "Sandy and I visited the other day."

"I remember. I just never got the name. What are you?"

"A friend."

He nodded, face suspicious. "How come you're so concerned about my sister? You wanna fuck her?"

"No, George, I don't wanna fuck her. I heard you say you'd do anything for her."

"And I meant it."

"She ever ask you and Dwayne to help her out of a tight spot?"

His face got confused. To cover it he hoisted the jug with his forearm and swallowed three long gulps. He set the bottle down, belched. "I don't follow you, Kruger," he said.

Thunder exploded the quiet. George came up off the stool. Dwayne yelled upstairs. Rain started to drum on the roof and against the windows. George sat back down. Said, "Man."

I said, "I'm talking about applying superior muscle to inferior muscle."

George didn't savvy, or pretended he didn't.

I said, "If she has a problem, does she ask you and Dwayne to take care of it? Like the night at Bobby's Tap, 'bout a year ago."

He shook his head like a small child denying a naughty to Santa Claus. "Oh, no. That was me, she never asked. I just went off the deep end that night. I got too high and I couldn't stand the thought of a greaser touching my sister."

"How bad do you hate Ronald Headon?"

"I'd like to kill him. I'd like to kill the son of a bitch."

I said, "No kidding?"

He tipped the jug again, drained it. He bowled it across the floor into the corner. As it rolled on the warped wood it made a hollow, ringing sound. He leaned forward, picked through the mound of butts in the hubcap. He found a smokable roach and clamped it in a clip he dug from his pocket. He bummed my lighter and toked. Breath held in, he said, "This should get me goin'."

He offered it to me. I said, "Not today, George."

He nodded like he understood.

I said, "Ronald cheats on your sister."

Still holding the smoke in he nodded fast, said, "All the time. For years. He beats her, ignores her, screws around on her. And everybody thinks she's so lucky, that they're so happy. People treat him like he's some kind of saint." He blew out the smoke. "It's because of the money. You give some of it to charities, you get this saint rep. Once you got that you get away with murder."

"Why doesn't she leave him?"

"I don't know." He sounded disgusted. "I tell her to all the time. Guess she's scared." He leaned forward until he was almost off the stool. His eyes were pink where they should've been white and sweat bubbles dotted his forehead. "You should hear the stories Sandy tells me. She doesn't tell anybody else. Only me."

I thought, "Buddy, she tells everybody," but I said, "She ever name names?"

"Of who?"

"The other women?"

He thought for some seconds. George wasn't a bright guy, but he was an experienced pothead and potheads learn to

compensate for being constantly out to lunch. Sometimes
they have to laboriously think things through, decide if what
they plan to do or say is what they'd do or say if they
weren't cruising the galaxies. I could tell George was asking
himself should he be answering these questions or not. His
face got a crafty expression. Looking at the roach clip, he
said, "Maybe she don't know the names."

"Ronald's other women enrage you, don't they?"

He didn't answer directly. He said, "But if I did do something to somebody, all anybody'd have to do is listen to
Sandy's stories and they'd say I did the right thing. I cry
sometimes after she goes home. Him and his bimbos." He
spat on the ashtray. "She raised me, we're as close as a
brother and sister can be, we *need* each other, but he
wouldn't let me live with them not even one day after I
turned eighteen. I was out the door. On account I was too
wild and didn't show enough respect. She tell you about
that?"

She hadn't, but I nodded.

"You *earn* respect, man. It's not a given. And that's one
man didn't ever earn no respect from me."

"You know a James Wylie?"

"Sure I do. Ronald screwed him over too. I don't know
the details, it was business I think. It was a long time ago, I
know that much. He's okay, Sandy says so too. He's partied
out here before."

"You and Sandy and James Wylie?"

He caught the startled tone in my voice and looked
quickly way. Pot paranoia was screaming at him now. He
said, "Not with Sandy. With me and Dwayne and some
other dudes. Dwayne's oldest brother, Buster, knows him.
He brought him out here a couple times when it was just us
guys sittin' around getting numb. One time, me and him
started rapping and I found out he knew Sandy and then he
told me about Ronald screwing him over. Small world,
right?"

"A global village. He tell you the story about him and
Ronald?"

"I don't remember."

"What's his opinion of Ronald now? He sound like he'd

like to get even?"

"I don't remember that either." He smiled. "I was fucked up."

"Wylie's missing. Got any idea where I could find him?"

"Maybe." I was surprised again and from the look he got on his face I showed it. He said, "Any this stuff gonna hurt Sandy?"

"Might help her."

"I'll look around, check it out."

"Don't miss any baseball practice."

"You think I'm lyin'? You think I couldn't find him?" He made impatient little bounces on the stool, pointed his finger. Shouted, "Don't you dare make fun of me, man."

"Chill, George, life's short. I'm not making fun of anybody."

He became calm in the time it takes to snap your fingers. He said, "Just don't talk down to me."

I took out the picture of Wylie and Andrea and handed it to him. He held it close to his face and studied it. His eyes narrowed.

"That's Jim alright. Feel sorry for him."

"Know the girl?"

"No."

"You sure?"

He stared at the photo a long time, then he whispered, "Bitch."

I grabbed the photo away, put it back in my pocket. "I think I found out what I wanted to know," I said. I wrote my home and office phone numbers and the phone number of the pay phone at the Jones Hotel on the back cover of a *TV Guide*, the only reading material and paper I'd seen in the house. I ripped the cover from the magazine and gave it to George.

I said, "I'm in and out of these places. You learn anything about Wylie, you call these numbers and leave a message."

He nodded.

"And you decide you wanna talk about the blonde in the photograph, call me."

"I don't know who she is."

"It might come back to you."

"She's one of his bimbos I suppose."

"You knew the answer to that before I did."

He told me the front door was nailed shut, I'd have to leave by the kitchen door. I passed the stairs as Dwayne came down. The man looked to be in immense pain. He followed me into the kitchen. I heard the refrigerator door squeak open behind me.

I stopped at the door, watched silver strings of rain splash into long puddles. Started to work up courage to make a dash around the house to the Caddy.

Dwayne rumbled, "Hey, buddy."

I turned around quickly, was just able to catch an end over end tossed can of Old Style. Dwayne turned sideways and ducked to get through the doorway to the hall. He lumbered back to the stairs carrying a five-pack.

# THIRTY

I was in the boonies anyway, feeling like Christopher Columbus. I got back to the highway. First gas station I came to I bought a map, asked the woman at the register to point to where we were, then I found where Oswego was. For forty-five minutes, wipers on high, nursing the can of beer, I traveled a succession of country highways. At twelve-thirty, I entered Oswego. It isn't big enough to get lost in twice.

I sat in the Farrell's driveway again, waiting out the rain, watching Bugs twitch his nose while he dreamed about whatever it is rabbits dream about. Opposite gender rabbits probably.

In the window nearest the driveway, a face peered through parted curtains. The curtains opened wider and a second face appeared. Then a short, chunky man with an enormous gut wearing black pants and a white T-shirt strutted onto the porch.

I rolled down my window.

"What're you doing in my driveway?" he shouted. He stuck his hands in the back pockets of his pants and cocked his head. He looked like an obese banty rooster.

"You Lisa Farrell's father?"

"What if I am?"

"Like to talk to you."

"Who the hell are you?"

"Dan Kruger. A friend of Lisa's."

He shrugged and went back inside. In a few minutes, I realized he wasn't coming back with an umbrella so I made a dash for the steps. The front door opened before I knocked.

Mr. Farrell's face was rough and round and a tangly moss of gray whiskers covered the lower half. His nose was meaty and shaped like a light bulb. Broken veins created tiny red blossoms on it.

He pointed me to a ripped blue sofa. He fell backwards into a well-worn Laz-E-Boy, hiked up the foot rest. "All My Children" blared from a television set on the other side of the room. He pressed down on the remote lying on the arm of the chair and the TV sound died.

A gentle-eyed woman with long thick hair brought out a six-pack of Bud and set it on the footrest. She was middle-aged, plump and her dark hair was liberally marbled with gray. She wore a discount store blue cotton dress. Facially, she didn't look much like Lisa, but she looked familiar somehow. The man glared at her back when she left the room.

He popped a can, held it out for me. I stood and reached to receive it. He tapped the top of a can before popping it open, staring at me the while.

"Didn't know if I'd find you home," I said, after a sip.

"Little early in the day to visit people you don't know. Most people're at work."

He grunted. Said, "I'm always here."

"Must be nice."

"Is it? What do you want, mister?"

"Lisa ever mention me to you?"

"Lisa don't mention shit to me. She in some kind of

trouble? This got to do with Andrea?"

"That's how I met Lisa. I'm trying to find out if David Stone really murdered Andrea."

"You defending that piece of slime?"

"His lawyer defends him. I work for him. Or used to."

"Same thing. That man is a twisted piece of work. Long-haired bum use to be Lisa's boyfriend. I hear tell he screwed Andrea right in front of my daughter. You ever heard of such a callous, perverted thing? He killed Andrea Gale all right. Fits his mental makeup perfect." He drank the beer in one long swallow, wiped his mouth with the back of his hand. Said into the other room, "Marge, bring us out some of that scotch."

I said, "I need to get some background on Lisa and Andrea. See if there's a name I haven't heard or an act somebody did that could of eventually led to murder."

He grunted again.

Marge Farrell brought out a half-empty bottle of Seagrams scotch and two dixie cups. She sat on the opposite edge of the sofa I was on. I held my beer up to Farrell, said it was fine.

He stared at his wife, face amazed. "What in hell you think you're doing?"

"If he's askin' about Lisa and Andrea, I'm staying. God only knows what you'd be tellin' him." She looked at me. "You don't think David Stone killed Andrea?"

I said, "Do you?"

She said, "Well, Lisa seemed so certain and the police arrested him. We just assumed—" Her husband drank a mouthful of booze straight from the bottle.

I said, "His lawyer believes he's innocent. Lately I'm inclined to believe it too."

Marge Farrell said, "Oh." She put two fingers to her chin and shut her eyes tight for a second.

I said, "Andrea's parents still live here? I'd like to talk to them too."

Farrell stared out the window at the rain.

His wife looked from me to him a couple of times, then said in a small voice, "Mr. Gale died a long time ago. Andrea was still in grade school. Her mother moved west,

Nevada I think, the summer before Andrea was to be a senior in high school. Just up and left. Told Andrea she could come if she wanted, but Andrea preferred to stay."

I sipped beer and nodded.

She said, "Andrea stayed here with Lisa and us for maybe three months. Then she dropped out of school and moved to Johnson City to live with a man."

"She was a senior when she dropped out?"

"We tried to talk her out of it, but—"

"Was her mother concerned about leaving her daughter behind? You contact her when Andrea quit school?"

"Her mother was a whore," Farrell blurted, still looking at the rain. "And so was she."

"Arthur!" The woman dug the nail of her left index finger into the palm of her right hand and scraped. She said to neither of us in particular, "Andrea had a lot of boyfriends, but that didn't make her a whore. Things are different today." She looked at me. "Even when she was young—twelve or thirteen—she'd get in trouble over boys. Her mother never set a good example so I can't fault Andrea. Way she was raised she must of thought promiscuity was normal." Mrs. Farrell meticulously smoothed out the formless dress. Her legs were bare. Thick blue varicose veins were bunched in the middle of her calves like a swarm of inchworms.

I said, "Lisa told me about her and David Stone. She said Andrea took other boyfriends away from her."

She said, "I can't believe that. They were too good of friends. Oh, they had their spats, but what good friends don't? I don't think they'd of stayed friends long if things like that happened."

"The girl was a whore," Arthur Farrell said again.

I said, "You remember the name of the man Andrea went to live with in Johnson City?"

She said, "Gee, I couldn't begin to."

"It was a beaner," Arthur said. He hadn't looked at either one of us since Mrs. Farrell sat on the sofa. "That girl'd bed down with anything."

"Torrance?" she whispered to herself. "Torres?"

"Eduardo Torres?"

She whispered the name to herself. "That might be it but

I honestly couldn't say for sure. She had so many boys."

I lit a Kool, let what I'd just heard sink in. Told myself not to get carried away. There's millions of Torreses in the world and this woman couldn't even swear Torres was the right name. But what if? I watched Mrs. Farrell carve her palm with her fingernail like there was something there that had to be dug out.

"Did you have any trouble with Lisa? When she was growing up?"

She said softly, "Really, I don't think that has anything to do with Andrea getting murdered." Arthur snorted and she glanced at him nervously, biting her lip. She said, "She can be a little high spirited, but she's young. And Andrea was always such an influence on her. In some ways I think Lisa was flattered that a girl that beautiful wanted to be friends with her. She did a lot of things she wouldn't of normally because of that."

"A little?" her husband jeered. "A little high strung?" He finally looked away from the window toward me. Said, "What business is it of yours anyway?"

"How'd you expect her to act?" Mrs. Farrell said, her voice low and hard. "With a drunken layabout like you for a father. Her friends laughing behind her back, making jokes. You don't work—"

"I worked for twenty-five years, woman, till I like to broke my back and you know it. You make it sound like I don't work 'cause I don't feel like it. Hell, I *deserve* time off after the years I put in." He resumed staring at the slithering raindrops on the window.

I waited a beat. This had the sound of a daily refrain, as common as asking to pass the salt, so I didn't feel as embarrassed as I normally would've. To Mrs. Farrell I said, "What about their jobs? They like working at Headon Engineering?"

"Oh, yes," she said. "They didn't have any college. Andrea had no desire to go after she quit high school and we couldn't afford to send Lisa." She stared defiantly at her husband.

"Lisa liked office work?"

"She did." She sounded like that surprised her. "She types

good and she takes shorthand. Knows how to operate those personal computers. Andrea never bothered to learn any of those things so she had to work the floor." Mrs. Farrell smiled to herself. She was a good woman, but not above a little parental gloating. She said, "Have you been going out with Lisa, or did you meet her because of the murder?"

I said, "I met her the day Andrea died. I don't see her much. She's busy moving into the new apartment your husband found for her."

"What apartment? I didn't find her no apartment," he said. "She tell you that? That girl lies worse than a TV preacher."

"You shut up!" Mrs. Farrell shouted. "Quit running down your own daughter in front of strangers. Show a little class. Just once!"

His forehead turned bright red and he puffed up like a bull frog. He pushed himself up from the chair, said, "Go to hell, woman." I braced for violence, but he stomped out the door, slamming it shut behind him.

"I swear that man is insane," Mrs. Farrell whispered.

"It's the alcohol," I said. "Some people, that's how it affects 'em."

"No, he's mean. Liquor makes it worse, but inside he's a mean and bitter man. No wonder Lisa refuses to stay here. I offered, but she only stayed two nights."

"Who got her that apartment?"

"I don't know. A friend probably. She told us she got a new one, didn't say how." She looked toward the porch. "Horrid man," she murmured.

I said, "When did Andrea and Lisa start working at Headon's?"

"Maybe a year or two ago. A man named James Wylie is a friend of mine. We went out together when I was young. He was older than me, but he was a nice man."

Suddenly it came to me why she seemed so familiar. She was one of the women in Wylie's box of memories. One of the early-Sixties photos. I tried to remember what vile things he'd written about her.

Mrs. Farrell went on, "He said they should apply there. He used to own a part of the firm, but he sold out to Ronald

Headon just before it took off." She shook her head sadly. "Story of that man's life." She looked at the porch again. "Story of every man I ever knew."

I was learning more than I could store. I said, "James Wylie hated Ronald Headon's guts. Why would he recommend Headon Engineering to anybody?"

"Because they needed a good job. He was helping them out, not Ronald Headon. When Lisa first went to Johnson City to live with Andrea, they stayed in a cheap walkup apartment, barely eating. They waitressed and such."

I thought, those two girls have never wondered where their next meal was coming from, but to Marge Farrell I said, "Andrea wasn't living with Torres anymore?"

"No. I don't suppose that lasted long. She probably moved in with him just so she could get out of this house. Who'd blame her?"

"You kept in touch with Wylie?"

"Over the years, a little. He's not always in the area. He comes and goes. He drinks too much, but basically he's a good man. Not like—" She nodded toward the porch. "Headon's pays good money. It's unionized, they got benefit books thick as a paperback novel. He said he could put in a good word with somebody. They applied and got hired within a week. I doubt he hates Ronald Headon all that much anymore. James is a gentle, forgiving man and that was long ago."

I shook my head. James Wylie must of about broke in two from the strain of pretending. I said, "When was the last time you talked to him?"

"About the time he recommended Headon Engineering to the girls. I probably called to thank him."

I said, "You know the names of other men Andrea or Lisa were friends with in Johnson City? Men who might have reason to get upset at them?"

"No, Lisa doesn't confide in me much lately. She used to. She's not proud of me now. She thinks I'm weak to stay with her father. He's gotten worse and worse the last couple years. I'm not weak, I just have nowhere else to go and nothing I could do. I'm trapped is what it is."

I said, "I know exactly how you feel. It's a scary feeling

and Lisa should understand that. Maybe one day she will." I got up. Said, "You've been a great help."

Arthur Farrell stood on the top step of the porch stairs, facing the house. His eyes were unfocused and he smirked as if to say, you've had it now, buddy. He held the empty scotch bottle by its shoulder. He raised it over his head, said, "You cheap, nosy prick," then threw it.

I swatted it to the floor with my forearm. He came at me. He threw a roundhouse left to my mouth. I tasted the spot with my tongue. No blood. I pushed him backward. He moved left and right, hands raised and bobbing. He kept up a steady muttering, but I couldn't make out any words. He sounded like Popeye.

I reached through his weaving fists, grabbed the collar of his shirt with my left hand and pulled him toward me. He was so drunk he let me do it. It seemed I had all the time in the world to decide where to punch. I shot a partially pulled right to his belly. It was like punching a bag of feathers; my arm disappeared halfway to the elbow. His face went slack, the talking ceased. I let go of his collar and he sat down so hard the porch shuddered. I stepped to the side. He folded his hands on his stomach, leaned forward and vomited.

I said, "You just wasted half a bottle of scotch, dumbass."

The door opened. Mrs. Farrell stood there. Her eyes canvassed the neighborhood. Her husband started to moan. He crawled to the corner of the porch, pulled himself up and leaned over the railing like he was puking on a boat. The rain muffled the sounds he made.

I said, "I'm sorry, he came at me. He's not hurt. I can't punch hard enough to hurt anybody."

She said, "I saw it."

"You'll be okay? He won't take it out on you, will he?"

"Of course he will. Oh God, look at this. This is a fine show for the neighbors, isn't it? Give them something else to gossip about. This is a refined town. I swear I'm afraid to show my face in it. You won't tell Lisa about this, will you?"

I said, "Of course not."

Farrell punched the side of the railing.

Mrs. Farrell said, "Leave, Mr. Kruger. Please?"

I did. When I got in the car, I said, "Bugs, you know what our lives've been lacking lately? Elegance."

# THIRTY-ONE

Halfway back to Johnson City, the rain suddenly stopped and I didn't have to concentrate on the road so much. I was ready to bitch. I said, "Suburbia can kiss my ass, Bugs. They can talk about Chicago weirdos and addicts and cheats all they want, but if what we're meetin' is anything close to the norm they got more fucked up people out here than any ten Chicago's. This is supposed to be picket fences and car pools and mothers making meat loaf. You seen any of that, Bugs? Hell, no. All I meet are drunks and liars. If I hung out with this crowd, I'd never even ask myself if I had a drinking problem because I'd be the soberest man in the bunch."

Bugs nodded sagely.

"I get lied to big-time by everybody. Nobody knows anybody, nobody hears nothin'. Everybody tells me what they want me to know and they assume I'm so stupid I'll accept it as gospel. Like I don't know how to check up on anything. Now I find out Andrea might of lived with Torres, which means Lisa knew him a lot better than she claims. Lisa knew Wylie too. For a long time. Sandy's brother admits he hung out with Wylie on occasion, so there's more there to look into. I got a feeling Sandy knows Wylie a lot better than she says. Least we found out why Ronald Headon's so scared and why his cop is harassing me. The five Polaroids I'm walking around with that could get me killed." I ran my fingers around my mouth a couple times, working away some frustration. "We still got a lot of work to do Bugs, finding out how all this stuff connects."

Bugs ignored me. He probably had the whole thing solved.

I stopped at the Princeton Men's Shop in downtown

Johnson City. The sign painted on the front window said it'd been in business since 1924, but judging from the dirty interior and the small amount of stock on hand, the Johnson City Mall would be singing "Another One Bites the Dust" any day. An old man with thin white hair like corn silk stood behind the cash register; I was his only customer. I bought a pair of white socks, a package of Fruit of the Looms, a navy chambray work shirt and a pair of 501 Levi's. Thirty-six bucks total. The old man never said a word from the time I opened the door until I walked out.

Down the street from Maury's was a laundromat. While my new clothes washed, I ate chili and saltine crackers at Maury's counter and listened to a group of male retirees gripe about baseball salaries. While my new clothes dried, I sat in the soap-smelly laundromat, read a day-old *Sun-Times* and listened to two female retirees gripe about how men their age only wanted to sit around and talk sports. Made me wish I could get old real soon.

Back at the Jones, I took a cold shower in the hallway bathroom, working up a skimpy lather with a piece of Ivory no bigger than a guitar-pick. Used a napkin-sized towel I found in Wylie's room to dry off. Put on my new duds.

Feeling as debonair as Fred Astaire on his wedding day, I called Lisa from the pay phone in the Jones lobby. She was glad it was me and suggested we meet at a place called the Beach Head. I said I'd rather see her new place. She hesitated. I said, "I'd like to see the apartment your father got you." I clumsily accented "your father" just like I wanted. She said to give her an hour.

Exactly one hour later, I pressed her doorbell.

Inside wasn't what I expected. It was spacious, tasteful and luxurious. The living room was cathedral ceilinged and had wall-to-wall mauve carpeting, a woodburning fireplace, and a loft that you reached via a circular flight of stairs. The kitchen was bigger than my living room. To me, any kitchen with an automatic dishwasher and a microwave is ultra-modern, but this one had a lot more than that. I think brochures would describe it as fully-equipped Eurostyle.

I said, "I know rents are cheap out here, but this ain't half bad for a working girl."

She told me to sit in the living room. Most of the furniture was from the Third Street apartment so I sat on the same sofa I sat on Saturday when Andrea Gale lay dead in front of me. Same sofa I sat on first time I talked to Lisa. She set a glazed ceramic ashtray in front of me and backed away. She had a look on her face like she expected me to start screaming at her. Maybe I was giving off bad vibes. She sat on a cushion on the floor with her back against the wall, under a painting of some trees.

She said quietly, "I just talked to my mother."

"Me too."

"I know."

"So tell me more about Andrea's immorality," I said.

She tried to smile. Said, "There's people worse, I guess."

"Or at least as bad. Lisa, you told me you never heard of James Wylie. Now I hear he goes way back with your mother and it was his idea that you and Andrea apply to Headon Engineering."

"You shouldn't of talked to my mother behind my back."

"You shouldn't of lied to me." I took out the photo of Wylie and Andrea standing in the snow and flipped it to her. It landed face down in her lap. Her eyebrows made an inverted V. For a second I thought she wasn't going to look at it, but then she turned it over. Her expression didn't change. She tossed it back to me.

I said, "You take that picture?"

"No!"

I took a stab. Said, "Andrea lived with Eddie Torres, right? Couple years back? Funny, I sure didn't get that impression from you. Also she *was* sleeping with Ronald Headon."

"How do you know that?"

I still wasn't showing the Polaroids to anyone. I said, "Never mind how, but believe me, I know."

She stared at the other side of the room. She said, "You don't stop, do you?"

"Part of the job description."

"You keep gouging and gouging. You can't leave a person alone. I didn't want to get involved in this mess, okay? Is that so hard to understand?" She looked at me finally. "Give me a break, can't you? Think of what happened to me since Saturday. I come home, find my best friend dead on the living room floor. Some man I never seen before is walking around my apartment. At first I thought you meant to kill me too. Then there's police all over the place askin' millions of questions. Later you tell me Torres is beating people up and nobody knows why. Then he gets murdered and the whole time you keep with all these questions."

"And you're just a girl, right?"

"I knew Andrea made it with any man who'd spend money on her. Yeah, I knew she was screwing Headon, okay? You satisfied? Maybe you can run and tell him I knew it and maybe you can get me fired. That would be great. I knew James Wylie and I knew he hated Ronald Headon. But none of this has anything to do with me. I just wanna be left alone and I want this to stop. The police arrested the killers. It's all solved. So why do you keep pushing and pushing like *I'm* a suspect?"

I said, "I never said you were a suspect, Lisa, but why didn't you tell me these things earlier? I find out on my own, makes you look like you got serious things to hide."

She wiped damp cheeks with the back of her hand. "I just wanted you to quit and leave. The more of this stuff you learned the more you'd stay around, and things'd just get worse. I want things back to normal."

"Things'll never be back to normal for Andrea. That's why I do what I do."

"I know that. I miss her and everything. I cry about it every night, but I've got to get on with my life."

"Well, don't feel like the Lone Ranger. Everybody wants me to quit and leave." I took a couple puffs on the Kool. "Was Andrea still seeing Ronald Headon as of Saturday?"

"I don't know, maybe. I told you things were a little cool between us since I found her with David. I don't think she was, but I'm not sure. Ask him."

"I did. He claims he barely knew who she was."

She faked a laugh.

"You lost other guys to Andrea and you stayed friends. Why fall out over Stone?"

"We didn't fall out. Things were just a little cool. See

what I mean? All these questions?"

In a sarcastic voice I said, "I don't know anybody named Wylie. Ronald Headon had the hots for Andrea, but he's harmless, he's got the hots for everybody. I'm sure he struck out with her. Andrea didn't go out with Torres except once or twice—if it was Torres. It was so long ago I don't remember." I crushed the Kool in the ashtray, took a deep breath. I was getting madder than I intended. Something was happening inside me I didn't like. In this job I get lied to all the time, but I never take it personally. This time I was. I took another deep breath and said, "Who got you this apartment?"

She cried into a Kleenex, blew her nose.

"Who you living with?"

She looked at me quick, then away. "I answered an ad in the paper. If I live with someone, that's my business."

We were silent a bit, then she started to cry hard. She said, "I just didn't want to get involved in all this, Dan. It's not my affair, it's not my problem. I shouldn't have to be involved. That's all. I didn't lie to cover anything up, I just lied hoping if you didn't learn anything you'd go away. Honest."

The tears were unfair. I held out as long as I could. I said, "Okay, Lisa. I just needed to be sure. The lies started to pile up and I got worried. I thought we were good enough friends you wouldn't feel you had to lie so much." I went to her, kneeled and patted her shoulder. "Forget all this. Let's go have a drink."

She made a small smile, blinked rapidly to flick tears away. She said, "I don't think so, Dan. I don't feel like it now. But call me soon, okay?"

I said sure.

# THIRTY-TWO

I drove back to the Jones Hotel. My brain felt like a centipede in wet cement. A hundred things wiggled furiously up there, but I was flat out stuck.

And sometimes you catch a break.

Cora was waiting for me at the front desk. She motioned me over, face excited. She whispered, "A man over there knows where Mr. Wylie is."

"I told you if you asked around we'd find him."

"I only asked a couple of men, but they asked some other men." She waved her hand at four men on the other side of the lobby watching the evening news. "The one in the dungarees and the white sweatshirt? That's Dix something. He's the most horrid man you could ever meet."

"I'd take bets on that, but what did he say?"

She blushed and lowered her eyes. "He came in just a little bit ago and says 'Cora, I hear you been askin' about your loverboy. I know where your loverboy is, your Jimmyboy.' I don't allow people to joke with me about things like that. I got a husband and the Bible says—"

I said, "Cora, your behavior with the guests is above reproach, everybody knows that."

"I told him Mr. Wylie was just a friend, not a boyfriend, and I'd appreciate it if he'd remember that. And then he said something I wouldn't repeat even to God."

"I certainly won't ask what it was, Cora. Where's Wylie?"

"He wouldn't tell me, but he knows."

Dix sat, arms crossed, on a folding chair fifteen feet from the TV. I pulled a folding chair away from the wall, sat next to him.

Dix was over seventy, didn't like to shave, and he badly needed a bath. He stared at Dan Rather. Dan was explaining the latest government position on unemployment. Seems they were against it, but sometimes it was necessary to let it rise so inflation could be controlled. Or something. I was glad the Prez worried about inflation so much he put people out of work every once in a while to make sure it didn't get too high.

Dix seemed to have other ideas. He grumbled at Dan.

I said, "Name's Kruger."

Dix said, "Dix."

I offered him a Kool. Said, "Dix, lady at the desk says you know where James Wylie is."

He took the Kool. I lit him. He glanced at me, then back at the TV. He said, "I seen you at Maury's."

"Probably."

"You had the chili."

"That's right."

"I'm partial to the liver and onions myself."

I said, "I'll try it next time. You *do* know where Wylie is?"

A commercial came on and he gave his full attention to me. "Sure I know. Guy lives on the other side of town told me. I was plannin' to joke with Cora about it. Rag her a bit. Those two were always over there talkin' and gigglin' like a couple of teenagers. She don't say jackshit to the rest of us, but she sure liked Jimmyboy. Anyway, I make a little joke and next thing I know the biddy's recitin' scripture to me."

"Some Christians get intense about stuff like that," I said.

"Way too intense for me. So I asked her did she miss hidin' Jimmyboy's salami at midnight? You should of seen her face." He started a hiccupy laugh that turned into a prolonged coughing fit. When he calmed down he said, "See, she's got a little room back there with a TV and a couch and all. Don't tell me he wasn't sneaking down come midnight for a little hide the salami."

I said, "It's a primal urge."

Dix said, "So she gets all indignant on me. You know what I say? Fuck her if she can't take a joke."

"Words to live by, Dix, but really, I need to know where Wylie is."

A look came over Dix's face. A look I see all the time. It's an "aware" look people get when it dawns on them they possess information that's valuable to someone else, usually me. The look means they comprehend the basic economic principle of supply and demand.

Dix said, "I didn't tell the biddy where he is."

"I know."

"She wants to see Jimmyboy she can find him herself."

"Dix, I'm gonna level with you. I don't give a fuck whether she sees Jimmyboy or not, okay? I care only about if I see him."

"Why you wanna see a bum like that so bad?"

"Bums are a hobby of mine."

He looked me over. Said, "You're a detective, am I right?"

"As rain."

"I heard some guys talkin'."

"Just a private, though. Telling me where Wylie is won't land him in the tank. You don't have to worry about your conscience." I pulled a sawbuck from my wallet, laid it on his lap. "If you got one."

He pretended not to see the money, said, "I usually don't rat on a guy, but you ain't the real law and I never liked Wylie anyway. Walked around here in his ancient suits and those big collar shirts, never talked to the rest of us stiffs. Actin' like he was some kind of monk, all quiet and serene like, but he drinks more'n any of us, then he spends his night slippin' the salami to the biddy over there."

"The address?"

He said, "1310 Altgeld." His eyes went back to the TV.

I walked to the desk, asked Cora where 1310 Altgeld was.

She said, "Did he tell you what he said to me?"

"He told me."

She turned fire red. "Oh, I'm so mortified. Can you believe he'd actually say such a thing to a decent woman? See what I was sayin' about these men?"

I said, "Cora, 1310 Altgeld?"

She screwed up her face. Mentally found Altgeld, started down it. She said, "What is it?"

"Not sure. A hotel. Mission maybe."

"Could be the Burlington House. Oh, I hope not. I hate to think of Mr. Wylie living in a place like that." She brought up the phone book and leafed through the B's. "Yep. The Burlington House." Her eyes misted and she chewed her bottom lip.

"Another hotel?"

"It's a hotel, but a bottom of the barrel one." In a low voice she said, "These men are life's losers. People at the Burlington House don't even play the game. They rent to people we never would. Drug addicts, prostitutes, worse."

"Where is it?"

"West end of town. The Spanish area. There's two blocks of nothin' but bars and secondhand shops and Mexican stores. And the Burlington House."

"Supposedly that's where he is."

She chewed her lip harder.

I said, "There's worse places he could be."

"You'll tell him I asked after him? Tell him he should live here, not at a place like that." She spread a *Johnson City Daily News* on the desk and bent over it. Her shoulders shivered.

I thought, "Lady, he's lucky to be living period."

I bought a bottle of Jack Daniels at the package store behind the Jones on the theory that destitute old rummies on the run love liquid presents.

Cora wasn't lying. The Burlington House made her place look like the Whitehall. Six stories of pitted, grungy, maroon-colored brick. The few windows had whitewashed wooden casings. No lawn, no parking lot, the only sign was handwritten on cardboard and taped to the front door. It said BURLINGTON HOUSE, ROOMS BY THE HOUR, DAY, AND WEEK. Spanish words were below, saying the same thing.

A wooden balcony extended off the second floor over the door. A reedy kid with blond hair hanging past his shoulders leaned on the railing and watched me cross the street. He coiled a strand of hair with his fingers. He grimaced like curling his hair was exhausting labor.

When I got to the sidewalk I asked up to him, "You know a guy named Wylie?"

His legs wobbled. He squinted to get me in focus. Suddenly his head fell forward and plunked on the railing like it was a rock held up by a pipe cleaner. He giggled, said, "Don't know the dude. Live here?" He pillowed his head with his arms. His hair slowly spilled over the railing, hung straight down. The early evening breeze fanned it.

"Think so."

He crumbled to the balcony floor, giggling all the way down.

The lobby was a telephone, a cigarette machine and a two-foot desk with high iron grille. A middle-aged heavy-weight with greased back hair and a dirty tank T-shirt moseyed out after I dinged the bell ten times. He displayed his eagerness to be of service by yawning in my face. He didn't have many teeth left and he'd just consumed beer and sausage. Also garlic. MOTHER was tattooed across his right forearm.

I said, "You got a casualty on the balcony."

"And you, you're the Johnson City Civic Improvement Committee?" He drummed the table with grease-rimmed fingernails. "It's only Baylor nodding out for awhile. His room has the balcony and he likes to get high there. Enjoys the fresh air."

I shrugged. "It's your joint."

"Yeah, it is. You want a room?"

"I'd sooner sleep on the street."

He spread his hands out, palms up. "Hey, Slick, it's a hotel. A guy comes in, I figure he wants a room. Stupid of me."

"Wanna see a man named Wylie."

"Got no Wylie's. What's the room?"

"I knew that I'd walk right to it. I wouldn't be having this lovely conversation, would I? He's a shriveled up old man. Few teeth, not much hair. No belongings. Drinks heavy."

"You just described ninety percent of my clientele." He scratched an armpit thoroughly.

I took out the photo of Wylie and Andrea Gale, held it up to the cage so the man could look at it. He whistled. "It's Jackson. What in hell's Jackson doin' with a gash like this?"

"She's his fiancée. He disappeared and she wants to know what to do with the Lamborghini. He here or not?"

"Might be." He got The Look.

I put two bucks on the counter.

His hand gobbled the bills like a frog slurping a fly. "Five-oh-nine."

I walked up five flights of wobbly wooden stairs, my breath on hold against the stench. I've climbed scores of sweat and urine smelly flophouse staircases over the years, but I never get used to the smell.

I started down the fifth floor hallway. The plaster walls were painted grass green, the doors black. The room numbers were shakily scribbled in white chalk.

There was noise behind every room. In the first two rooms, drunken couples argued. After that it was clashing cultures door to door. Loud boom box music; rap, salsa, hillbilly. No Mozart. A middle-aged black man staggered past me in his underwear. Never looked at me.

I knocked softly on 509. Heard rat-like rustling inside. Thirty seconds went by. There was heavy breathing on the other side of the door.

I said, "Wylie, open up."

"The name is Jackson. You got the wrong room."

"Open it, Wylie."

"Who is this?"

"A friend from the Jones Hotel. I got some Polaroids for you."

He was silent for a bit, then said, "Gimme a name."

"I'm gonna break down the damn door you don't open it." I'm tough as Robocop when I deal with shrunken old alkies.

"Come on, mister," he pleaded. "Gimme a name."

"Dan Kruger. Lisa Farrell sent me. I brought along a good buddy of yours named Jack Daniels. He's dyin' to see you."

There was another wait, then he released the bolt, opened the door cautiously, ready to slam it if necessary. One eye peeked around the corner. I grabbed the doorknob, pulled the door away from him.

And finally stood face to face with James Anthony Wylie.

# THIRTY-THREE

The only light in the room came from a low-watt bulb in a bedside lamp. Wylie wore a white shirt and pants and in the dimness he looked like a shadowy ghost. His head was like a skull, his arms mere bones covered with grayish skin stretched tight.

I said, "Wylie, I been looking for you all week."

His eyes were fearful. "Could you give me the bottle? Please?" He put his hand out, palm up.

I said, "I wasn't looking for you so I could give you a bottle of booze. You gotta earn it. For he who does not talk, neither shall he drink."

But there is a prime-the-pump theory. A card table was set up under the window against the far wall. A dixie cup was on the table. I walked over, poured two fingers of Jack into the cup, gave it to Wylie. He drilled it. He had a prominent Adam's apple and while he swallowed it bobbed like a marble sliding down a string.

I sat down next to him on the bed. I put one of the Polaroids on his lap. He made a whimpering sound. I said, "Andrea Gale and Ronald Headon." I laid the picture of him and Andrea next to the other one. "Andrea Gale and James Wylie. I wanna know the connections."

He said, "Christ, how'd you get these pictures? This is my property. You're from Headon. I knew it."

"Wise up, Wylie. The guy Headon sends won't bring along a full bottle. But if I found you, he can too."

"What are you? Why'd you come here?"

"I'm a private cop. I started a job for David Stone and I like to finish what I start. Police say he killed Andrea Gale. You don't think that, do you?"

He jerked his head no, tapped his lips. Said, "But you're a professional at locating people. That's why you found me. Maybe Headon won't."

"You didn't even leave town, Wylie. And Headon's got

real law working for him. The surprise to me is nobody's
been here yet."

Wylie cringed like a dog watching his master pick up a
stick.

"You could've at least blown town, for Chrissakes."

"How? I got no money. I had to touch a friend to afford
this dump. My check don't come for another week."

"You plan to hole up in this room forever?"

He massaged his forehead. "Honest to God, I don't know
what I'm gonna do. I've racked my brain, but—" He stood,
the two photos sliding to the floor, and started to pace the
room. The white pants were corduroy and the legs zipped
against each other as he walked. "I wish I never thought of
any of this." He stopped and leaned against the radiator.
Made soft sucking sounds with his mouth.

I said, "Little late now for should of's and could of's."

"I've always had somewhere to go, no matter how bad
things got. But now this is it. Lookit this scummy room.
Nothing in here belongs to me except what I got on. This is
a fine way to end up, isn't it?"

"Don't count yourself out yet, Wylie."

"How'd you get those photos?"

"I rented your room at the Jones. By the way, the sign-in
lady says you should come back. She misses you."

He almost smiled. "Cora's a fine woman." He stared at
the floor for a second, then said, "What do you want? I got
no money."

"Only thing I want is answers."

"Can you help me blow town?"

"Tell me what I need to know, I'll see what I can do."

"He killed Andrea. He'll kill me too."

"You don't talk, I give him the photos and tell him where
you are."

"He might kill you."

"I'll take my chances. Why'd you leave these photos at the
hotel?"

"I was afraid to go back after I heard about Andrea. I
was out with friends when I heard about her. If he knew
everything he'd of had someone waiting for me. I came
straight here. I needed time to think."

"You've had a week to think, you're still here."

"I don't trust anyone. Give me another drink, okay. I'm feeling sick. I haven't been feeling good lately." He reeled toward me. With one hand he dabbed at his mouth, the other was extended in supplication.

"After I hear about the photos, James."

I made sure the bottle stayed in view. Wylie stood in the middle of the room. He thought things over. He started to shake like it was fifty below. His eyes bulged like golf balls. He was scared to talk, but he *needed* a drink.

He backed against the radiator again, lowered his eyes. "Andrea Gale and me were gonna sell Ronald Headon the pictures."

"I always love it when blackmail gets described as buy and sell. Like paying for dirty pictures is the same as buying zucchini at the A&P."

For the first time since I walked through the door, he showed some fire. "You don't know much about the man, do you? It would've only been justice. What goes around, comes around."

"Meaning?"

The fire vanished. "Nothing. He did me rotten a long time ago."

"Why'd you take so long to get even?"

"I was young enough then I figured I could still salvage something. Start over here or somewhere else. But I got older and things never got better. Kept getting worse. Every time I look back, I realize what he did was the turning point. It kind of preyed on me. If I'd stayed a partner in Headon Engineering I'd be rich today."

"But Headon'd be only half as rich. He was looking ahead."

"That was the turning point," he repeated.

"Maybe you should quit lookin' back."

"At my age, my condition, that's all I got to do. Wonder where things went wrong."

So why was I always doing it at my age? I said, "You're lucky you got someone else to blame. Most people in this position got only themselves."

He kept looking at me, said nothing.

I said, "So explain how it came down."

"I knew Andrea Gale and Lisa Farrell since they were little because I knew Marge Farrell. Lisa's mother?"

"I know her."

"I watched the two of 'em grow up like in three or four year intervals. They thought of me like I was an uncle or something. I come back from the West Coast two years ago and found they were living in Johnson City. They remembered me and I got to know them better. I'm not always in such a poor condition as this. I told them to apply at Headon Engineering. I knew they'd get hired. Headon put a buddy of his in personnel whose main job is to see that good lookers get hired. Not a lot of people know that, but I do. Headon has a passion for young girls—has ever since I've known him—and he likes to have a supply on hand. Knowing that I devised this private revenge fantasy. As I got to know Andrea and Lisa better, I realized there was a chance they'd go for my scheme. I never thought I'd have the guts or the opportunity to go through with it. Never thought I'd find anyone who'd join up with me. But I gradually realized from talking with Andrea and Lisa that if enough money was involved, those two would do anything. Those girls wanted theirs and they wanted it now."

"Lisa Farrell knew about this?"

He shook his head. "This scheme, no. This was Andrea and me. Looking like she looked, Headon came on to Andrea soon as she walked through the door. She played hard to get for awhile, then started seeing him. About two months ago, I described my fantasy to Andrea as a kind of what-if type thing and told her what I thought we could make. I was a little hesitant because what if she genuinely liked the guy, you know, but Andrea went for it like it was the greatest idea since the wheel. I figured we'd get enough money we could both leave Johnson City. She talked about that a lot. She said she was sick of the town, sick of small-time romeos, sick of Lisa hanging on to her life."

"She said that about Lisa? She was tired of her?"

"Yeah. Their friendship had really deteriorated. Lately, they never got along. Andrea said Lisa hung around her so much and for so long, she felt suffocated."

"I heard Andrea was a master at extracting money from her boyfriends. Why didn't she just string Headon along?"

"He isn't the most generous man in the world. There were gifts and small amounts of cash and he paid for everything when they were together, but that was all."

"So you took the Polaroids?"

"Yeah."

"Where were they taken?"

"The Roosevelt Inn outside of Dearborn."

I shook my head.

"Dearborn's a small town about twenty-five miles north of here. The Roosevelt's a roadhouse hotel. Headon always took Andrea there. It's in the country, a secluded spot. It's got a reputation as a one-night-stand kind of place. Headon and Andrea would eat in the dining room downstairs, go to their room for an hour or so, then leave. That was Ronald's idea of a date. There's a covered hallway that runs outside all around the place, but except for the roof and a railing the hallway is open to the elements. I waited under some stairs while they ate. It was cold as hell, I remember that. When they got in the room, Andrea told Ronald she wanted to do it with the lights on, opened the curtains and turned the radio up loud. I snapped photos with an instant camera she gave me."

"When was this?"

"About a week before she was murdered."

"What were you gonna pop him for?"

"Thirty-five grand. Five a shot. Andrea wanted more."

"How much more?"

"A hundred."

I whistled.

"I know. She was the greediest human being I ever met, that's why I was pretty sure she'd go for the idea in the first place. It's also why I didn't trust her worth a damn. If she'd gotten hold of all the photos, she'd of froze me out and asked for the hundred. So I made sure she didn't get all the pictures. I hid five of them in my room."

"It was almost by accident I found 'em."

He shook his head sadly. "Last Saturday, I was at a bar with friends when I heard she'd been murdered. God, I never once thought he'd kill. I was certain he'd pay up. They were Polaroids, so he'd know there wasn't any negatives. All he had to do was pay the money, we'd give him the photos, and it was all over. Thirty-five grand to him is tip money. Soon's I heard about her, I ran like hell. I been in this room since. I admit it, I'm scared to death. I'm afraid to go out. I only been out twice to get some drink." He moved closer to the bed and in the light I could see the sweat glistening on his whiskered face. His shirt was soaked. He said, "Please, pal. Let me have the bottle now. It'll help me think."

I said, "Why were you so sure he'd pay?"

"Because he has a reputation to protect. He thinks nobody knows about his girls. That it's all a big secret. Only people don't know the real Ronald Headon are those church people and the business community. Something like this would cause scandal, maybe Sandy'd even divorce him. I thought he'd be glad to pay. We asked for so little."

"How many pictures you take?"

"Seven. I told you—five grand apiece. Thirty-five G's."

"I only found five."

"I gave two to Andrea. She mailed one to Headon two days before she was murdered. She enclosed a note telling what we had, how much we wanted and when we wanted it. We wanted the money Sunday night, we'd be gone Monday morning."

"Where were you goin'?"

"West Coast again. I bounce back and forth. I like it there, but this is home to me and after a while I always come back. I can never figure out why once I get here."

"Where was Andrea going?"

"New York City, I think. She planned to find a rich man to take care of her. She said once she'd learned all the gold-digger lessons she could here and now it was time for the Big Leagues." He made another whimper. "Lord, I never thought he'd kill over this."

"Blackmail stresses people out," I said. "They get irrational. Did he know you were the other half of the 'we'?"

"I'm sure she told him. I can't afford to assume he doesn't know it was me. Besides, there's a reason he'd suspect me for this."

"What?"

"Nothing. It was a long time ago." He beat his fists against his knees. "We thought we'd be safe so long as he knew there were more photos, and then we planned to leave as soon as we exchanged the rest of the photos for the money. But he up and killed her right out of the box."

"Did Sandy Headon know about any of this?"

"I think so."

"Why do you think that?"

"You know a man named Dwayne? Lives with Sandy's brother, George?"

"Yeah, the catcher."

"Dwayne's got a older brother named Buster."

"I heard about Buster and how he introduced you to George and then you and George got chummy and found out you had so much in common. Mainly you both hate Ronald Headon. Frankly, I'm skeptical about it all."

"But that's what happened. Buster lives here in the Burlington House. I've known him for years. Buster was with me when I heard about Andrea. I said I needed a new place to stay, I didn't say why. He said to come here, gave me the week's rent. It's cheap and out of the way. I heard of the place, but I never thought I'd end up living in it."

"Buster know about the blackmail?"

"No. He knew something was going on, but he didn't know what. Night I moved here he and I shared a bottle of Schnapps on the fifth floor steps. Like it was just a funny story, he told me he'd been at the farmhouse a few days earlier when Sandy drove out and her and George went into the kitchen and started talking. Next thing George went insane, saying now for sure he was going to kill Ronald. Buster didn't know what it was all about, but I knew right away. George worships Sandy and Buster said he was screaming he was going to kill Headon and the bitch. I figured it had to be the photo Andrea mailed to Headon. Somehow Sandy had gotten hold of it. I wish George would of killed Ronald, but he simmers down fast as he blows up."

I motioned him over, splashed a drink into the dixie cup. He sloshed most of it over the edge before he could get it to his lips. I needed a drink myself, but all Jack Daniels does to me is make me puke.

I said, "What a pair of amateurs."

"Andrea sent the photo to him," he whined. "I told her to wait. We had the photos, that was the important part. I said we could take our time, wait until we worked out a foolproof plan. But she said no, we do it now. That's how she was. She couldn't wait."

"What about Lisa? You said she didn't know about 'this scheme.' What'd that mean?"

"It means Ronald Headon came on to Andrea and not Lisa. It means she didn't know about these pictures. After I told them how easy it would be to get hired at Headon's and they got the jobs, Lisa bought me dinner to thank me. I told her the kind of guy Headon was and how he'd messed my life up. I didn't mention my idea to her at all, but damned if she didn't propose the very same idea to me."

"An identical plan?"

He nodded. "She said if Headon came on to her, she'd get naked with him, we'd take some pictures, sell him the pictures. I'm telling you, mister, those two girls had no scruples. I mean, Andrea was worse, but not by much. Anyway, Headon never came on to Lisa, which was strange because he came on to every girl with any kind of looks so Lisa must of thought the whole idea just faded away. Andrea would never of told her because Lisa would've angled to get some of the money."

I whispered, "Dammit."

Wylie rubbed his palms up and down the inside of his thighs. He said, "You believe what I'm saying, don't you? I wouldn't lie about this."

I said, "I believe you, Wylie."

He kept up the rubbing. His eyes were locked on the bottle. He even licked his lips like a thirsty drunk in the movies.

"Why'd you sell your half to Headon? He didn't just pull a fast one, did he? You wouldn't cook up a hardass scheme like this twenty-five years later over a fast one."

"I won't tell you about that."

"You want the bottle?"

"Please?" His voice cracked. "Come on, pal. I told you

about the pictures."

I walked to the window, opened it, made like I was going to pour the Jack out. "I think what happened then ties in with the Polaroids."

He said fast, "Listen, Headon and that cop buddy of his—"

"McCoy?"

"Yeah, McCoy. They did something to me when Headon wanted to buy me out. It involved pictures too. That's why I said, what goes around, comes around."

"Tell me what happened."

Wylie said, "Just know that what they did was embarrassing enough, rotten enough, that twenty-some years later I wanted to get back at Headon for it."

I stood by the window for a bit. Wylie kept with his nervous massage on his legs.

I said, "Wylie, talk. It's ancient history, I won't tell a soul. I could give a shit about it except it relates to what's going on now."

He stared at me, at the bottle, at the floor. It was a long minute before he said, "I passed out at a party and they staged some photos of me and a teenage queer." He looked up at me, sincere and ashamed, and said, "I ain't queer. I never even experimented that way when I was in the Navy. Lots of the boys did, but I never did. They hired some fag from Chicago, got me drunk, took me to a bedroom, and staged some pictures. See, I didn't really wanna sell my half. I say so now, but I wanted to make that company work. I put a lot of time and money into it."

"So this was like a hostile takeover?"

"Yeah. He made an offer and I said I wasn't interested. I thought that'd be the end of it, but he kept insisting. Then him and his buddy McCoy stage these *pictures* and he tells me he'll mail them to my friends if I don't sell. McCoy was there. He chuckled the whole time. Like it was funny, a big joke. Headon told me not only did he want my half, he didn't much like me either. That I'd rubbed him wrong too many times. Fact, he disliked me so much he'd love to embarrass me in front of the whole town. I had no idea he felt like that. We had our disagreements, but what partners don't? I remember McCoy said, 'You want all of Johnson City knowing you're a queerboy? You're forty, you never married. Everybody'll believe it.' I knew something was up. They wouldn't of done something like that unless something big was gonna happen. I should of done something, but I was so scared, I just signed the papers. I mean you should of seen those pictures." He shuddered. "I settled for less than we talked about. To them it was just a big joke. Couple weeks later I read in the paper about this huge Defense Department contract awarded to Headon Engineering."

"You should've gone to the police."

"McCoy *was* the police. Besides, that was a different time. You didn't even want there to be a hint of—" He stopped and looked at the floor again. "I mean in a town this size, everybody would've known. And how can you fight pictures? What can you say?"

I walked over, handed him the bottle. Said, "Bend the brain, Wylie, you need it."

He slanted the bottle toward the ceiling and poured a third of it down his throat. He gagged twice, sealed his mouth with his free palm to keep the alcohol down. The sweat on his forehead became Niagara Falls. I tossed him my smokes. Had to light him up because his hands shook so bad he couldn't get the cigarette and match to meet.

After a long drag he said, "God, I feel like hell."

"You look like a recruiting poster for A.A., Wylie."

"You said you'd get me out of here."

"I'll be in touch."

He tipped the bottle again.

"You sure Andrea sent him only one of the Polaroids?"

"Pretty sure. She only had two."

"Means there's one Polaroid unaccounted for."

He said, "That's not good, is it?"

I said, "I don't know if it's good or bad. And one other thing. I get another chance at polishing a car roof with Ronald Headon's face, I'll be sure I leave a permanent impression."

Wylie said, "What?"

I told him to skip it and left.

# THIRTY-FOUR

It was 8:00 P.M. I drove back to the Jones.

I walked to the package store. Bought a tall bottle of Christian Brothers brandy and a carton of Kools. Brandy and tobacco helps me think, always has. I'd worry about sobriety when this mess was over.

Back in the room, I lay on the bed, Bugs at my side, and smoked and sipped and thought.

This case was not progressing the way a case should progress. The more you learn, the clearer a case is supposed to get; you eliminate suspects, you develop theories. This case, the more I learned the muddier it got. Obviously, the killings tied in with the Polaroids, but if what Wylie told me was true, everybody involved had either known about or seen the damn things. Ronald Headon, which meant McCoy, Sandy Headon, George. They all had their reasons not to want those Polaroids made public.

And one thing angered me more than confused me. Lisa Farrell coming up with the same scam on her own. She would've done exactly what Andrea did. It made me mad because I'd fallen for the Little Miss Innocent bit.

So even though Wylie was convinced it was Ronald Headon or McCoy, I wasn't so sure. I tossed the night away, mulling it over.

By ten the next morning, after a beer and a doughnut, I was ready to face Cora. She was at the desk. I said, "James Wylie needs your help."

Cora said, "What can I do?"

"Loan him as much cash as you can. He needs to get out of Johnson City fast."

She clucked and oh-my'd, went back to her room, returned with five fifties. "That's all I can spare. Is it enough?" Two-fifty would get Wylie to Chicago and keep him in a room with plenty of Dog for two weeks. I promised to get him out of town. After that he was on his own.

She said, "Is his life in danger?"

"He did a very stupid thing and he didn't do it very well."

Her mouth quivered. She said, "Oh, Mr. Wylie."

I was two blocks from Altgeld when I heard the sirens. Three squad cars were parked in front of Burlington House, their light bars swiveling blue flashes on and off the brick wall.

I hit the steering wheel, quietly said "Fuck."

At the front door, a uniformed cop was telling a passerby, "Just a dead bum in the alley."

"OD?" the man asked.

The cop said, "Yeah, overdose of knife." The civilian laughed.

McCoy leaned against the sign-in desk. The heavyweight greaser who loved his mother was on the other side. Soon as he saw me, he pointed and said, "Him!" McCoy beamed like the guy had said "Cheese." He said, "I been waiting for you, PI."

The hotel man said, "This guy here left around eight o'clock, minus the bottle. Jackson, who you say is really James Anthony Wylie, came down maybe an hour later, bums a quarter from me, and makes a phone call." He pointed to the phone on the wall next to the cigarette machine. We all looked at it like we'd never seen a telephone before. "He was on the horn for two, maybe three minutes. Then he heads back upstairs."

"He call you?" McCoy asked me.

"Why would he call me right after I got done talking to him?"

"Like you'd tell me if he did."

The deskman went on, "About eleven-thirty he comes back down and now he is well oiled. Smashed to the gills. He's singing and weaving and he's got that shitface ear-to-ear grin. He says he can't be late for a very important date and he's out the door. That's the last I seen of him till an hour ago one of the bums comes in all hyped up and says look in the alley."

McCoy crooked his index finger, said, "Come round in back, PI." We walked around the building in silence except for the clicking of the pen in his trench coat pocket.

Wylie lay on his back on wet gravel behind a line of garbage cans. His head and torso were under a rusted out trash compactor that looked like it hadn't been used this century. McCoy and I hunkered down to take a look. The back of Wylie's head rested in a mud puddle. His arms were flung out like he'd died singing "Mammy." The wooden handle of a carving knife pointed straight up from his chest.

We stood. McCoy smiled at me. I smiled back. Considering we couldn't stand each other, we did a lot of smiling back and forth.

Two uniforms stood a few feet from us, bored, waiting for the meat wagon. A murdered wino in an alley behind the cheapest fleabag in town doesn't rate very high on a cop's prestigious crime list. One asked the other where they should go for lunch.

McCoy said, "See how the dumpster and all the garbage cans hide the body? That's why it was here all night and part of the morning before it got found." He smiled again.

"Somebody was shrewd," I said.

Above us, a tired voice called down, "He leave any cigarettes?" We looked up. On the third-floor fire escape landing, six men watched us with dull eyes. They hunched into themselves, shivering against life. They seemed as bored with what was going on as the three cops. But it was free entertainment. Then again, so is daytime television.

McCoy said, "You hear that? They want his cigarettes."

I said, "Don't blame 'em. They're two bucks a pack in the machine."

McCoy said, "You asked all over town about this bird for a week. You finally found him, paid him a visit, now he's dead."

"And you've spotted a trend."

"Yeah, that's exactly what I've spotted. You go see Andrea Gale, she's dead. You go see Torres, he gets dead. You go see James Wylie and here he is in this alley. You ain't plannin' to come see me I hope."

"If it was that easy."

"I wanna see you run to Snow now. Complain how I'm harassing you."

I said, "I bet you been looking for this guy too. I found

him first because I knew who to ask. There was one person who wanted to see him as bad as you and me, but for different reasons. Your friend the sweet little old lady at the Jones. You mighta asked her, but that bully stuff backfires sometimes, McCoy. She told me because I'm a nice guy and she genuinely liked James Wylie."

"Why would I wanna see this derelict? What'd you and the derelict discuss?"

"Little this, little that. He got a bit nostalgic, started to reminisce about the past. His past kind of ties in with another man's present. I think maybe you could even hang Wylie's murder on this other man. You and the man did a job on this poor loser a long time ago. I imagine you and this man been doing jobs on a lot of people over the years. So maybe it's not only the man you can hang it on. You wanna hear the man's name? You want I should start talking about the man's budding porn career?"

He turned his back to me and prodded Wylie's leg with his shoe. Said, "Shove off, PI."

"Think I'll stick around. Maybe my friend Snow will show up and we can talk about harassment."

"Snow show up for a derelict? Shove off, I said!" He said it loud and there was enough anger and fright in his voice that the two cops swung their heads our way. They watched with interested faces.

I'd already said too much; now McCoy knew I knew about the Polaroids, but I added, "I wonder who would wanna see a harmless old drunk dead? Who'd have a reason, McCoy? And what would the reason be?"

"Beat it, PI. I fucking mean it."

At the sign-in desk, the greaser recited the story of James Wylie and the phone call and the "important date" to a baby-faced patrolman who scribbled it down in a steno pad. The greaser pointed at me again when I walked in, said, "Him."

I said, "You keep doin' that every time I walk in the door, you're gonna give me a complex."

A young Hispanic man with enormous biceps and a wispy mustache sat on the fifth step on the stairs, drywashing his hands, watching the cop and the desk man.

I stepped up and sat next to him, said, "What's up, guy?"

"I find an old bird named Jackson stabbed out back 'bout a hour ago. I gotta talk to the law about it." His voice was thin and weirdly pitched. His head bobbed back and forth like he was grooving to a riff only he heard.

"They say who did it?"

"Nobody knows, man. I heard Homer over there say a private detective visited Jackson and afterward Jackson made a phone call, then later he split. Never come back. Homer says Jackson was so drunk he couldn't of found his ass with both hands."

"You friends with Jackson?"

"Nah. I nodded to him in the hall one time when he was waiting to use the can. He was only here a week and he never left the place. I heard he hardly ever left his room. Kinda odd, but—" He shrugged. Lot of odd in a place like this. The kid said, "Guy named Buster in 410 took him a bag of sliders and a bottle once in a while."

"Anybody talk to him besides Buster?"

"He kept totally to himself, man."

"Buster around?"

"He's in Wisconsin, I think. Or Minnesota. Left two nights ago after he got a phone call about a job." The kid looked at his fast moving hands. "I got to mellow out. I was up all night on pills so I started in on a little Tequila this morning. Needed to get numb so I could sleep. I wanted some air so I walked out back. Thought long as I was there I'd check and see if maybe some butts or booze was in the barrels—sometimes there is—and there was Jackson. I could only see his legs so I thought it was somebody passed out and maybe I could lift his butts, but then I bended down and looked underneath the trash bin and I saw the knife." He shuddered. "Never seen a murdered man before."

"First time's always a shock, 'specially if you know the person. They mentioned a motive?"

"Not to me," he said, shaking his head. "But who'd rob an old feeb like that? That man had *nothin'*. Had to be some crackhead, man. I'm telling you those people'll kill you for a quarter. Even destitute people aren't safe from crackheads." His legs jiggled double time.

I took the bottle of Valium from my pocket, shook out two. Said, "This'll help."

He nodded thanks.

I nudged the rookie cop on my way out. "McCoy wants me out of here. He'll tell you what Wylie and I talked about. I'm at the Jones Hotel should an honest cop wanna talk to me. If you got such a thing out here."

He didn't look up from the pad and he didn't bother to act indignant.

# THIRTY-FIVE

Wylie was dead and they knew I knew about the Polaroids now, so things would be coming to a head. I had to move fast. Last night, I'd looked at this case from every angle I could think of. What Wylie did after I left him made one of those angles look right-on now. His murder reinforced it.

I felt a vague guilt about Wylie's murder. Why did I wait until the next morning to get him out of town? I track the guy down, get him trashed enough to make the phone call that lures him out of his hiding place, and then he gets hit. I was sure I knew who he called, hoped I could prove it. I kept telling myself, you didn't know he was going to make the phone call, but fact was, he made it and he made it because of my visit.

Out loud I said, "Dan, Wylie pulled his own chain when he snapped the photos of Andrea and Headon. You didn't make him do that."

I called Sandy Headon from a pay phone. I said, "It's early afternoon. Don't tell me Ronald's home now."

"He's not."

"Stay there. I'm on my way."

She started to argue, but I slammed the receiver.

She opened the door before I pressed the bell. She wore the same fuzzy pink robe she'd worn the morning I met her.

Both hands were wrapped around a tall glass.

She said, "What's so important?"

I brushed past her, headed down the hall to the room with the giant TV and the fireplace and the Tiffany lamps and the state-of-the-art stereo system. Also the Hydraulic Hideaway Bar Table. She tagged behind, saying, "Where're you going? What do you want?"

"A drink."

She sat in the chair by the fireplace. I poured some brandy, swallowed most of it. She stared at me as I stood by the cabinet, letting the Spanish brandy make its warm circle.

I said, "Why didn't you tell me about the Polaroid?"

"What?"

"The picture of your husband and Andrea Gale."

She said, "Damn you," very quietly.

"You knew the whole time. You knew about the picture, you knew about the blackmail letter. Why didn't you tell me?"

She looked up at me, astounded. "Some man I never saw before in my life knocks on my door, starts asking personal questions about my marriage like it's any of his business and I'm supposed to say, 'Oh, yes, I'll tell you all about it. See, my husband was screwing this bimbo and she had pictures taken. She wanted money for the pictures. But guess what? She got murdered.' Did you honestly expect me to tell you that? Only reason I spent any time with you that day was to see how much you knew."

"And to introduce me to George and Dwayne. In case I needed to be taken care of, they'd know who to do the job on."

"That's not true."

"You told me your husband was sleeping around, why not tell the rest?"

"I only told you what you would of found out on your own. Ronald's sleeping around is hardly a secret in certain circles in this town. If I'd denied everything I'd of ended up looking like a fool."

"What about the stuff you told me on the way back? More BS?"

"No. I was too high on the ride back. Sometimes pot and booze makes me maudlin and I talk when I shouldn't. How'd you find out about the picture?"

I sipped more brandy, tried to recall details of the conversation we'd had on the way back from George's. But I'd been too high too. All I could remember was I felt sorry for her afterward. But that probably had been the point. If I felt sorry for her maybe I wouldn't dig any more.

I said, "You were afraid you knew who murdered Andrea Gale, but you weren't sure. If it was Ronald it'd mess up, maybe finish, this life-style you're convinced you can't live without. If it wasn't Ronald, it might of been brother George, and you couldn't stand to see your baby brother— the only person in the world who gives you unconditional love—go to jail. And there's a third possibility, right? I don't blame you for feeling afraid, it's a no-win for you."

Sandy said, "All this is to you is a job, a puzzle. You don't give a shit about the people who have to live with it."

"Don't I? If you'd told me half of what you knew, James Wylie might be alive now."

She looked up quick. "He's dead?"

"Very."

Her color faded, the glass slipped from her hand, hit the carpet. The liquor made a dark circle as it flowed out. She said, "Because of all this? Why?"

I said, "You know why. Because he took the photo. It was his idea. I know you're all protecting your asses, but if anybody'd told me the truth, Wylie might be alive now. But everybody's got something to hide. Everybody sits around waiting for me to give up and go home, assuming sooner or later people'll stop keeling over and things'll get back to normal. Well, none of you people is gonna see normal again. Ever."

"You ever stop to think," Sandy said, "maybe I don't care who killed those people? I don't *care* they're dead? All you're trying to do is mess up my life."

I walked over, kneeled in front of her. Said, "Sandy, your life is already messed up. Big time. How much did you know about your husband and Andrea Gale?"

Her eyes watered over, she shook her head.

"You might as well talk. I've figured out most of it and I'm going to the police."

She said, "Refill my glass? Scotch."

I did. She drank three gulps of it, staring at something beyond me, something only she could see. In a tiny voice she said, "I found the picture and a blackmail note in an envelope in the bottom of his underwear drawer last Friday. I was furious at first. I thought Ronald'd had the photo taken for a souvenir or something. Proof of conquest. But then I read the note and I got scared. I went hollow inside. I didn't know who else was involved or what it meant. I took it to George's Friday afternoon."

"Why?"

"I wanted advice, but of course he went totally berserk. This was like the first actual proof either of us had seen. We knew he'd screw anybody he could, but he was always discreet. This was so blatant. I mean, *pictures!* George kept ranting about revenge, but he cooled off real quick when I explained the note said there was another person with photos. We discussed what we should do. When I left, we still hadn't decided. Next morning, she was killed."

"Did George kill her?"

"No!"

"The truth, Sandy."

Quietly, she said, "I don't know. I asked him and he said no. I didn't press him. I just told him to pretend he'd never seen the photo."

"What about Dwayne and his brother, Buster? They were there, right?"

"They were there, but we certainly didn't let them know about the picture. They were in another room. I'm sure they figured it had to do with Ronald from the way George acted, but they didn't know what or why."

"George would do anything for you. Would Dwayne do anything for George?"

She looked away. "I don't know."

"What did you do with the photo?"

"Burned it. The picture and the note."

"Why'd you do that?"

"What was I supposed to do? Keep it for the family

album?"

"Did you know Wylie was in on the blackmail?"

"Not until after you showed me the picture of him and the blonde. I should of thought of him before that. He's been friends with those two for a long time."

"Two?"

"The blonde and her roommate."

"Lisa Farrell?"

"Yeah."

"What do you know about her?"

She took a long drink. She belched and then for a scary second her face tightened into a fright mask. Her eyes narrowed, she snarled and exposed the tiny teeth. Then it was gone. She put her free hand on her cheek and started to rub it.

I said, "I wondered why you told me Wylie was at the Jones Hotel. But at that point you didn't know he was involved. You thought you were sending me off on a wild goose chase. Away from your husband and your brother."

She said, "The note said two people had photos, so Ronald wasn't to try anything because even if he did there'd still be more photos. Once I learned the blonde lived with this other girl, this Lisa Farrell, I assumed she was the second person."

"Did Ronald know you found the Polaroid?"

"He must of. He couldn't say anything about it because he's pretended all these years that I never knew what was going on. It was almost funny, him walking around the house, giving me these side glances, trying to figure out if he'd misplaced it or I'd found it. I acted normal as could be, it left him between a rock and a hard place."

I said, "No wonder he freaked when he saw us together. He suspected you had the photo, then I show at his office asking about the dead girl that's in the photo. Twenty-four hours later we spend the day together."

She smiled. "He was scared to death."

I said, "He probably thought you and I were cooking up another blackmail scam. He was gonna get it from two sides. Did you know about Ronald and Andrea Gale before you saw the photo?"

"I know he fucks girls who work for him. I don't know

names. I only learned her name because she was stupid
enough to sign her first name to the note. George did some
checking Friday night and we found out she and Lisa Farrell lived together."

"Was Ronald making it with Lisa too?"

"Probably. The more the merrier."

I waited a second, said, "Sandy, did you kill Andrea
Gale?"

She pulled her knees up to her chest, wrapped her arms
around them and rested her chin on her kneecaps. Pink
toenails peeked from beneath the bottom hem of the robe.
She started to get the look she'd had the morning we met.
The slip-sliding away from the real world look. Too much
stress mixed with too much booze do that to some people,
especially people who didn't inherit strong emotional genes
to begin with. And this week had been nothing but stress
and booze for Sandy Headon. When it happens to me, I
suffer anxiety attacks. Some people, like Sandy, have to get
away. Just "go" or freak-out. Like an animal who feels pain
and thinks if he runs like hell the pain will stay in that spot
and he'll be free of it. If they can't physically leave the spot,
mentally will do.

She said as though to herself, "But this was the first one to
try blackmail. Imagine that. All the years, all the girls, all
the money he had. First one had enough brains." She
paused, no doubt thinking about all the years and all the
girls. She whispered, "He had to kill her."

I said, "Who's 'he,' Sandy?"

Her face went slack and she detached. Her eyes glazed
and saw nothing. I kneeled and grabbed her knees, gently
rocked her back and forth. After a bit she drifted back,
looked me in the eyes. She said, "Look at me, Daniel," and
grinned her wacko grin.

I said loudly, "Enough, Sandy. Who had to kill her? Your
brother or your husband?"

The grin still there, she said, "Either way I lose, don't I?"

"Did you kill her?"

"I lose that way too."

"Did Ronald leave here last night? Late?"

The grin went away. "Ronald never came home last

night."

"Not at all?"

"He called to say he had too much work and he'd stay at the office. He does that all the time. He's got a foldout couch in a room behind his office. God only knows what secretary worked late with him."

"Ronald has more to worry about right now than which secretary to sleep with."

Sandy said, "Was that the only photo? Were they bluffing about more photos?"

"These people were first class chumps, but they weren't so stupid they'd send the only photo they had before they got their money."

"How many more are there?"

"Six." She didn't need to know five of them were a foot away from her. And that she'd never have to worry about them.

She winced, then groaned like she had a stomachache. "He should just pay the money."

"Pay who, Sandy? Both people are dead."

"Will the other photos show up?"

"You're not grasping the issue here. It's not just dirty pictures and blackmail anymore. He can't buy the photos and then everything goes back to normal. It's murder now."

She shrugged. Her brain had decided enough was enough.

I said, "Do you think Ronald killed these people?"

She shrugged again. She embraced herself tighter and started to shiver.

I stood up. Said, "Don't get any drunker, Sandy. I've stirred things up enough, police are gonna have to check on the Wylie-Headon connection. They're gonna talk to you. McCoy can't keep a lid on it anymore."

Sandy looked sad. Started to detach a little more.

"And for what it's worth, I'm not completely sure who killed these people, but I'm sure it wasn't you. I don't think you're guilty of anything except being very lonely, very unhappy, and very very scared."

And who of us isn't that most of the time?

# THIRTY-SIX

Snow sat in a squad car in the No Parking zone in front of the Jones Hotel. He got out when I walked around the corner from the lot in back, stood by the car door.

I said, "Lady here says the Fire Department fines your ass good for parking there."

"I told you once, fuck the Fire Department. Where you been?"

"Driving. I was depressed."

"Being a harbinger of death would tend to depress a person. Kruger, we got to talk."

"Let's retire to my suite."

Cora's eyes were red. She said, "Is it true?" I nodded and she said, "Is it because of me finding out where he was?" I said, "Of course not. We'll talk about it later." I returned the two-fifty. She started to sob.

"Noble," Snow said as we climbed the stairs. "Easing the old woman's conscience like that."

"He was her only friend." When we passed the floor's bathroom I said, "Bidet's in there should you need it."

He sniffed when he got inside the room. Said, "Damn, this is some fine accommodations. The rodent come with the room or'd you have to provide it?" He stood in front of the window, hands in coat pockets. "You PI's sure got the life."

"Sit down," I said.

He looked around. "On what? I wouldn't sit on one thing in this room. Just being here is vaguely insulting."

I said, "Suit yourself," and sat on the edge of the bed. "I thought you'd be other places. Like trying to find who started the open heart surgery on James Wylie." I pulled Bugs up from the floor and started to stroke his back.

Snow said, "You wanna hear something funny? Least I think it's funny in a pathetic sort of way. Our detective on this murder today? He takes you to the alley to view the stiff, right? Apparently you said something to him that caused him to chase you off. After that, he paces around, ignoring everything that's said to him. Then he *kicks* the goddamn stiff like he's trying to boot a seventy-yard field goal. After that, he splits without a word of explanation to anybody, including the incredulous cops standing there watching him do all this."

"Sounds like a man with a troubled mind."

"Sure does." Snow shook his head for a bit, watching me and Bugs. He said, "You're talking to an honest cop, hear what I'm sayin'? It's brick wall time, Kruger. I warned you what could happen if you didn't share, but I'm such a decent man I'm gonna give you one more chance. I wanna know what's going on and I wanna know now."

I dropped into a bass voice. "Way it stands now, it's Stone for Gale, Baker for Torres."

He made a face. "Okay, rub it in all you want, but tell me what you know."

"For openers, McCoy is no family man."

"No shit," he said, all sarcasm. "And here I was about to nominate him for National Cop of the Year. I'm not here just to talk about McCoy. I wanna know about these dead people keep turnin' up right after you talk to 'em. We aren't used to three murders a week in Johnson City. That's half our yearly average."

"McCoy can tell you more than I can."

"I wanna hear what you know."

"Stone's innocent, Baker too."

"Maybe now I believe that. So who's guilty?"

"I think I know, but I'm not positive."

"You got a PI hunch," he said.

"This sneering tone you've adopted here does not become you, Snow. Maybe I got a hunch, maybe it's more than a hunch. Anybody ever talk to Ronald Headon about Stone's allegations?"

"We will now." He picked lint off his coat. "I'm gonna ask politely one more time. What've you got on this?"

"Give me till tomorrow."

"Tomorrow?" he pointed his finger at my face. His voice rose. "Dammit, I got three murders in one week and it appears one of my detectives is doing a major league cover

up on 'em. You probably know why and who, but you want
me to wait till tomorrow?"

I kept petting Bugs, said nothing.

His breathing gradually returned to normal. He said,
"How'd you get so far on this and we didn't?"

"You just said it. Your guy wasn't even trying. McCoy's
buddy was involved so he fixed this like it was a busted pipe.
He's a goddamn accessory. And you let it happen."

"All I had were some wild charges by an alleged murderer
trying to save his ass."

"What about me?"

"You're a cheapskate PI in it for the money. If Stone had
accused Ronald Reagan and hired you, you'd of insisted
Ronald Reagon looked guilty to you."

"You blew us both off."

"I didn't know you from Adam. Look at you. You dress
like a damn street person. Chicago cops tell me you're a
lowlife alkie pill-popper, for Chrissakes. Why shouldn't I of
blown you off?"

I smiled and even Snow managed a feeble grin. I said, "I
bet next time a lowlife alkie pill-popper from Chicago gives
you a tip, you follow it up."

"I hope to God there ain't a next time. What do you know
about McCoy?"

I said, "He's crooked as a boomerang. Probably in every
way, shape and form, but what I'm interested in is his
arrangement with Ronald Headon. McCoy and Headon go
way back. I'm sure Headon pays him, but maybe friendship
and loyalty play a part too. Whatever, when Headon has
dirty work to be done, McCoy does it. He helped him get
rid of an unwanted business partner with a filthy trick when
they were still boys. Turns out that partner was James
Wylie."

"You been real curious about James Wylie lately. That
why?"

"Just found that out last night."

"And he turns up dead today." He tapped his square
white teeth with his index finger. "I always figure what's
past is past and nine-tenths of all rumors are bullshit," he
said softly. "But so many stories float around about McCoy,

I figure he's as bad as you say. Most persistent one is that he's got an arrangement with a couple of Puerto Rican hookers downtown. The ancient scam where the girl gets a John in the rack and the cop busts in, badge first, and shakes the John down to avoid the bust and consequent scandal."

I said, "That one'll work with ninety-nine point nine percent of all married men."

"Supposedly he's done it for years."

"Sounds like a thing he'd be up for. I mean, if he plays personal cop for an old friend to the point of framing two innocent men for murder."

Snow said, "Doesn't say much for his moral fiber."

"No, it doesn't," I said.

"You saying Ronald Headon killed these people?"

"Not necessarily. Just that he's involved."

"McCoy might of killed them then."

"Might of."

"Christ. He lucked out having someone easy the first two times. Stone and Baker. But who was easy for Wylie?"

"Me, if he could swing it. Some out-of-touch wino if he couldn't. Maybe he'd let that one slide. Who'd care about an old drunk? But he found out I knew the deal. He found out I knew Gale, Torres and Wylie are all related, and you give me one more day I'll show you."

"They were all killed by the same person?"

"Think so, but not positive."

"You might be number four."

"Possible. Not probable. Two of these people were like lambs going to slaughter."

"Tell me more."

"Tomorrow. If I don't have it nailed tomorrow night, I'll tell everything I know and you can knock yourself out. But I'm so close that pouring the real law into it might backfire. These people are running scared as it is."

He gave me the badass stare. I winked again and he grinned without wanting to. "Okay, Kruger, tomorrow. But only because I'm a nice guy."

"It's only cause you got no choice. What's Stone and Baker sayin' lately?"

"Stone's braying like a mule about how we're trying to

frame him. Appears he's right, which is a damn shame because I've developed a robust hatred for the man. Baker don't say shit, 'cept 'I can't remember, man, I can't remember.'"

"He ever say why they beat up Stone and me?"

"Says Torres told him to. I smell McCoy and Headon behind that too, if Headon was sniffing around Andrea Gale like Stone maintains."

"You should talk to McCoy and Headon."

"We will when we find them."

"Headon's wife can tell you a good story. If she's sober enough. Go easy on her though, she's fragile in the mental department."

Snow cocked his head, said, "Hmmm."

# THIRTY-SEVEN

I called Lisa. No answer. Drove to Heaven-in-the-Round. The Camaro was there, I didn't know if that meant Lisa was. I backed the Caddy into a spot a row behind the Camaro and down a bit.

Half a pack of Kools later, she walked briskly, a workout bag slung over her shoulder, around the corner of the building to the Camaro. She exited the lot, going east.

I followed. She drove fast, but I was able to keep her in sight and only drove over the limit when she turned and was briefly out of sight.

We went downtown. She jerk-turned into an alley between a Mexican Restaurant and a Typewriter Repair Shop. I did the same and got to check out the backsides of the boarded-up buildings I'd been driving by on the street the last week. It was grim back here, too.

She made another turn into another alley. In the alleys, I felt as conspicuous as a naked man at a quilting bee. Good thing I had the Caddy and not the Skylark. I stopped, let her get farther ahead of me, then put it in "D," drove slower. When we came to crossing streets, first she, then I, poked grill snouts out slowly, until it looked safe, then floored it across. The Seville's wheels slipped into old streetcar tracks and hummed on patches of century-old brick that poked through the asphalt.

After five blocks in the alley, she whipped into a parking lot. The one in back of the Blue Palm. I kept going, stopped as far from the bar as possible.

Lisa parked by the back door of the bar. She walked to it, carrying the bag. She fumbled with keys for a few seconds, then went inside.

I drove to the end of the alley, up Grove Street, took a right to the front of the bar. Yellow police paper was still stapled to the front door, the neon palm tree and the beer sign were black. I drove to the rear, parallel-parked on the other side of a battered pickup truck in the far corner of the lot. The truck hid most of the Caddy, but I could see the back door and Lisa's car.

Other buildings backed onto the alley and the parking lot, but only Lisa's car, the truck, and I were back here. The lot was dark except for one high-pooled arc light directly in the middle.

Ten minutes passed. A teenage boy and girl exited between two buildings on my left, walked in front of the Seville, never seeing me. The girl was willow skinny with long, limp blond hair. The boy was tall, curly-haired, and walked with a full-of-himself swagger. The girl wrapped her arm around his waist. His right arm disappeared to the elbow into the back of her black jeans. His hand rapidly massaged the base of her tiny butt. It looked like a mouse doing pushups under a blanket; she was so light he was half-lifting her off the ground. She giggled loudly. I resisted the idea of tapping the horn. They'd jump a mile, but so might Lisa. They turned into the drive that sided the Blue Palm.

Five more minutes passed. I smoked another Kool. Thought about going to the door, knowing it was a stupid idea.

As I was stubbing the Kool out, a brand new bronze

Seville entered the lot from the drive the boy and girl had exited. The Seville parked next to Lisa's Camaro. Ronald Headon got out, went inside without even a look over his shoulder.

I shut the car door gently, sprinted in a crouch to the bar. I put my ear against the door next to the Employees Only sign. Nobody was on the other side. I tried the knob, the door was unlocked. Feeling like a man following sharks into a sunken ship I opened the door and slipped inside.

Stood in blackness. Heard nothing.

My sight gradually adjusted. In front of me was a narrow hallway ten yards long. It connected the parking lot door with another door. I went to the second door, put my ear against it, listened hard. Still nothing. I opened the second door. There were four steps bathed in the weak light of a naked bulb hanging from a cord. I went down the steps.

I was in the hallway that led to the Blue Palm office. The stairs I'd followed the bartender down on my first visit were on the other side of the hall. I heard voices coming from the office. My back brushed flat against a wall of beer cases as I moved slowly toward the voices. An inch of orange light bled from beneath the closed door. I got to it, held a lungful of air and listened.

Lisa was talking in a loud angry voice. "Don't give me that shit, Ronald. You're the one who killed her, not me. That's all I need to know. Now Wylie's dead too."

Headon said some sentences I couldn't make out.

Whatever he said, Lisa wasn't buying. She said, "Then your cop buddy is. No way are you walking from this free and clear. I'm your ball and chain, your life sentence, Ronald. And you and I both know it's better than jail. All I want is money. Nothing else you got is worth a damn."

Headon droned some more.

Lisa said, "Why'd he tell us to meet here anyway? Three cars parked behind a boarded-up bar isn't too smart."

I didn't care for Lisa's last sentence at all. I backed silently down the passageway, went quickly up the stairs. Got to the parking lot door.

McCoy and I collided as I opened it.

He reacted first. He twirled me around, hiked my left arm

up my back. Without a word we step-marched that way down the stairs and to the office. He used my face to push the office door open.

Lisa was behind the desk. She gasped when she saw me. Ronald Headon sat on the ripped-up couch, looking dejected and whipped, his inner power source on "off." There was no change in his expression when he looked at me. His face was like a droopy flag.

McCoy pushed me onto the other end of the couch. He put his hand in his coat pocket, tigthened it around what I assumed was his revolver. He said, "I don't know what you two been discussing, but this yahoo no doubt heard all of it. Kruger, I told you and told you to quit this thing. How'd you know about this?"

"Called a tail, McCoy."

Lisa said, "Daniel, why couldn't you stay out of this?" She sounded sad. A little.

I said, "Snow says it's okay to be here. He and I got everything worked out."

McCoy swore.

I said, "I know how stressed out the three of you are. Don't do something you'll regret later."

McCoy stepped toward me, smashed the side of my face. He said, "The hell with Snow." He looked at Headon. "He knows about the photos."

Headon looked at me, eyes shiny bright. A little juice started to surge his body. He said, "Let me punch him around. I owe him." He hit my face like a girl playing tag. I said, "Ouch, you brute," and he turned red.

McCoy said, "Shuttup! Ronald, I'm about ready to start in on you. It's gone too far. These people keep dying and I'm the chump has to find somebody to fit. Who I got ain't gonna cut it downtown anymore when those other photos turn up. And if this guy's seen 'em, they'll turn up. Count on it. You're about a step and a half from Joliet, thanks to this jackoff."

Headon said, "Watch what you say, McCoy. I didn't kill Torres or Wylie and you know Andrea was an accident." He stared at the cop and his pink face hardened until he looked almost menacing. But in seconds that look faded away and he was back to resembling a little boy about to be spanked.

McCoy said, "If you didn't kill 'em, your wife or her air-head baby brother did. Or this golddigging little tramp here. I told you I didn't wanna know all the details, the less I knew, the dumber I could play if it fell apart. But I thought it was just gonna be Andrea Gale, Ronald. I didn't think these bodies'd keep turning up. Now Kruger's linked us to Wylie. Wylie must of showed him the Polaroids. If Kruger talked downtown, there's gonna be hard questions asked, Ronald. I told you this would only work so long as no more photos turned up. Our only chance was if we found Wylie first or if Wylie'd stay so scared he'd get rid of the other photos. He didn't." He turned to me. "You actually saw the photos?"

I shrugged. Thought, please don't frisk me.

"You talked to Snow about the photos?"

"Not a word."

He looked at Headon. "He's lying."

Fear started to fill me like a drug high gone bad. I suddenly realized these people were playing it by ear. They were just as confused as Snow was and scared to death on top of it. I probably knew more about all this than they did. Confused, scared to death people frequently commit totally irrational acts. I concentrated on keeping my composure.

I checked out the room. The orange light polished the centerfold pictures on the wall. I thought about those glossy pictures being the last things I'd see before I died. I told myself there's worse things to see just before the eternal night kicks in than young snatch with huge breasts, but that wasn't a soothing thought.

I said, "Let's talk deal. Ronald, you're already paying McCoy and Lisa. Make me an offer. I can get you the Polaroids and I'm cheap as hell."

"Shut up," McCoy said.

Headon blurted, "I think it's you." He was talking to McCoy. "You're the cop. You're the one with the most to lose." He looked at Lisa. "Although you'd lose plenty too."

That enraged McCoy. He started for Headon. I came up off the couch. McCoy punched the back of my head. I fell forward to my hands and knees on the floor, dazed. An electrical cord lay in front of me, under the corner of the desk. I pulled it.

The room went black and all hell broke loose. Headon yelled, Lisa screamed. I heard a heavy scraping sound, sensed Headon was pushing the desk and Lisa against the wall, trying to clear a path for himself to the door.

I got a grip on McCoy's knees. Swearing, he punched my head again and I lost my grip. I groped for his ankles, wanting to get him down on the floor.

There was a gunshot. So loud it filled the room with noise, reverberated from wall to wall. Above me there was a grunt. A body fell on me, pinning me flat.

The smell of gunpowder settled over me like a tangy blanket. I tried to buck the body off. I screamed, "Get up!" aware it was a stupid thing to say to a person with a bullet in him, but my brain screamed, "You're a sitting duck!" and I was merely reacting.

A terrified, raspy male voice husked, "Let's go, dammit." Lisa screamed again.

There was a second gunshot. The sound of it sealed my ears. Then a million-color kaleidoscope exploded in my brain. Warm, sticky liquid oozed down my ear onto my neck. As the colors intensified, nausea slugged my stomach and I gagged.

Then I heard a buzzing like a trillion crickets were in the room. My body went numb and I dived from all the colors down into solid black.

# THIRTY-EIGHT

Zig zaggy white lines flickered through dim orange light. I wanted to open my eyes, but my eyelids were rusted shut. Took forever to get them up.

I was lying on the couch. A moon-faced cop stood inspection straight just inside the door. He made nervous swallows and avoided looking my way.

Somebody moaned. A few seconds later I realized it was me. My head felt like an overripe pumpkin with a hot iron bar for a stem. A thick, crusted scab pinched my ear and the back of my neck.

I moved my head to the right. Clanging alarms and air raid sirens went off. Pain shot across my head, nausea flooded back.

Below me, on the floor between the desk and the couch, McCoy lay face down. The back of his head was wet and matted and flat. There was a puddle of blood under him.

I tried to sit up. The nausea came harder and I gagged violently, fell back and shaded my eyes with my arm.

The cop said, "Please don't move, sir. Ambulance is on its way."

"This isn't like it seems," I mumbled. I wanted to explain everything, but my thoughts were getting tripped up somewhere between my cerebellum and my tongue. Things were loose up there, rolling around like so many steelies and cat's eyes. The ache in my head grew until it couldn't get worse. Then it did. I said, "Where's Snow?"

The cop said, "Lieutenant Snow wants to talk to you."

"And I wanna talk to him. Where is he?"

"Downtown talking to Mr. Headon. What went on here anyway?"

"Read about it in the paper."

I heard voices in the hall. Two paramedics and another cop entered the room. This cop looked real pissed off. I wanted to ask why, fell asleep before I could.

Next morning I woke up again. I was in a bed under a white blanket in a high-ceilinged room. Next to the bed, Snow dozed in a turned-around wooden chair, his chin resting on a folded towel on the backrest.

I cleared my throat, said, "What the fuck, Snow?"

He shivered awake. His eyes were bagged and bloodshot, but when he saw I was awake, he grinned. Said, "I been waiting for you to wake your lazy ass up. While you been getting all this beauty sleep some of us been awake all night, busting our chops."

"Some of us need more beauty sleep than others."

"Ain't *that* the truth."

I looked around. The noise and the pain in my head was much subdued from the last time I was awake. White cloth stretched on metal poles partitioned us from the rest of the room. The smell of pine disinfectant was heavy. Too heavy. I gestured. "What is this?"

"Called a hospital. You're okay, I think. You got a mild concussion and they plan to keep you for observation. You had a lot of blood on your neck and head when everybody got there. They thought the worst, but turns out the blood was all McCoy's."

Snow picked up a styrofoam cup from the floor, swallowed some coffee. He lit a cigarette, belched. His all night caffeine and tobacco breath mixed with the disinfectant stink and I had to shut my eyes.

He said, "I hate to say this, so you're only gonna hear it once. Enjoy it. You were right, everything's connected." He toasted me with the cup. "I'm truly amazed, but you were right."

I said, "That's twice."

"Ronald Headon turned himself in eleven o'clock last night. They called me at home, I went right down. Man was a nervous wreck, babbling about him being blackmailed and now his buddy was dead. Said there was nothing else he could do. Yesterday I talked to his wife like you suggested. Very bizarre, but interesting conversation. I related it to Ronald Headon and he crumbled like a Ritz cracker. Started telling us all kinds of things, ending with the board meeting you crashed at the Blue Palm, a joint he owns, by the way."

"That's why they met there?"

He nodded. "That's why. So we send cops there. Find McCoy dead and you underneath him, out cold. Like I said, first report they phoned in said you were a stiff too. I'm glad you're not."

"Makes two of us."

"Bet Headon don't make three."

I said, "He admits to murdering Andrea Gale?"

"He admits to that, but the rest of what he's sayin' I ain't likin'."

"How so?"

"I'll get to it. He says the Gale murder was an accident. He thought they had a thing goin', found out she was in it only for the blackmail. He says sure, he sometimes played around with the help, but he fell in love with this one." Snow made the deep chuckle again. "And maybe he did. I saw some photos of the girl. She was a fine-looking woman. Uninhibited too." He removed the five Polaroids from his coat, held them in front of me like they were a poker hand.

I said, "I found those last night, right after you and I talked."

"You're a liar, but not to worry. Long as we got 'em now I play it your way. You outworked us. I got no beef with that so long as it ends up okay." He put the photos back in his coat pocket. "Back to the murder. He says he went to Gale's apartment Saturday morning angry as hell because he'd gotten one of these little snapshots in the mail. Said he'd never been to her apartment before, he's a discreet man, but he was so heartbroke and angry he threw caution to the wind. He had to see her, talk this new development over. As he's parking his car, he sees David Stone rushing out of the building. Now he's past heartbroke and angry, he's irate. Figures she's screwing this punk Stone while puttin' the screws to him. Like I said, he fell for the flooze and now he's hurt and angry and jealous and all that neat romantic stuff."

I said, "Love *is* grand."

"Makes the world go round. Might explain why this world is so fucked up."

"You're cynical."

Snow said, "No, divorced. Anyway, Headon rushes to Gale's crib in this irate frame of mind so of course immediately he and Gale exchange words. She laughs at him, says he can't do a thing to her. Reminds him there's another person involved, there's more photos. This is a man of prestige getting his heart and his wallet handed to him by a concrete-walking assembly line flunky. You know, he's thinking she should be grateful to him, but she's busting his balls. He lost it totally. He admits to having a hair-trigger temper."

"I've seen it."

"He's seen yours too, what I hear. Anyway, he starts swinging and next he knows, he's gone too far, she's dead. Being the decent, law-respecting community pillar he is, he gets the hell out of there. After beating on her ass for awhile. He says he didn't do that, but he did. Funny isn't it, a man of prestige like Headon will admit to murder, but he refuses to admit he's a little kinky."

"He talk about the other murders?"

"That's the part I'm not likin'. He's got 'em all solved, but it ain't with him as the killer."

"What's he sayin'?"

"For starters, he claims either you or the Farrell babe knocked McCoy off."

"I've never owned a gun in my life. If I did how could I shoot a man in the back of the head when he's layin' on top of me?"

"Told you I wasn't likin' any of it. He won't even admit he had Stone worked over. Hell, he *owns* the Blue Palm where the two bozo's worked, he admits to bein' head over heels over the girl, but he denies knowin' 'em, or hirin' 'em. But he's guilty. He figures right down the line, A to Z. How about he had Stone stomped because he thought he was Andrea's blackmail partner?"

I shook my head, said, "No way. Timing's way off. Stone got beat up days before Headon ever saw that picture."

Snow said, "Yeah, I was afraid you'd say that."

I said, "He probably just wanted to scare Stone off. If he'd genuinely fallen for Andrea, he'd of checked up on her and found out about David Stone."

Snow said, "So the kid was a rival for her affections. That works out. Establishes passion early on. The kind of passion that would lead a man to beat a chick to death when he finds out she's blackmailing him and not in love with him. To a man like Headon, it'd be personal humiliation and you mix that with passion." Snow sipped more coffee and smiled. Things were falling into place for him and it felt good. I knew the feeling.

He said, "We got a witness who saw Headon leave the building at the time of the murder. The dead girl's roommate, Lisa Farrell. We picked her up little after two A.M. for questioning after Headon told us she was at the Blue Palm meeting. She tells us she saw him leave. Says he threatened her and she's afraid of him, he's so rich and she works for him and she needs the job, blah blah blah. That's why she never came forward. *He* says the girl's been shaking him down and in this case I believe him because first of all, she never called the police, she went straight to Headon. You officially 'found' the body. And second of all, why else would she be at the meeting unless Headon had to include her as part of any deals? But we'll get it all worked out."

"Why'd they go there anyway?"

"Headon says McCoy called, all scared, and said they had to talk. Said things were too hot to meet in public. Headon called Lisa Farrell, seeing as how she was involved." He tapped his teeth. "How much of this did you know?"

"I was on the right track."

"Headon says he didn't kill Torres and Wylie and I'll get to that in a second, but you claim they're related and I say you're right." He ticked off the reasons on his fingers. "Torres was a threat because Headon had hired him to work Stone over. That meant when Torres figured out why—and he would of, that it had to do with Headon being nuts about Andrea Gale—he had to die when Gale turned up dead. And Wylie? Sandy Headon thought the other person was the Farrell girl, but Headon assumed right from the getgo that Wylie was the partner, the two of them being old enemies. So he figures Wylie has the other photos. Only thing is Wylie is nowhere to be found. But soon as he is, that's all for him."

I said, "Thanks to me, right?"

"Don't blame yourself for that, partner. This whole mess was his idea."

"What about Wylie's phone call? I'm sure he didn't call McCoy."

"I don't think he did either. I don't know who he called. I think that call was only important in that it got Wylie out of the hotel. They probably knew he was there and were waiting for him to step out."

I said, "Possible."

"McCoy was covering it all up for Headon or, and I hate

to say this, was doing the actual crimes for him, but I think McCoy'd had it up to here."

I said, "McCoy knew it was over when I told him about the Polaroids. Until then, nobody but the people involved knew about the pictures and they hoped Wylie would be so scared it would stay that way. That was the one good thing about Andrea's death from their point of view. It scared Wylie so bad he went underground. Those pictures put Ronald Headon smack in the middle of everything. And that put McCoy smack in the middle because he was covering for Headon. Like he told Headon when those pictures went public, there'd be some hard questions asked and everything would come out."

Snow said, "So Headon killed him at the Blue Palm meeting out of sheer panic."

I said, "There was a lot of panic in that room. No trust, lots of panic."

Snow said, "Headon saw it all coming apart. And here's where we get to the bullshit part. Like I said, Headon's got it all covered. That's what he must of been doing from the time he left the Blue Palm until he turned himself in. Inventing his story. He's saying McCoy must of done Torres and Wylie. He admits he paid McCoy to 'do things' for him over the years. But he's saying McCoy killed these people just to *please* him. Like he didn't want McCoy to do it, but what could he do? I say, why would McCoy know to kill these people—especially Torres—unless Headon told him to? But to hang the Torres and Wylie killings on McCoy, he had to kill McCoy so it would be his word against a dead man's. And for McCoy's murder, it's his word against you and the babe's. And it was pitch black in that room. Nobody could see a thing, right?"

"Not after I pulled the plug."

He rubbed his eyes. "McCoy had two slugs in him. One in the chest, one in the back of his head. Think the second one was meant for you?"

"Probably. McCoy and I both knew what he didn't want known. He must of thought he got me with the second bullet, then slammed my head with the gun butt on his way out to be sure. Did you find the gun?"

"Hell, no." With his thumb and fingers, he made little circles on his chin. "You see what he's doin', don't you?"

I said, "Sure. He's angling for a manslaughter on Gale and he's gonna dazzle us with bullshit on the rest. His upstanding, community pillar word against a dead man, a party girl, and a cheap Chicago PI. A jury might suspect he did it all, but if there's even the shadow of doubt—." I wasn't liking this either. I said, "If it works, he'll get off with maybe two to five."

"Or less."

I said, "Hell, Andrea Gale *was* blackmailing him. Jury might think she had a beating coming and too bad the beating got out of hand."

Snow's hand moved faster on his chin.

I said, "What's the chances of making it stick the other way?"

"With a lot of work, maybe fifty-fifty. But I don't know if we could get a conviction in this town." He crushed the cup, dropped it to the floor. "You gotta testify. Seeing as how everything ended up okay, I'm gonna forget how you strung me along and lied to me and didn't share with me and we'll be great friends. Lisa Farrell and Sandy Headon still got some talkin' to do. I might ignore the fact Farrell was shaking Headon down, build her up as the scared kid she wants us to think she is, get her to testify that way."

There was a long silence, then suddenly Snow beamed. He said, "You know, we say all this, but I still wouldn't wanna be in Ronald Headon's weejuns. It ain't just a community pillar's word against you guys. We get this testimony and introduce these pictures and it's a conniving, adulterous, murdering community pillar's word against you guys. Get him put away for a long time."

I said, "They ever had a black mayor in this town?"

"Hell, no. Why?"

"You pull *that* off, you might wanna consider it."

He stood and winked.

# THIRTY-NINE

I rested awhile, replayed the week the right way.

Snow thought he had it A to Z, and I played along.

But he didn't. His was a good theory, but if you played it from a different angle, started from a slightly different beginning, it made better sense.

At three-thirty, I signed an Against Medical Advice form while a protesting nurse witnessed it. I still had a raging headache, but I was conscious and cognitive so nobody could stop me from signing myself out. I called Snow from the hospital lobby, asked him to give me an hour, told him where I'd be.

Lisa's Camaro was in the lot. When I knocked on her door it opened so fast it was like she'd been waiting for me.

She was sobbing. She locked her arms around my neck, pressed her body into mine. She said, "Oh, Dan, isn't this terrible? I had to keep this a secret from you and everybody. Last night I was so scared for you. Those two men were like—animals. I've been terrified for a week, terrified of Ronald Headon and that McCoy creature."

I gently unlinked her arms and went inside. I sat on the couch I always sat on. Lisa followed and sat on the chair across the room. Her eyes were round as doorknobs. Her lips quivered. "Oh, Dan." She was Mary Astor in *The Maltese Falcon* but I doubt she knew it.

I smiled, said, "You're good, you're really good." Just the way Bogie had.

"What're you talking about?"

"Murder. Four of 'em. And I'm looking at the murderer."

She swallowed, tried to grin, like I was suddenly going to laugh and say, "Just kidding!" But I wasn't kidding and she knew it.

I said, "Sorry, girl, but everything points to you. Seeing you at the Blue Palm last night clinched it. You even had keys to the place."

"But—"

"Police think your only involvement was shaking down Ronald Headon. They think he killed Andrea and master-minded the rest of it. But even if he could beat a girl sense-less in a rage, that doesn't mean he could kill in cold blood, or order it done. The fact he didn't kill you when you shook him down tells me he wasn't the type. And one thing practi-cally screams out. Headon and McCoy would of had about as much chance of getting near Eduardo Torres at an after hours party of hardcore derelicts as I have of flying to Mars. But you could of led Torres into that office with a knife and an iron bar in your purse and Torres, drunk, naked and horny as a goat, would never know what hit him."

"McCoy killed Torres."

"McCoy had too much to lose. His sugar-daddy deal with Headon was set up a long time ago. It was mutually beneficial and lucrative, but McCoy was still a cop, he had limits. There was lots he'd do for Headon, but he wouldn't kill for him. He spelled that out last night. And the others? Sandy Headon hates Ronald and his bimbos, but she's addicted to her life-style. She's like those people who detest their job, but're scared to death they might lose it. After her initial anger over the photo, she wanted him to pay up and forget about it. And if George and Dwayne had tried any of this, they'd of screwed it up so bad the whole world could've figured it out."

She kept with the Astor look, all vulnerable innocence. "But Headon confessed. And I saw him leave the apartment. I didn't say anything because he threatened me and gave me money to keep quiet. I'm guilty of that, but—"

"Quit it. Nobody but nobody believes that. Police think you saw Headon leave, went to the apartment, found Andrea dead, and instead of calling them, went straight to Headon to hit him up for hush money. They might of played it your way to get you to testify the way they wanted, but they wouldn't believe it. But the thing is, when you went into that apartment, Andrea was still alive. Beat up, maybe unconscious, maybe just groggy, but she was alive. Stone pushed her around, Headon beat her up, but you finished her off. Talk about bad luck, I'd hate to see

Andrea Gale's horoscope for last Saturday. In one morning she encountered one after the other three people who felt nothing but rage toward her. I mean 1, 2, 3. Stone, Headon, Farrell. What're the odds?"

"You're babbling."

"You saw Headon leave. No doubt he was terrified and practically ran to his car, a petrified look on his face. You went inside and found Andrea beat up on the floor. I've learned a lttle about how your mind works. James Wylie was no saint, but even he was amazed at how devious you girls were. He told me how you came up with your own blackmail scheme independent of his. I can't prove it, but I think you knew about their scam, which meant you knew they were getting money and you weren't. That plus your resentment and hatred of Andrea boiled over. Andrea was lying helpless in front of you, there was a patsy all set up. You made a spur of the moment decision to kill her. After you killed her, you had to live with the consequences and that meant more killings to cover loose ends. I don't know if you felt sick about it afterward or if you ran with it. But I gotta admit I admire the sheer gall of blackmailing Headon for a murder you committed."

Lisa stood and walked to the fireplace. Looking into it, she said again, "You're just babbling."

I said, "You seen your chance and you took it. That's an old Chicago alderman cop-out when they get caught with their hand in the till. And I sympathize a bit. When I found five photos of Andrea and Headon having sex, know what my first thought was? Blackmail Headon. Jumped right into my head. But my thought passed. You acted before yours could. You finished off Andrea, went to see Headon who no doubt hightailed it straight to his office to call McCoy. You told him you'd seen him leave and you'd found Andrea dead. You told him nobody else knew and it could stay that way. The man was scared to death of scandal. To hush up a murder, he'd pay whatever you asked."

"Stupid, stupid," she muttered.

"I'd say it was brilliant if you'd gotten away with it. This all came to me in pieces. Like doing a jigsaw puzzle. Sometimes you have to turn the puzzle around or look at it upside down. Like when I flashed to the fact it was you who hired Torres and Baker to beat up David Stone. Had to turn it upside down to realize that. Andrea already had Headon hooked. You knew about that. Lots of dough for her to extract there. Then on top of that she took Stone away. As always Andrea got whatever she wanted. Having Stone beat up felt good as revenge, plus it made Headon look like a goon because Andrea would assume Headon'd paid for it."

"But we got beat up too."

"*I* got beat up. You got slapped because you made too much noise. You played the role of scared onlooker too well. Only reason you spent any time with me was to set me up or find out what I'd learned. You were afraid I'd figure out you killed Andrea or that Headon killed her. The second possibility would of been almost as disastrous for you as the first. You wanted Headon to stay innocent as bad as he did because you wanted his money to keep rolling in. At the Crazy Alm, you arranged for the two punks to follow us out while I was in Gant's office. After you got home, you called Headon, told him I still planned to nose around. He applied pressure to Dennison and got me fired. Dennison wasn't afraid of McCoy, but Headon was a different story. Then for good measure, Headon sent his errand boy, McCoy, to scare me off."

"But why would I want to kill Andrea? She was my friend since grade school."

"I heard things this week. A little from your parents, a little from Wylie, a little from you. It all added up. When you talked about Andrea Gale, you couldn't keep the bitterness or the envy out of your voice. Your mother suggested you felt inferior next to her. We're talking fifteen years of feeling like an ugly duckling hanging out with a swan. A swan who got whatever she wanted, whenever she wanted. Anyone in that situation would eventually get bitter. They wouldn't admit it, maybe not even to themselves, but the bitterness would build up. Eventually become hate. Wylie told me the friendship was in tatters. Andrea told him she was tired of you. She wanted to leave Johnson City partly to get away from you."

"That's not true."

"Understand, I don't think you'd of ever killed Andrea in cold blood. Devise a plan and act it out. But one day you came home and the opportunity was there and you acted before you could think."

"It's not true. I swear it."

"Your mother was afraid you killed her after I told her I thought Stone was innocent. I sensed it when I talked to her. She told me some things, but when it dawned on her you could be the guilty party she started to lie. Like she claimed to know nothing about Andrea taking men away from you. She knew you were capable of killing Andrea and she wasn't about to supply reasons."

"No one is going to believe this."

"Thing you shouldn't of done, Lisa. You shouldn't of pulled off her pants and beat her butt and legs like that. You tried too hard to make it look like a man did it. Headon admits he beat her upside the head. But you had to get cute and make it look like he went sicko and took his time. No wonder he's so indignant. He'd deny that part forever. He probably thinks the cops are making it up to make him look like a perv."

"But you were there. You saw me come in."

"I saw you come in the second time. You'd left, leaving the door unlocked because with Andrea dead who else would be coming? Headon and Stone wouldn't of gone to the trouble of leaving the door unlocked, but a person who lives in an apartment in a security building and is just running out, they might. You got rid of whatever you used on her, found Headon and told him he was screwed, then you came back to 'discover' the body. But you didn't know Andrea had hired me the night before. At first I thought she did that to put the fear of God into Baker and Torres. Now I think she wanted a hired gun in case the blackmail deal got ugly. God knows Wylie wouldn't be any help and she had no way of knowing I'm not a hired gun type PI. But I was a PI and I'd told her I was down on my luck. I must of sounded like a guy who'd do about anything. You freaking out was no act. I genuinely scared the hell out of you. Finding a strange man wandering around the apartment. I mean, how much did I know, right?"

She smiled nervously and shook her head. "I can't believe you're saying these things, Dan."

"Know when I first asked myself if it was you? When you drove into Chicago. I couldn't figure out why. Must be my self-esteem is too low, but I refused to believe you came all the way in just to see me. Then after the game you started asking questions to see what I'd turned up. And that comment you made about Andrea being immoral. You had that last Polaroid and you were fishing to see if I knew about it."

"I came in to see if you were okay."

I laughed. "Nice try. This whole thing was set up perfectly for you. McCoy had a killer, David Stone, courtesy of Cleo Bell, to account for the murder. You hated Stone so you were getting revenge there. You had big bucks coming in from Headon to make sure his name stayed out of it. The only negative was me poking around."

"But the other murders."

"You screwed up there too. Snow is right about Torres. He *was* killed because he knew who hired him to work Stone over. You. After you killed Andrea, you worried Torres would start thinking. I'm not sure he knew how, but you knew him better than me. He knew you hated Andrea and David so much for what they did to you that you paid him to work Stone over. If he went to the police, told 'em who really hired him they might look at you a little different, they might of learned what I learned, might of come to the same conclusion I did." I stopped and thought for a second. "But that was a senseless murder, Lisa. Eduardo Torres would of never gone to the law and the police weren't paying much attention to anything Stone was saying. They figured McCoy had a handle on things. But you were new to murder. I'm sure you've lain awake every night wondering what little slipup might screw your deal. Even the smallest detail looked enormous to you."

Lisa looked away. Said, "Dan," then stopped.

"Everybody thinks Headon hired Torres to work Stone over. I'm sure Andrea thought so too. She probably accused him. When Torres turned up dead, Headon didn't want Andrea's accusation to get out, so he told McCoy not to poke too hard into it. If he did, Headon's name would come up.

McCoy said not to worry, Baker was tailor-made. And I'm willing to give McCoy the benefit of the doubt on that one. Maybe he thought Baker really was guilty."

Lisa walked toward the kitchen. I lit a Kool, kept my eyes on her. She stopped under the loft, turned hard to face me. She opened her mouth, but said nothing.

I said, "Wylie's who I feel bad about. Before I left him, I mentioned one Polaroid hadn't turned up yet. Afterward he got trashed on the Jack Daniels, started to think. Like I said, I'm sure you have the last photo. The police never found it. And Headon wouldn't of known Andrea had it or where to look if he did. He was in no condition to think about things like that right after he realized he'd killed her. Or thought he had. I think you found it on her or knew where she kept her valuables and found it there. Maybe you found it before all this happened and that's how you knew about the scam. Whatever, Wylie concluded you had it too and, knowing you, figured you'd use it. That didn't bother him, he wanted no part of those photos by then. But the man was drunk and desperate for money to blow town. You'd been his friend a long time and he thought you'd help him out. After all, it was his photo, his idea. He should get something out of it. So he called you, set up a meeting. He hoped you'd loan him some gone money. Or if he was in an ugly mood maybe he threatened to tell the police you were the second person Andrea talked about. I'm not sure what an old drunk desperate for money would say, but whatever it was it made him another person who could link you to this. But killing him was another mistake because McCoy and Headon wanted him to stay lost.

"You shoulda just given him some money, he never suspected you for the murders. He was certain it was Headon. When he turned up dead, McCoy had to find someone to fit for that and he was getting sick of the whole mess. Headon knew from the start Wylie was the other person. He might of told McCoy that much. But Wylie had dropped out of sight, nobody could find him. And believe it, they hoped it was permanent." I smiled. "Wonder what those two were thinking? Wylie was right, Headon would of paid the thirty-five grand and been done with it, except he was in love and that made him lose his temper and he thought he killed Andrea. He had to figure somebody was setting him up on the rest of the murders, probably you, but he couldn't say a word. Even now he won't say it was you. It's easier to blame a dead man. When McCoy knew I'd seen the photos, maybe had them, he knew he couldn't keep Headon out of it. It wasn't just Stone's wild accusations now. He called Headon to tell him he couldn't cover anymore. Headon set up the meeting at the Blue Palm and called you, you being part of the deal. The part of the deal he thought was protecting him from a murder charge."

I stopped, thought to myself: Damn, Kruger, this *does* make sense. I smiled to myself like Snow had.

I said, "McCoy knew *he* was innocent. He knew Headon had killed Andrea, accidentally of course, and he knew the photos were the reason. I'm not sure what else he knew except that Headon wanted the subsequent murders covered up. I don't think McCoy knew who he was shielding. Could've been Headon or Sandy or George. He might of asked Ronald what the hell was going on and Headon told him to fix it and not ask questions. You went to the Blue Palm last night intending to kill McCoy. You got there first so you could be behind the desk, with the gun in your lap. Headon told you McCoy was panicky. He was the last loose end, the last person who could ruin things for you. Put you or Ronald Headon in jail, cut you off from the money. And you wanted it down to you and Ronald Headon and lots of free money." I drew deep on the Kool, blew the smoke out. "He was the last person except for me that is."

I gazed around the apartment, looked up at the loft. "Looks like it would of been worth it if you'd pulled it off. You almost did."

At the end, she'd been staring at me as I talked, a mixture of fury and fear in her eyes. Suddenly she bent forward, hands on knees, and wailed. A hoarse primal scream of pure rage. I felt very sorry for her while she screamed, because the sound she made was that of a woman who realized her life was essentially over. There was no future. She punched her knees twice. Shrieked, "I *will!*"

She ran to the kitchen. I expected her to. When she came

back, she held a butcher knife in her right hand. I dropped
the Kool, picked up an end table, held it in front of me, legs
toward her.

She stopped fifteen feet away.

I said, "I understand Andrea's murder. You gave in to a
moment of passion, of insanity almost. If you'd stopped
there, I don't know what I would of done. But the rest of it
was only about greed and saving your skin."

We stared at each other. She didn't move. Her face went
slack, her breathing became labored. She said, "Dan?" once,
very soft. Then, "Let me?"

I shook my head no. Said, "Lisa, I can't."

There was a hard knock on the door. Lisa jumped, swung
her head and stared at the door like it was yet another
friend who'd betrayed her.

Keeping the end table between me and Lisa, I moved fast
to the door, pulled it open.

Snow had four uniforms with him. Lisa screamed, "No,
Dan!"

The men drew their guns. With a sinking sense of déjà vu
I heard a cop say to Lisa, "Ma'am, *please* drop the knife."

For ten seconds, she looked from one to the other, then
she let go of the knife and collapsed to her knees, sobbing.

They put her face down, cuffed her hands behind her
back.

Snow said, "You'll tell me about it, right?"

I said, "Tomorrow."

"What's the matter with now?"

"I'm talked out."

"Maybe you should go back to the hospital."

"Don't worry, I'm not gonna run out on you. I'll tell
everything first thing tomorrow."

"What about now?"

"Now I'm going back to my suite at the Jones. Gotta tell
my partner what happened. Tonight I'll be sitting at the
Crazy Alm drinking Diet Pepsi—I hope—and putting my
best moves on a girl with black lips and no hair."